ELEMENTAL WARS

BOOK 3 ELEMENTAL GAMES

TAMAR SLOAN

HEIDI CATHERINE

SEQUEL HOUSE

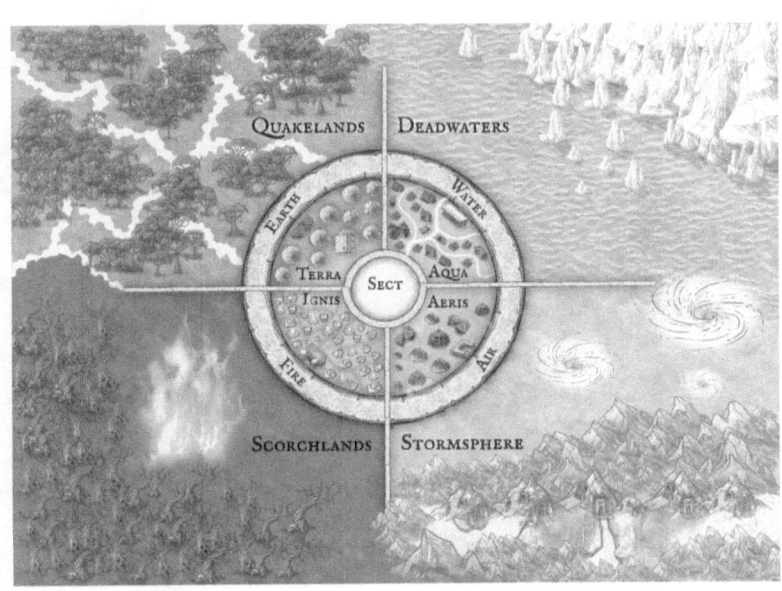

ONE

HAYZE

H ayze doesn't know where to look first. All four walls are moving, shearing away at the top as they fall outward like a box unfolding.

There's no time to process that Aura chose to end the Elemental Games.

That she chose the Alliance.

Chose him.

Because the four panels crash to the ground, revealing what was waiting for this exact moment.

Armed guards, clad in sleek black armor, form an impenetrable circle around them, and high-tech drones hover overhead, their ominous hum filling the air. Behind the guards, four large screens float where each Element's wall stood, the leaders' smug faces on each one.

Hayze, Aura and Pace create a tight, protective center, their backs pressed against the other. They execute a slow turn, confirming what's already obvious.

They're surrounded.

"Congratulations," Avalan croons. "You've won the Elemental Games."

"Liar," Hayze spits. "We were never meant to end the Games, let alone win them."

"The aim was to see what you're capable of," Cyclonis responds, his aged face dominating the screen. "And we've achieved that."

"You have no idea what we're capable of," Pace growls.

The drones hovering above twitch and shift, several spinning so their lenses are focused on him. Hayze maintains their slow turn, hoping between the three of them they can keep an eye on the triple threats—the armored guards, the drones, and the leaders with an agenda they haven't figured out yet.

"If we won, what's with all the firepower?" Aura demands.

The guards don't twitch, but the guns held tightly across their chests are unmistakable in their deadly threat.

"They're a precaution," Infernos responds. "Until we know whether you'll accept your honor."

Hayze almost sneers at the word. Honor. It doesn't matter how they try to dress up the Games, they're nothing but a tool for the elite to ensure their control.

"What did we win?" he asks, glaring at the leaders as they slowly pass his line of sight. "A lifetime of roasted kelp? A round trip of the capitals? A virtual reality trophy?"

Oceania's face twists. "You never did think big, Fire boy."

Avalan inclines her head as if her headdress is a crown. "You will know your destiny once you pledge yourself to us. To what must be done."

"Not cryptic at all," Pace mutters.

"Which is?" Aura calls out.

"You're destined to be the most powerful force of all," Cyclonis intones.

Oceania nods. "The hope for the future."

"The solution to humanity's survival," Infernos says.

Avalan lifts her chin. "The ultimate weapon in this war."

The final words hang in the air as ominously as the drones.

"Did you guys practice that?" Hayze asks dryly, unimpressed by all the big talk.

The leaders haven't answered Aura's question. What do they want with the teens who've unlocked their Elemental powers?

"Enough!" Infernos roars. He leans forward, his face dominating the screen. "Do you accept?"

Hayze, Aura, and Pace stop their slow turn. The leaders gaze down on them from the four points of their compass. The guards don't twitch a muscle as they grip their weapons. Even the drones still, seeming to hold their breath.

"No," Aura states flatly. "Not until you tell us what you're planning."

Not until they know exactly what they're signing up for.

Infernos sighs. Oceania shakes her head. Cyclonis closes his eyes as if he doesn't want to watch what's about to happen next.

Avalan waves her hand, disappointment etched in the lines around her mouth.

The guards and the drones move simultaneously, contracting around Hayze and the others. The teens respond instantly, each unleashing their Element.

Hayze and Aura blast out two fireballs. Pace throws a torrent of water.

The drones divide into three, two shooting white foam, one its own fiery projectile. The pale froth intersects Hayze and Aura's attacks, instantly dousing their fire balls. One second the blazing comets are streaking through the air, the next they're nothing but a dirty splatter on the floor. The third drone's fiery shot slices through Pace's water attack, rendering it to steam.

Hayze, Aura and Pace freeze in shock. Their attack was neutralized in a blink.

Tide's words when they were ready to fight the leaders in the pod room filter through Hayze's mind.

You don't think they'll be prepared this time? They've spent years planning this, ensuring they can control what they create.

The ramifications of that have barely sunk in when a hail of bullets rains down on them.

"We are Fire!" Hayze screams.

He spins and shoots out a wall of flames, Aura at his back doing the same. Pace crouches down at their feet, covering his head. They create a shield of fire around them, one that renders the bullets coming at them to molten lead. The projectiles fall to the floor, peppering Rateen's dead body only a few feet away, nothing more than harmless, misshapen blobs.

Yet the barrage doesn't stop.

In fact, it intensifies.

Black dots bloom over the blazing shield, blossoming as the bullets melt, then disappearing as they drop to the floor.

"We have to get out of here!" Aura shouts.

"Before you cook me," Pace gasps, sending a burst of water at his face and torso.

They can't stay here, fending off endless attacks from the guards and drones. And Pace can't withstand the heat like Hayze and Aura can.

"There has to be a door," Hayze says, lifting his hands a little as if that will make a difference to the wall of fire Pace is surrounded by.

Aura moves so she's shielding Pace. "I saw one between Avalan and Infernos's screens."

"Then that's where we go," Hayze grits out.

"Up above!" Pace cries.

Six drones appear at the top of the tunnel of fire. White foam shoots from their underbellies, coating the sides. Extinguishing their shield.

"Like heckus!" Hayze roars.

Lifting his arms, he creates a ceiling of fire above them. The foam lands on it, creating pale patches, but with some extra focus, they vaporize. Hayze allows himself a second to breathe. They're safe.

Except they're now surrounded by flames. Pace is crimson-faced and gasping. "I...can't..."

Hayze and Aura glance at each other, realizing this isn't an option, no matter how effective it is. Which means they have no choice but drop the fiery shield and hope they can reach the door in time.

"Get ready to run," Hayze grinds out.

Pace looks both grim and relieved as he raises his hands, his body coiled and waiting as he crouches beside them.

Hayze and Aura clench their hands into fists, muting their powers. They're already moving before the wall of fire dissipates. Running. Ducking. Fighting for their lives.

The drones react first. They drop as one, ready to neutralize any attack they unleash.

A group of guards launches at them. Pace drops to one knee and presses his palms to the floor. A sheet of water shoots out toward the guards, crackling as it turns to ice. The guards go from running to slipping and falling in a heap.

Hayze glances at Aura. "Let's show them the power of unity."

He shoots fire at a drone above them. The machine quickly responds with a ball of foam, turning the attack to slush.

Except the drone's not ready for Aura's fireball as it follows a split-second later. The flying machine explodes, its fiery metal carcass dropping onto a guard. They both crash to the ground, lifeless.

Hayze sees the door Aura described in the gap between Avalan and Infernos's screens. The two leaders are watching on, grimly and silently. Waiting for this to end in three deaths. The guards realize what the teens' intentions are and quickly converge, creating a wall of black armor between them and the door. The drones hover above, ready to protect from any Elemental attack.

Hayze, Aura and Pace break into a run. Hayze and Aura attack with fire. Pace unleashes a barrage of water and ice.

Some guards drop. Some drones crash to the floor.

Yet there's always more of them. Attacking. Firing. Protecting their own.

Hayze and the others gain a foot, only to be beaten back as the guards and drones attack mercilessly. Bullets slice the air. Fire is abruptly extinguished. Water is immediately vaporized.

There are too many drones.

Too many guards.

There's no way they'll escape this place alive.

A drone swoops low, shooting out a small black projectile. A net explodes outward, black and webbed and crackling with electricity, then wraps around Pace. He drops, screaming as the electrified weave crackles everywhere it touches his skin.

"Pace!" Aura cries, quickly dropping beside him. She shoots out a controlled dose of fire and it catches the edge of the net. The flames eat the web fast, crawling over the black rope and freeing Pace. He leaps to his feet, but weaves dangerously. Aura steadies him.

Throughout it all, Hayze becomes a canon of fire. He shoots fireballs of every size at any twitch of movement, guard or drone. There are cries as some hit, other blazing balls become defenses as they swallow bullets. When a drone shoots a net at him, he incinerates it even as he knows there will be many more. That once two of them are simultaneously overpowered, this will be over.

They may survive this. Only to be taken as prisoners.

Hayze looks toward the door. It's only yards away, but it may as well be miles with all the guards and drones in between.

They might have ended the Elemental Games.

But they're no closer to freedom.

"Assholes!" comes a voice from behind them. "It's time to meet the Alliance!"

Hayze and the others spin to find a dozen, masked people standing several feet away. Someone throws a jar with a flame dangling from a wick. It lands at the nearest guard's feet and explodes, engulfing him in fire. His screams are cut off by the roar of the remaining guards.

As they attack.

The newcomers scatter, ducking bullets and drones. "Get out of here!" one of them shouts, waving their arm in the direction of the door.

"They're here as a distraction," Aura gasps.

They're here to ensure they get away.

Yet Hayze and Aura hesitate. They can't let these people die doing this.

"Come on," Pace cries, shoving them forward. "If I can leave my father behind, you can do this."

Hayze breaks into a run a second before Aura does. They both know Pace is right. If he can allow his father to sacrifice himself for this, then they need to honor the people of the Alliance's readiness to do the same.

This time, their Fire and Water attacks are enough to get through the divided guards. The door comes closer, foot by foot. Behind them, there's a volley of bullets and a cry is abruptly cut off. Someone just lost their life fighting for this. Fighting for freedom.

Pace yanks the door open, and Aura follows. Hayze right behind. The small space they find themselves in has Hayze realizing they're in one of those rooms that moves up and down between floors. He uses the split second before the doors close to give the bird to the scowling images of the four leaders on their screens.

The unsettling weightless feeling blooms and the shots and cries fade away as the room rises, even as Hayze knows the fighting continues. That rebels are dying so they can be here.

Pace looks at the rows of buttons on the wall in front of him, breathing hard. "Tempo's somewhere in here." He turns to Hayze and Aura. "We have to find her."

Hayze and Aura don't need to look at each other to know what their answer is. He reaches out and presses the topmost button. He has no idea if that's where Tempo is, but they can start there and work their way down.

"We won't leave the Sect without her," Aura promises Pace.

They can't leave Tempo behind. They can't leave any of the others behind.

It's time to unite the Elements.

So they can never be used as a weapon in this war they've found themselves in.

TWO

AURA

The small room shoots up so fast, Aura's certain her stomach drops to the floor.

She chose to side with the Alliance.

And now the Alliance has chosen to side with her.

They risked their lives for Aura, along with Hayze and Pace, with many of them losing the gamble. She can't let them down. This is their chance to find Tempo. Then they can not only end the Games, they can end this entire nightmare.

The doors spring open to reveal an empty white space.

Both Aura and Pace look to Hayze. He's the only one who's witnessed Tempo hooked up to the machines keeping her alive. All Aura has seen is his sketch of that heartbreaking scene in the dirt of a cave that never existed.

"It didn't look like this." Hayze presses another button, sending the doors sliding closed again.

"What *did* it look like?" Pace asks. "Where is she, Hayze?"

"She was in a room."

"Helpful..." Pace taps his foot.

"Let me finish." Hayze rolls his eyes. "There was a corridor outside it, with four doors, one for each Quadrant. I went through the Water door that eventually led me to Aqua."

The doors slide open again to reveal another white space.

"We need to find that corridor," says Pace. "Simple."

Hayze nods, although Aura can see doubt in his eyes. Nothing is ever as easy as it seems when it comes to the four leaders and the traps they set.

"It was high in the Sect," says Hayze.

"Then we need to go back up." Pace drags his hands through his dark hair.

"But there was nothing up there," says Hayze, his finger hesitating on the button. "We agreed to work our way down."

"We need to check properly," says Pace, desperation leaching into his voice. "We didn't even look."

"Okay." Hayze nods, pressing the button for the top floor again. "We'll go back and search."

"We'll find her, Pace." Aura puts her hand on his back as she feels the small room moving up again. "It's going to be okay."

She notices a flash of jealousy cross Hayze's face but keeps her hand where it is. Things are complicated between her and Hayze right now, and as much as she doesn't want to add to that, she needs to support her friend. She knows how it feels to have the person you love torn from your side. Pace is living in torment. Aura never experienced greater pain than when Hayze was swallowed by lava.

"I won't stop until I find her," growls Pace as the doors slide open.

"Nor will we," Hayze adds.

"That's right." Aura steps away from Pace and slips her hand into Hayze's. He grips her tightly. They have so much to repair in their relationship, but she already knows without doubt that's what she wants to do.

Rebuild. Together.

The more she's finding out about the world, the more difficult she's realizing it is to live in. But it wouldn't just be difficult without Hayze.

It would be impossible.

They step out into the white room, looking for a door or another path to take.

"Over here!" Pace shouts as he runs into an expanse of whiteness that swallows him up.

"Where is he?" Hayze asks, pulling Aura forward. "He disappeared."

They follow Pace into the whiteness, crossing over an invisible barrier that instantly reveals the room in its true form. Spinning around, Aura looks back to where they just came from, wincing as bright light projects into her eyes.

"It's a control room," pants Pace, drawing Aura's attention back. He moves to a large desk in this otherwise bare room that doesn't even have so much as a window or door.

Aura and Hayze join Pace, finding a panel on the desk with dozens of buttons labeled with intricate symbols.

"Not another guessing game," groans Hayze. "Which bu—"

Pace presses a button without waiting for a consensus, and a rope ladder drops from the ceiling, revealing a hatch above it.

"How did you know which one to press?" Aura gasps.

"The picture on it looks like a ladder." Pace shrugs. "Come on!"

"It's too easy," says Aura, as Pace begins to climb. "It's never that easy."

"Maybe I'm just smart," Pace calls back.

He might be living in torment, but at least his ego seems intact.

"You go next," says Hayze, not needing to discuss if they

follow him. Separating isn't an option. Their power comes from sticking together. And that's with only two Elements. Once they rescue Tempo, they can free Jewel and the Air teens, making them even more powerful again.

Aura climbs the rope ladder as Hayze holds it steady, reminding her of when they climbed to the safe zone in the Quakelands. When she reaches the top, Pace grabs her from under her arms and hauls her up into a long corridor.

"Hurry!" says Pace. "Where's Hayze?"

"Give him a sec—"

Hayze climbs through the hatch and blinks.

"Is this the same corridor you saw last time?" Pace asks, hopping from foot to foot.

"Ah, it's hard to tell." Hayze smoothes down his leather trousers and Aura forces herself to look away from how his muscular thighs fill them out.

"It could be any corridor," says Aura. "It looks like the one we were trapped in during the Games."

"We're not in the Games now," Pace growls, not prepared to listen to any answer that doesn't lead him closer to Tempo. He takes off down the corridor, his determination to find her tugging at Aura's heart.

"We have to let him do this." Hayze links hands with Aura and they chase after Pace's desperate footsteps.

It's with enormous relief that Aura sees a door at the end of the corridor, which means it's not the same corridor as the one in the Games. Her cheeks flush. Real life doesn't have endless corridors. Just like real life doesn't allow you to die and bring you back again. They need to be extra cautious about whatever awaits them on the other side of this door.

Pace flings it open.

"This is it!" Hayze cries from over Aura's shoulder. "Look! A door for each Quadrant. Tempo's through the unmarked one at the end."

Aura glances to her left and sees two doors marked with the symbols for Air and Water. The two on her right are marked with Earth and Fire. She looks at her hand bearing her Fire tattoo, feeling a pull toward the door with the matching symbol. That door would lead her to her parents, and they have so much to talk about...

But that time isn't now.

This is about Tempo. The girl who spent the last days of her life believing she was Aura. Which bonds them in the same way Hayze is tied to Pace. She just hopes if they find Tempo that she's willing to let Pace into her life. Because Aura remembers only too clearly how much animosity she'd held for Hayze when she woke up on the raft and thought Tempo's past hurts were her own.

Pace charges at the door at the end of the corridor and opens it, his hands springing up ready to defend against attack.

Aura follows, gasping to see three beds—the empty one Hayze had broken free of, the charred remains of Geo's bed, and...

"Tempo!" Pace gasps, running toward the girl with hair the color of flames and a heart that belongs in Water. "I came for you."

She lies completely still and unresponsive. Aura desperately hopes they're not too late. It would be agony to find her after all this time, only for her to be—

"Tempo!" Pace begs as he gently taps her face. "Please, wake up. I'm here."

To Aura's surprise and relief, Tempo's eyes flutter open. A tsunami of emotions washes over her face as her memories of her real life flood back to her. Everyone in this room knows how that feels.

Confusion mingles with fear. Love wars with hate. Then surprise slips beneath a wall of pure exhaustion.

Tempo frowns at Pace, turning from him to look at Aura. That's where she anchors her gaze as she reaches out.

"You're Tempo from Water," says Aura, stepping forward and taking her friend's hand. "And Pace loves you so much. He's fought hard to get back to you."

Aura glances at Pace to see hurt etched across his features. This is the reunion he feared. It wasn't the one he wanted. But Tempo is far from being out of danger just yet. She's extremely weak, possibly only moments from death claiming her permanently this time.

"We need to get Tempo out of here," says Hayze, hovering nervously in the doorway. "Before they come after us."

"She's not strong enough to move." Pace remains firmly by Tempo's bedside.

Aura winces, knowing both Pace and Hayze are right. Tempo is hanging on by a thread. If they move her, it could be too much. But if she stays here, she might also slip away. Or worse still, be killed by the leaders. She would have been better off if she'd been left in her pod. At least there she would've been fed with a constant stream of nutrition, instead of being left to die in a lonely bed.

"We don't have a choice," says Hayze. "It's more dangerous for us to leave her here."

"Tempo." Aura squeezes her hand. "We have to move you. Is that okay? We'll look after you."

Tempo shifts her eyes to Pace, her distrust for the guy she was made to believe she loved perfectly clear. It's potentially a blessing she's far too weak to speak.

"You trust me, don't you?" Aura asks. "Nobody in the world

knows me better than you do. Not even Hayze. You've been inside my head. I won't let anything bad happen to you."

Pace lets Aura talk, his love for Tempo greater than his need for her to love him in return.

"She just needs time," Aura says, talking to Pace, desperately hoping Tempo lives long enough for that to happen. "She'll understand."

"I hope so," he whispers, grief tearing at his soul. "Tempo, what happened was between our parents. We were only kids. I love you."

"A Game," she whispers. "Not real."

"It was real to me." A tear rolls down Pace's cheek. "The danger we were put in was fake, but everything I felt for you was true. Every kiss, every touch, every brush of my skin against yours was real. I love you. And I'd go through the Games a hundred times again if I had to. Because it brought me to you."

Aura lets Tempo's hand fall, feeling like she's intruding on something too private, too beautiful, for her to be there. But as she steps away, she sees Tempo shake her head at Pace, and Aura's heart shatters.

Hayze pulls her to his chest, and she accepts his comfort. Surely Tempo can forgive Pace, just like Aura did in the Games? Like Tempo herself had when she thought Hayze's betrayal belonged to Pace.

"Tempo, please," Pace begs. "I love you. Can't you see that? I know you love me, too."

But Tempo's either too weak or too confused to answer. Her breathing becomes ragged and her eyes close once more.

"Tempo!" Pace gently shakes Tempo as she slips even further away from them. "No, Tempo. You have to hold on!"

Hayze holds Aura closer, and she finds herself holding her own breath as Tempo draws in a huge gasp of air. Her eyes fly wide, and she stares up at Pace. She takes another desperate breath, then her head falls to the side as her eyes glaze over.

"Tempo!" Pace cries. "No, Tempo!"

Aura's seen enough death in her life to know it's no use. And her shattered heart crumbles to painful shards that stab her in the chest.

"She's gone, Pace," Aura chokes out, leaving Hayze to return to his side, only for him to push her away. It's not Aura he wants. It's the girl who made it clear she didn't want him, right before she died.

"Oh, Tempo." Aura shakes her head, giving her the respect she deserves. She shared so much with this girl that stretched far beyond simply their memories. The only consolation is that Tempo's last moments were surrounded by people who love her. That alone makes everything they went through to get here worth it. Tempo wasn't just a pawn in a sick Game. She was a living, breathing human, worthy of a better life than what was handed to her.

Pace leans over and scoops Tempo up in his arms, holding her close as he sobs. There's only one death that's cut Aura more deeply, and that was when she thought she lost Hayze. But unlike Tempo, he returned to her. This almost makes her wish they were back in the Games. Because at least there they had a chance, even if it was only one of them.

Hayze holds up a hand. "I hear footsteps!"

Aura races to his side and they take a few steps away with their hands raised, creating a barrier between the door and the bed. If the leaders want to get inside, they're going to need to get past their Fire powers first. Pace is worse than useless right now.

The door flies open, banging against the wall with a boom.

Aura lets out a loud gasp when she sees someone she never

thought she was going to lay eyes on again. Someone who not long ago, she killed...

Rateen.

She's wearing the same long black robes as last time, only now they're not burned. More than that, she seems in perfect health.

"You're alive," says Hayze, taking the words from Aura's lips. "How?"

Rateen stands with her hands by her side. Aura and Hayze keep their defensive pose, having learned the hard way just how lethal this old woman is.

"Welcome to the Sect," says Rateen. "I've been waiting for you."

Aura glances at Hayze, wondering if he realizes these are the exact same words she used last time.

"Waiting for us to do what?" Hayze asks, clearly deciding to play along until they figure out what in the heckus is happening here.

"Waiting for you to see sense and hand yourself in to the leaders, of course." Rateen smiles. Then her gaze shifts to Tempo, lifeless in Pace's arms. "Oh. We lost another one, did we? That's a shame."

Pace lowers Tempo gently to the bed. "It's worse than a shame. Who are you? How can you be here when we all just saw you dead?"

"I am but a humble servant," Rateen says. "I came to check on our patient. But I see that's no longer necessary."

"How. Are. You. Here?" Pace shouts.

"She's not real," Aura says, ice sliding down her core as the truth dawns on her.

"She is!" Pace grabs Rateen by the arms, his grief clouding his ability to care about the consequences. "She's flesh and blood. Just like us!"

"We're not real." Aura shakes her head.

"Have your powers scorched your brain?" Pace steps away from Rateen, instinctively returning to Tempo. "Of course, we're real."

"She's right," says Hayze, shock seeping into his eyes. "In the Games we felt real. To ourselves and each other. When I kissed Aura, I felt the warmth of her lips and the beat of her heart, just like I have all my life. But we weren't real. And nor is Rateen. Which means..."

"We didn't end the Games," says Aura. "We're still in them."

THREE

HAYZE

"It's still virtual reality!" Hayze roars in fury. He spins one way, then the other. The Sect is nothing but a fake. "None of this is real. The room. Rateen." He looks at Tempo's lifeless body. "She may not even be dead!"

Pace's hand brushes her pale face, looking torn. Accepting Hayze's words means everything he just went through was for nothing. A lie. At the same time, it means he has the chance to do this moment again.

That Tempo could survive.

Rateen inclines her head. "The only way out is to pledge yourself to the leaders."

"Like fractal," Hayze growls. "Enough is enough."

He lifts his hands and aims them at the old woman.

No more.

"Hayze..." Aura starts, reaching out toward him. But then her hand drops as her face tightens.

She realizes it's the leaders who have to stop, not Hayze.

All it takes is a thought, a single twitch of his fingers and a fireball explodes from his palms. It grows exponentially over the short distance, flares from red to yellow to blue as Rateen's killed for the second time. She's instantly incinerated. Relegated to ash and smoke.

"Statement made," Pace says, sounding a little awed.

Hayze lowers his hands, searching for a hint of remorse but not finding one. Rateen is as fake as everything they endured in the Games. She was a means to an end, a program sent to relay a message, possibly triggered by them entering this room. Well, Hayze just sent a message of his own.

"Come on," he says to Aura and Pace. "We have to get out of the Sect altogether."

Aura nods, her face grim as she skirts around the ashen remnants of Rateen. Yet Pace remains where he is.

Hayze stops, his hand on the door. "It's not Tempo. It never was."

Aura takes a step back toward Pace. "The only way to find her is to leave."

Pace hesitates, clearly hating the thought, even if it's nothing but a mirage of the girl he loves. Then he leans down, brushes a kiss across her forehead, and breaks into a run.

The moment they exit through the door, a wail pierces the air. The walls flare with flashes of red, pulsing in time to the alarm.

Hayze clenches his jaw as he rams into the nearest exit— the door to Earth. They've been manipulated again. The leaders expected them to go to Tempo all along. That's why Rateen was waiting for them, already programmed with what she was going to say. The leaders were testing them once more. They wanted to see what they'd do.

And according to Avalan, Cyclonis, Infernos and Oceania, they just made the wrong choice.

They step into the small room that Hayze already knows is going to carry them down to the Earth chamber. It's not until the doors shut behind them that he lets himself exhale. He draws Aura to him and presses a kiss against her temple, then freezes. In the rush of adrenaline, he forgot so much remains unresolved between them. He just made an assumption.

Aura splays her hands over his chest as she looks up at him. He gazes at her, unmoving, breath once more trapped in his chest. The faint smile that graces her lips is captivating. The way she presses up on her toes, bringing her face closer to his, is downright mesmerizing.

The soft press of her lips to his chin is *everything*.

"They're going to pay for this," Pace growls beside them, vibrating with fury.

Aura lowers back down but stays tucked into Hayze's side. He senses her sigh more than feels it. Their moment's over. Because the battle is far from over.

And he has no doubt she's thinking the same thing he is. Pace just went through the loss of Tempo, believing their lifetime of resentment and hatred never had the chance of being resolved.

The leaders have a lot to answer for.

Hayze frowns as he looks at the white doors that will open once the room stops dropping seamlessly through the Sect. The fake Sect. Everything that happened the moment he woke up in the room flashes through his mind—Geo, Tempo, the leaders, his memories rushing back. But one moment flares the brightest. Geo dying. Except...

The. Sect. Is. Fake. Virtual reality, just like the Games.

Could the Earth boy still be alive?

Which also means the Alliance members who came to save them may have survived. Somehow, they must've plugged into this the moment they entered the Sect.

Has every death the teens have had to endure been nothing but a simulation?

The room glides to a stop and tension contracts around them. "We'll have company when the doors open," Hayze growls under his breath.

Aura nods, her body tightening. Pace flexes his head from side to side.

Every muscle in Hayze's body is a coil ready to spring.

The doors are silent as they move, revealing the Earth chamber. Massive, monolithic stones punch through the floor, carved with intricate, ancient trees and mystical landscapes. The air, rich with the scent of soil and moisture cradling the leaves which hang everywhere, not rising, not falling.

And beside every stone, on every walkway is a black-armored enemy, with several drones hovering above them.

"We can't die," Hayze shouts, breaking into a run.

"Hey!" Pace calls out. "Save some for me!"

Hayze unleashes a volley of fireballs, and each one is neutralized by foam just like he expected. The roar of more fireballs is also what he knew would follow. Aura's right behind him, a weapon in her own right as she takes out several drones.

Gunshots erupt. Bullets slice through the holographic leaves, shooting straight toward them. A battle cry explodes from Pace as he releases blast after blast of water and ice. Hayze and Aura are a whirlwind of fiery flames.

Just like with Rateen, there's no hesitation. No regret.

This is a *Game*, after all.

Drones are annihilated. Guards drop, frozen or scorched. Most of the bullets never reach them, the nets raining down trying to capture them are incinerated.

But some get through.

A searing, sharp pain pierces Hayze's shoulder. Another explodes through his thigh. Yet, he keeps running. Keeps attacking. Keeps protecting Aura, just as she's protecting him.

They weave through the monoliths, using them as shields, their focus on one thing.

The door out of the Sect.

"Above us!" Pace shouts.

Hayze looks up, registering several armored men on top of a monolith, their guns pointed down. Their arms jerk and a second later, a rapid burst of shots sounds.

"We can't d—"

Hayze's words are cut off as multiple bullets shred the existing wound on his thigh, turning it from a single puncture to a mess of blood and flesh. He screams even as he tries to tell his mind this isn't real, then stumbles. Aura cries out, quickly followed by Pace's shout. Hayze rolls and turns, his heart convulsing in his chest. A net has wrapped around Aura and Pace, its black webbing crackling and sparking everywhere it touches. It presses against Pace's face, and he drops to all fours, screaming in agony, while Aura tries to hold it away from them.

"I...can't..." Aura gasps.

She's being electrocuted. She can't use her Elemental powers.

Hayze leaps to his feet, staggers, then drags his lifeless leg toward them. Reaching out, he grabs the net and cries out. Electricity, white hot and lightning fast, shoots up his arm. His muscles contract, meaning he holds the black webbing even tighter. Ignoring the jagged burning ripping up his arm, he yanks the net off, gritting his teeth against the pain. One flash of energy and it incinerates in his hand.

Aura collapses and Hayze catches her. Pace rolls onto his side, groaning. He reaches up to touch his face, then stops. Blood is running down the right side, soaking the collar of his suit, weeping from the mangled lines across his face.

More shots hit the rock beside them, making them duck.

"Come on!" Hayze says, reaching out a hand to Pace and hauling him up. "Don't forget—"

"I know. I know," he croaks. "Apparently we can't die."

No matter how much it feels like it.

"Hayze!" Aura gasps, pointing up.

Another net is spreading its black wings as it drops on them.

Hayze annihilates it with a fireball. "Run!" he shouts, taking Aura's hand and doing just that.

Except his leg is a dead weight. It drags along the earthen ground, gouging a line through the rich soil. He's just set his jaw against the pain when Aura slips under his arm. "Almost there," she tells him.

Hayze uses his Fire powers to protect them as Aura half carries, half drags him toward the door. Pace remains at their back, freezing the dozens of nets that fly at them, each one desperate to catch the teens on the verge of escape.

The walls of the Earth chamber are covered in perpetually growing vines. They sinuously twist and coil up, glistening and serpentine. The moment the teens come close, they converge on the door, covering it and protecting it.

"Like heckus," Hayze snarls. He shoots out a stream of fire, ignoring the strange high-pitched screaming as the vines burn.

They crumble away, turning to ash just like Rateen did, revealing the door. Hayze swipes his Fire symbol, and it opens, exposing the same small room he entered the last time he left the Sect.

Assuming it was real.

The doors close, cramming them into the small space. "Close your eye—"

There's a flash of white and it feels like Hayze's brain was just bleached dry. The opposite doors open and the three teens stumble out, blinking as they adjust to the gray world they find themselves in.

Hayze straightens, squinting. They're on the other side, the earth and trees of Terra stretching out in all directions, breathing hard and uninjured. He looks down at his leg, the echoes of agony still ricocheting through him although his thigh is blemish free. Pace touches his face, finds it smooth and unharmed, then pulls his hand back to look at his fingers. They're dry. Free of blood.

"I don't think I'll ever get used to that," he snarls.

"No one should," Hayze says, curling his hands into fists.

Having a lie forced upon you isn't something anyone should endure.

"We need to get back in," Aura says, her voice hardening. "So we can really end this."

Hayze scans the white expanse of the Sect, then looks up. Dark storm clouds frame the pale dome, low and ominous. "We can't enter through those doors," he says, his gaze dropping once more as realization hits him. The moment they do, they'll be reconnected to the virtual reality.

Pace frowns. "Then how do we get in?"

For the first time, Hayze wonders what the Sect really looks like. The true Sect. "We make our own entrance," he states flatly.

Aura tugs her shoulders back. "One door, coming up."

Without needing to communicate, they lift their hands. Take a few steps to the side. Exhale. And blast the wall of the Sect.

Hayze injects all the fury, the fear, then an extra dose of fury into the fire pouring from his palms. He thinks of the leaders and everything they've put them through. He thinks of Geo and Tempo, who they have no idea are alive or dead. Of

Jewel, Atmos and Skylus, still trapped in a lie. He thinks of the rebels who are willing to risk their lives for a better way.

There's a crackle, a shudder, and the sound of grating and grinding. The flames on the wall of Sect burn brighter as a puddle of white pools at its base.

"Pace?" Aura says as she and Hayze drop their hands.

"Coming right up." One blast of icy water and the flames are extinguished, revealing a hole large enough for them to walk through.

They move forward without hesitation. With conviction.

Ready to face the next battle in this war for freedom.

Hayze steps through first, followed by Aura and Pace. They all stop, gravel crunching under foot.

Up above, lightning splits the iron sky. A gust of wind buffets them.

But they don't move.

The real Sect, the true center of the Quadrants, has left them frozen in shock.

FOUR

AURA

Aura rubs her eyes, certain she's dreaming.

A decrepit building looms before them like a relic of times gone by. At least a dozen stories high, its concrete exterior has white paint desperately clinging to it, peeling away in ragged sheets. The windows are either broken or boarded up with rusted sheets of tin, their frames weathered and warped as they succumb to the ever-increasing harshness of the elements.

"Is this real?" Aura asks. "This can't be the Sect."

"We're not in virtual reality," says Hayze, his own eyes wide. "There was no flash of white. No pod. This is happening."

"Which means we *can* die," says Pace, having heard Hayze tell them they can't so many times, it plays like a mantra in their heads.

Hayze nods. "We need to be careful."

"And perhaps dial back the killing a little," Pace adds with a grin. "Now that it's real."

Hayze shakes his head, a smile of his own playing on his

kissable lips. It's always a relief to see Pace's sense of humor return. He must be confident he'll find Tempo again and that this time things will be different between them. Aura's not so sure. It may not be their real bodies when they're in the Games, but they still think like themselves. Pace will have a battle ahead to win Tempo back.

But first, they need to find her.

Hayze takes a step forward only for Pace to put a hand on his arm and draw him to a stop.

"What if it's a trap?" Pace asks.

"Their traps work better in virtual reality," says Hayze. "We're more powerful than they are. They can't use any of their fancy tricks on us here."

"I thought you wanted to find Tempo?" Aura asks, confused.

"I do," he says quickly. "Which is why I want to be sure we keep safe. We can't find her if we're dead."

"I don't think they're going to kill us," says Aura. "They've invested too much to simply wipe us away."

Hayze nods. "I was thinking Geo might even be alive."

"Whoa." Pace's eyes flare. "Now you're really messing with my head."

Hope lights in Aura's chest that Hayze could be right. She always liked the boy from the Earth Quadrant. He may have been quiet, but she always felt like he had so much more he wanted to say. Now, maybe they'll get the chance to find out what.

"Let's do this," she says, marching forward with Pace and Hayze racing to catch up.

The ground has weeds growing through the cracks in the pavement as nature tries to reclaim this space as its own and there's debris scattered everywhere. This couldn't be more of a stark contrast to the gleaming white building of the virtual reality Sect. It seems the leaders have put far more effort into their fake world than the one they're forced to live in.

Pace jogs ahead, reaching the double door at the entry first. He pushes and they swing open with a loud creak. Aura winces, half expecting the cracked glass in the frame to shatter. But it holds steady, as does the rapid beating of her heart.

Hayze puts a protective hand on Aura's back as they step into the building and are hit with a musty stench that's a concoction of both dampness and decay.

"It's dark in here," Pace whispers. "Can you make us some light?"

Hayze removes his hand from Aura and creates a flame in his palm. An eerie glow casts across the lobby, revealing chipped tiles on the walls and pools of murky water on the floor. A wide staircase stretches out in the middle of the space lined with threadbare carpet of an indistinguishable color.

"This place gives me the creeps," says Hayze with a shudder.

"Surely Tempo's not somewhere in here?" Aura looks around with an expression of horror. "This place is abandoned."

"We have to check," says Pace.

Aura nods as she holds her nose. "Agreed. But can we do it quickly?"

"Come on." Pace has already taken a few steps up the staircase. "I need your light."

Aura follows, knowing Hayze won't move until she does. She grabs the handrail, quickly deciding that's a bad idea when it wobbles, threatening to give way. They head up to the first floor to find a corridor that goes both left, right, and straight ahead.

"Not this again," Pace groans.

"This way," says Aura, pointing at the carpet that's completely worn away in the path that goes to the left.

"Frenius," says Hayze, using the word he'd invented for being a freaking genius.

Aura shakes her head affectionately, having always enjoyed the way he creates words. Even when he thought he was Pace this habit had stayed with him it was so deeply entrenched.

They follow the passageway to another set of double doors, these ones made from metal with a cloudy window at eye-level in each one.

Again, Pace is the first to push his way through, his determination to find Tempo renewing the energy in each of his steps.

"What is this place?" He blinks at the desk in front of them. There's another long corridor behind it with multiple doors feeding off both to the left and right. Dim lights flicker from the ceiling and Hayze lets the flame in his palm extinguish.

"It's a hospital," says Aura.

"How do you know what a hospital looks like?" Pace raises one eyebrow.

She indicates a sign above the desk that reads *Hospital.*

"Told you she's a frenius," says Hayze.

"If you only need to be able to read a sign to reach those heights, we're all freniuses," Pace grumbles. "Especially Atmos."

This makes Hayze laugh and he slaps Pace on the back. "You know, I kinda miss that guy."

Pace groans. "You couldn't possibly. I had a wart once that I miss more than him."

Shaking her head, Aura moves behind the desk and slides open the top drawer. "Let's see what we can find here before we go searching."

Pace turns to her abruptly, all thoughts of Atmos vanishing

to the very Quadrant his nemesis is from. "I'll go for a quick search while you're doing that."

"No." Hayze steps in Pace's path. "We need to stay together."

"Then let's search first," says Pace, trying to push past him. "Tempo could be in there!"

"Fine," Hayze puffs, not seeming to want a fight. "Go. But be fast. And don't do anything stupid."

Pace has gone before he can either agree or disagree with that request. Hayze moves immediately behind the desk, his hands going straight to Aura's waist instead of the drawers they're supposed to be searching.

"Hayze!" She spins around to face him. "We have a job to do."

"I know," he says, leaning forward to kiss her. "But first..."

Aura doesn't resist him. Her body won't let her. She leans so instinctively into Hayze that she knows she couldn't stop herself if she tried.

"I miss you," he says between kisses that are desperately trying to ignite into more.

"I'm right here," she laughs against his warm lips. "And this time, I'm real."

He moans as he deepens his kiss, his tongue searching as his hands trail down the curve of her back. Her own fingertips run to his chest as she aches to undo his leather vest and throw it far away, never to be seen again.

"You're too real," he says, pulling back. "As soon as we're alone properly, you're in so much trouble."

She laughs, hoping that's going to be sooner rather than later. "Something to look forward to. Because, you know, you're really *hot*, Fire Boy."

He shakes his head as he groans. "I'm the one who makes the bad jokes around here."

"Actually, that's me," says Pace, returning down the corridor.

Aura and Hayze glance at each other, glad their friend hadn't returned a minute earlier. The last thing his broken heart needs is to witness a passionate moment between the two of them.

"Any luck?" Hayze asks him.

"Obviously not." Pace rolls his eyes. "Or I wouldn't be back here looking at you two, pretending you weren't just sucking each other's faces."

Aura pokes out her tongue while Hayze gives Pace a playful tackle.

"Find anything yet?" Pace asks, shaking himself free of Hayze.

Aura quickly opens another drawer, pulling out a leather-bound book. Unlike everything else behind this desk, it's not covered in a thick layer of dust. Flicking it open, she frowns as she sees what's written on the first page in decorative text:

Elemental Games

"Found something," she whispers, turning another page.

"What is it?" Pace and Hayze quickly come to lean over her shoulders so they can see.

"First Elemental Games," she reads, pointing to the top of the page. Underneath the curly script is a list of eight names:

Fire Quadrant — Enya—Day 1
Fire Quadrant —Leo—Day 1
Water Quadrant—Nile—Day 1
Water Quadrant—Brooke—Day 1
Earth Quadrant—Eve—Day 1
Earth Quadrant—Stone—Day 1
Air Quadrant—Sora—Day 1
Air Quadrant—Jonah—Day 1

"What the fractal is that?" asks Hayze.

"You mean, *who* the fractal," Pace points out. "I've never heard of Nile or Brooke. You know Enya or Leo?"

Aura shakes her head as she turns another page.

Second Elemental Games:
Fire Quadrant —Soleil—Day 1
Fire Quadrant —Elio—Day 1
Water Quadrant—Cosima—Day 1
Water Quadrant—Sage—Day 1
Earth Quadrant—Elowen—Day 1
Earth Quadrant—Clay—Day 2
Air Quadrant—Hudson—Day 1
Air Quadrant—Delta—Day 1

"There were more than one Games," growls Hayze. "Just how long has this been going on?"

"And what's with the days?" Pace asks, pointing at Clay's name with the *Day 2* beside it. "What did Clay do that was so special?"

"Probably lived an extra day than everyone else," says Aura, feeling ill as she continues flicking the pages.

"I thought you said they don't want to kill us," Pace points out. "That they've invested too much into us to wipe us away."

"Yeah..." says Aura, not feeling so sure about that now that there's evidence to the contrary sitting right in front of them. She continues to turn the pages, unable to believe just how many entries there are.

"Hold on," says Hayze when Aura gets to the forty-first Games. "Look at that name. *Paloma.* Wasn't there a girl with that name who went missing from our village years ago?"

Aura gasps. "You're right. There was. She was older than us."

"I'm guessing she was exactly eighteen," says Hayze. "And now we know where she went."

Aura stares at Paloma's name with *Day 6* scrawled beside it. As she turned the pages, the numbers increased but never beyond double digits. It seems the earlier iterations of the Games were even more deadly than the ones they faced themselves.

She reaches the final page that's been filled out, her stomach contracting to see a very familiar list:

Fiftieth Elemental Games:
Fire Quadrant—Hayze
Fire Quadrant—Aura
Water Quadrant—Tempo
Water Quadrant—Pace
Earth Quadrant—Jewel
Earth Quadrant—Geo
Air Quadrant—Atmos
Air Quadrant—Skylus

The three of them stand in silence, staring at the list that means so much more than just a collection of names.

"We don't have days recorded," says Pace. "Why not?"

"Because we're not dead?" Aura shrugs.

"I knew Tempo was alive," Pace nods. "I can feel her in my heart."

"They might not have filled it out yet," says Hayze. "It's dangerous to assume anything."

"It's also dangerous to lose hope," Aura says quietly.

Hayze drops his hand to her back and nods. "That's true."

"But she's not here," Pace groans, glancing down the corridor. "I already looked."

"She has to be here somewhere." Aura points at the book.

"Why else would they keep the record of our deaths in this very drawer? We're just not looking in the right place."

Pace pulls back his shoulders and nods. "Come on, frenius. You lead the way this time."

Aura rolls her eyes, feeling the pressure behind his words, even if they were spoken in jest. She looks to the floor, noticing how frayed the carpet is in all directions. That will be of no help. This time, she needs to listen to her gut. Either that or check every possible option in this decaying excuse of a hospital.

"Tempo," she murmurs, as she runs down the corridor. "Hold on. We're coming."

FIVE

HAYZE

Hayze breaks into a run, following Aura just as a crack of thunder rumbles through the building. It has him instinctively ducking but not slowing.

Finding Tempo is their focus.

They've just reached the stairs when Hayze registers a sign.

In case of storm, enact basement protocol.

He glances at Aura, seeing she's read it too. As if to emphasize the point, a flash of lightning blasts the stairs in radiant white. Another roll of thunder ripples through the building. Hayze and Aura instinctively step away from the cracked glass that used to be the window along the left side of the stairs.

"I suspect that's why they have a basement protocol," Hayze mutters.

A gust of wind rattles the glass shards as a spray of water slips through, hitting them like needles of ice.

Pace stops beside them, barely seeming to notice. "Tempo's probably in the basement. It's the safest place in this crumbling box."

He doesn't bother waiting, streaking past, his usual impatience meaning he takes the stairs two at a time as he heads down. Hayze and Aura follow, both flaring a flame in their hands as their footsteps are muted by the damp air. The smell of mold and decay is almost overwhelming.

They've just caught up to Pace when he rears back. "It's flooded," he gasps, the sound of splashing water bouncing off the walls.

Hayze lifts his flame and sees a pool of water stretching out. The stairs descend into blackness, the green slime coating their surface suggesting they've been underwater for quite some time.

Aura squats down as she tries to peer ahead. "It looks like the water's swallowed the whole of the Sect's foundation."

Hayze can't help but glance up. The entire building has been undermined. He tenses, feeling like they're surrounded by Mother Nature's fury. "All that's left is to go up," he says grimly.

And defy the warnings to find somewhere enclosed and safe during a storm.

"Tempo's here," Pace states flatly. "I can feel it."

He darts back up the stairs and Hayze and Aura follow. There's only one way to find out if he's right.

They pass the first floor with the disturbing evidence that the Elemental Games have been going on for far longer than Hayze has considered. Other teens, forty-nine batches of eight, have endured this before.

And none of them survived.

They reach the second floor and are greeted with another area similar to the one they just left—a corridor that goes left, right, and straight ahead.

"We split up and search," Pace says, turning right and disappearing into the gloom.

It's an unspoken agreement that Hayze and Aura stick

together. They take it in turns to open the endless doors down the corridors as they keep alert, finding each room the same, containing nothing but rusted beds and mold.

They return to the stairs. The window is boarded up, but the lightning show beyond the weathered wood is unmistakable. The blazes of light, the rumbling thunder that vibrates the very air, the faint metallic tang that sticks to Hayze's tongue.

He tucks Aura in close. "Mother Nature figured she'd flood us from above as well as below."

She sighs, giving him a quick squeeze. "The virtual reality Sect was almost safer," she says wryly.

Hayze can't help but chuckle. He runs his hand up her spine and slips it over her shoulder, conscious their fiery kiss from minutes ago still heats his blood. This isn't the moment to be thinking of the chemistry the Games seems to have amplified, possibly because they've walked on a knife edge between life and death since they started. But he still does.

They've almost lost each other more times than should ever be branded into a person's memory. Hate, lies, secrets, and the very Elements have tried to come between them.

And love triumphed each and every time.

It would be nice to have a moment to appreciate that.

Pace appears, panting. "Nothing."

"We didn't find anything, either," Aura says.

"Then we keep going," Pace says grimly, walking past them and ascending the stairs to the next floor.

Hayze and Aura follow, staying close to the wall as the storm rages outside. With each violent gust of wind, each blinding streak of lightning, each furious explosion of thunder, the walls seem a little thinner. The foundations a little more unstable.

Yet they repeat the process on the next level. They split up and navigate the corridors. They open door after door.

The third floor is empty.

So is the fourth.

And the fifth.

"Next one," Pace pants as he heads for the stairs.

Hayze doesn't point out they're running out of floors. After this one, there will be nowhere else to go.

This flight has a window that's half glass, half boarded slats. They're part way up the stairs when lightning cracks, then cracks again. And again. A wall of wind and water hits the side of the hospital with a tsunami of force. The window implodes, shards of glass and wood spraying the stairwell.

Pace ducks, covering his head. Aura screams as she and Hayze curl around each other. He spins them so she's pressed against the wall, biting back a cry of his own as something impales his shoulder.

"Come on!" Pace shouts, breaking into a run as the gust dies down.

Hayze and Aura follow, conscious they need to be as far from the window as possible. They take the stairs two at a time, bursting onto the top floor a moment later. They keep running, barely aware of their surroundings as they move away from the walls that no longer feel like they can protect them.

As they slow and then come to a stop, as the adrenaline fades, two things assault Hayze. The realization that this floor is a wide expanse of nothing.

And pain.

Sharp and lancing, it has him gritting his teeth. He reaches back, grimacing when his fingers come back coated in blood.

"Hayze, you're hurt!" Aura cries.

She rushes to look at his shoulder as Hayze glances over. A

shard of glass protrudes from where his arm meets his shoulder, catching the flashes of lightning that haven't abated.

Aura's hands flutter over it. "It needs to come out."

Hayze tenses, then instinctively groans. He locks his knees as the pain of the small movement threatens to take him down.

"We need to take care of this," Aura says, glancing around.

Except the first realization returns, just as undeniable as the pain—this floor is empty of anything.

It stretches out, free of walls or furniture or giving a damnatus what that means for the three teens now standing here.

Pace strides forward, stops, then turns. "It can't be empty!"

There's no need to point out that's exactly what it is. Tempo isn't here.

Pace spears his fingers through his hair, gripping it. "She has to be here!" he shouts.

Aura frowns. "We need to go back down. See if we can find some bandages."

Hayze reaches over and his fingers brush the shard of glass. "I've got it."

He pinches it and pulls. The only thing that comes out is a garbled groan of agony.

Aura places her fingertips over his, then gently pulls his hand away. "This is real, now. We have to be careful."

"I'm still going to pretend it's fake," Hayze says, trying to grin. "It's not like I've been shot in the leg multiple times."

"You weren't," Aura points out, even as she almost smiles back. She sobers as her blue eyes settle on his face. "I'm going to have to take it out."

Hayze's mouth twists. "I thought you might say that."

Outside, the storm batters the building. The lightning is so frequent, Hayze no longer needs to light the room with his fire.

The garish walls flare with neon light bright enough to make them squint.

He draws in a breath that shudders more than he'd like, then locks every joint. "Do it."

He's barely finished the monosyllabic words when Aura moves. With a short, swift jerk, she yanks out the shard of glass. Hayze's back arches as his shoulder spasms and his mind rebels. Agony tears at him, ricocheting down his arm, through his gut, wiping his mind of everything but pain.

"I'm sorry," Aura whispers.

He shakes his head. "You didn't—"

White hot pain flashes at the site of the wound, and Hayze bites back a scream with sheer force of will. He folds over as his hand instinctively reaches for the point where the agony is pulsing as if it's alive.

His fingers don't brush shredded flesh. They touch puckered, dry skin. Hayze blinks in astonishment.

Aura cauterized the wound.

He turns to find her eyes are big in her pale face. "I..."

Hayze straightens, conscious this hurt her almost as much as it did him. "I know. You had to." He takes a step toward her when something crunches under foot. He glances down, registering the shard she pulled out.

Scowling at the blood-streaked glass, he kicks it. The shard skitters across the floor, illuminated by the lightning that's only intensifying. It spins toward the opposite wall.

Then slips right through it.

Hayze, Aura, and Pace freeze. They stare at the wall that looks solid yet has no substance.

"No," Pace groans. "We can't *still* be in the Games."

A sick, black feeling spreads in Hayze's gut. He fingers the cauterized wound, blinking at the pain that he's now second-guessing. Surely not...

"No," Aura spits. "I'm not doing this again."

She strides forward and Hayze rushes to join her. But then she's running, the lightning illuminating her as she doesn't hesitate when she reaches the wall.

And disappears.

"Aura!" Hayze cries, finding Pace beside him as he also bursts through whatever the fractal is posing as a wall.

They find Aura just on the other side, as if she stopped in her tracks. Which is exactly what Hayze and Pace do.

They stand side by side, realizing this world isn't an illusion. But the wall is.

So it could hide what's on the other side.

"Tempo!" Pace gasps, rushing forward. He passes seven metal-framed beds before reaching the one she's lying on and falls to his knees. "Tempo," he whispers.

Hayze and Aura follow, standing behind him as he gently takes her hand. She's even more pale than she was in the Games. Her lips are almost gray, her freckles little more than a patchwork of faded dusk.

Pace reaches up, hesitates, then brushes her cheek. "It's me, Pace," he murmurs, the false reality they've already been through possibly replaying in his mind. The one where Tempo not only can't forgive him but dies. "We have to get out of here, Tempo. You need to wake up."

Tempo doesn't respond.

"Tempo, baby, please wake up," Pace pleads. "We need to make this right."

Hayze wonders if he's talking about the Games or their past. Probably both.

Tempo doesn't move. Barely breathes. As if each one is a little less than the previous...

Aura slips her hand into Hayze's and he squeezes, glancing at what else they found. There are seven other beds lined up beside Tempo. Hayze knows in his bones that each group of eight teens once lay here. Their names are branded in his mind.

Enya, Leo, Nile, Brooke, Eve, Stone, Sora, Jonah.

Soleil, Elio, Cosima, Sage, Elowen, Clay, Hudson, Delta.

These beds were waiting.

But for what?

"Tempo, please!" Pace cries, now gripping her shoulders. "You're not dead! Don't let them take you!"

He lifts her a little and her head flops back, her body as lifeless as her responses.

Pace looks up at Hayze and Aura. "We have to go back in." He says the words as a statement, but the tremor of desperation, the hint of begging, show he knows he can't do this alone. "We need to talk to her!"

Hayze glances at Aura, who nods. They can't reach Tempo. She's locked in a reality they can't access. One where she's dead.

But this is bigger than that. The Elements will have to work together if they're going to survive this, let alone win.

Hayze repeats Pace's words, even as he can't quite believe he's saying them. "We have to go back in."

CHAPTER
SIX
AURA

Aura runs beside Hayze as they chase after Pace, who's cradling Tempo's unconscious body against his chest. He leads them out of the decrepit building and through the hole they blasted in the wall surrounding the Sect.

"We're back in Terra," Pace puffs, seeming surprised to find the world exactly the way they left it. Ancient trees stretch across the horizon and Aura feels a pull, knowing Jewel is hidden out there somewhere in a pod.

"We'll get to Jewel as soon as we can," Hayze whispers, knowing Aura almost as well as she knows herself.

She nods, sending a silent promise to the trees. As soon as Tempo's safe, they'll go to Jewel. And Geo if he's still alive. Then they'll find Skylus and Atmos. Nobody survived the previous Elemental Games, but this time things will be different. They'll all make it if they can.

Pace looks down at Tempo's gray complexion, his own face turning pale. Tempo's only just hanging onto life. If they can get her into virtual reality, they can explain to her what's going on. Only then does her body have a chance. If her mind is strong, then her body will follow.

"Come on!" Pace runs to the door they used when they exited the virtual Sect. With any luck, that will also be exactly the way they left it.

Aura and Hayze are right behind him and they crowd into the small room they now know connects them to the virtual world, ignoring the fact it also connects them to something else.

Danger.

But Tempo is worth the risk.

A blinding white light steals Aura's vision. It doesn't matter how many times she gets put into a virtual reality world, she's never going to get used to that.

"Put me down!" Tempo shouts, squirming in Pace's arms. "Like, now!"

Aura blinks as her vision returns and sees Pace set Tempo down, only for her to run immediately over to Aura, using her as a human shield.

Pace's hands fly to the air with his palms exposed. "I would never hurt you."

"Keep away from me." Tempo glares at Pace, making his nightmare come true. He shrinks back against the wall, his expression just as broken as his heart.

Aura reaches out a hand and touches Tempo's pink cheek. She looks impossibly healthy, which unfortunately, is because it's not really her. "Welcome back."

"Welcome back where?" Tempo clutches the sides of her head. "What's going on? Why did I think I was from Fire? Why did I think I was in love with *him?*"

"Because you are," says Hayze somewhat defensively. "You just don't realize it yet."

Tempo crosses her arms, a permanent frown etched on her forehead. "Hard to realize what isn't true."

They step into the Earth chamber, which shows no sign of the battle that took place when they passed through here last time.

"You two walk ahead," Aura says, giving Hayze a gentle push. "I need a minute with Tempo."

Hayze seems hesitant but takes a step beneath the giant trees and monolithic stones, bringing a forlorn Pace with him. They all know Aura's the only one Tempo will listen to. They keep a short distance ahead, just enough space to give them the privacy they need but close enough if anything unexpected should happen.

Aura takes a deep breath, knowing it's an impossible task to fill Tempo in on everything that's happened in the short space of time it will take to pass through the Earth chamber. "Are you listening?"

Tempo nods, looping her hand in Aura's arm as they walk.

"So, everything I'm about to say is going to sound crazy, but I swear every word of it's true." Aura puts a hand on her heart. "I need you to listen and ask questions at the end. Got it?"

Tempo nods again, her eyes narrowed as she turns to study Aura's face.

"When you were a baby, your parents made a deal with the leaders. You were given life in exchange for them having access to you on your eighteenth birthday. There were two of us taken from each Quadrant and we were the fiftieth lot of teens for this to happen to. Every other set of eight has died. They infused us with powers and we were put into a virtual world to harness them. But this time was different. The leaders messed with the system to see if we could harness more than one power. You were given my memories. I was given yours. Same with Hayze and Pace. But now you know who you really are, right?"

"I'm Tempo from Water." Tempo pulls back her shoulders. "Daughter of Marina and Bayou."

Aura smiles. "And you remember being in the Games? You were crushed by a pile of rocks."

"Of course," Tempo says on a shudder.

"Good." Aura touches her hand. "So, when you died in the Games, your mind thought you were really dead, and your body started to give up in the real world. Pace insisted we find you. He loves you."

Tempo grimaces. "He doesn't love me."

"He does." Aura tightens her grip on Tempo, willing her to listen. "His parents wronged your parents, but his love for you is true. If it weren't for his persistence to save you, we'd never have found you."

"Are we in the Sect?" Tempo asks, steering the conversation away from Pace as she glances at the enormous boulder they're passing.

"No." Aura shakes her head. "This is a virtual simulation of the Sect. We're not real. We found you in the real Sect and brought you here so we could talk to you."

"You put me back in?" Tempo's eyes flare. "How could you—"

"If we didn't, you'd be dead by now," Aura snaps. "For real this time."

"Where are the others?" Tempo asks. "Why is it just the four of us?"

"They're in their capitals in pods, hooked into the Games," says Aura. "Which we think we ended, but it's hard to know for sure. Now that we have you, it's time to get them out."

"You're right." Tempo narrows her eyes. "This does sound crazy."

"How else do you explain knowing every single thing about me?" Aura asks. "Including the fight I had with Hayze the night before we turned eighteen. And you forgave Pace for that when you thought it was him. That's how I know you love him."

"Going by that reasoning, I actually love Hayze," says Tempo, back to her feisty self.

"Hold out your hands," says Aura, remembering how Hayze had convinced her he was telling the truth when he returned to the Games. "Make a cup with them."

Tempo humors her, doing as she's told. "Now what?"

"Fill them with water," says Aura, bringing up her own hand and sparking a flame.

"How did you do that?" Tempo's eyes are wide.

"The same way you can." Aura points at Tempo's cupped hands. "Go on."

Tempo stares at her hands and slowly but surely they fill with water. She gets such a surprise that her hands spring back and the water splashes on the floor.

"You're more powerful than you think," says Aura, smiling widely. "You should see some of the incredible things Pace has manifested now that he knows what his true Element is."

"His parents wronged my parents," Tempo says, her expression hardening. "Do you know what happened? Has he told you?"

Aura remembers being in the Games and not being certain what transpired all those years ago. That's the place Tempo's still at. She nods, biting down on her lip as she finds the words.

"Pace's parents stole from yours," she says. "They took the edrian the leaders gave your parents in exchange for having access to you. It was half the cost of entry to a life in Aqua."

Tempo glowers. "How could—"

"They wanted a better life for Pace," says Aura. "It doesn't make it right, but they were desperate. And that decision had nothing to do with Pace. He's been trying to make things right. And his father has helped us several times, saving our lives in ways he'd never have been able to if he hadn't been a trade master."

"I don't love him, Aura," says Tempo. "I can see you want me to, but I don't. Now I understand why I felt so much rage toward him even when I thought he was the love of my life."

"Give it time," says Aura. "If anyone knows how you feel, it's me. Don't forget when I woke up on the raft, I felt exactly like you are now. And Hayze won me over eventually."

Tempo nods. "That doesn't mean the same will happen with me."

Hayze and Pace reach the door to the small room that moves between floors, and the doors open.

"Come on," says Hayze. "We'll show Tempo where we found her."

Aura and Tempo follow them inside.

"Hey, look." Hayze points to a tiny sign above the buttons. "*Lift.* I think this thing's called a lift."

"Appropriately named," says Aura as the small room jerks into motion, causing her stomach to lurch. They travel upward and Aura presses herself to Hayze's side, as Tempo avoids Pace's gaze.

The doors spring open and Aura peers out to see they've arrived on one of the empty floors, which is nothing but a wide expanse with a dark corridor feeding onto it.

They step out and Pace puts a hopeful hand on Tempo's back, his face lined with hope. She immediately brushes him away.

"Give her time," says Aura. "I've explained what I could."

"I love you, Tempo," he says. "Even if you don't love me. I love you."

Tempo rolls her eyes. "Yeah, Aura covered that bit."

Aura tries to remember if she was ever that awful to Hayze. She definitely remembers rolling her eyes a few times on the raft.

"What do we do now?" Aura asks. "Do we go back to reality and see if Tempo's strong enough to make it?"

"We need to give her enough time," says Pace, blocking their path to the lift. "To make sure she's really strong."

Aura knows he's buying time in the hope Tempo will return just a little of his affection. Which is not going to happen anytime soon. They can't wait forever while Jewel and the others are in danger.

"We have to keep moving, Pace," says Hayze. "There's nothing for us here."

"Aura! Aura!" comes a familiar voice, followed by fast footsteps.

She spins around to see Jewel running to her with her arms outstretched.

Even though Aura knows Jewel isn't real—that she herself isn't real—she opens her arms wide and catches her friend in a warm embrace.

"Is it really you, Jewel?" she asks, pulling back to look at Jewel's sweet face. "Or are you another NPC?"

"A what?" Jewel furrows her brow. "It's me. I was in the Games with Atmos and Skylus. We were trapped in darkness for eternity. Then suddenly we were here in the Sect. I'm so happy to see you."

"Me, too." Aura's eyes prick with tears of happiness and surprise. She never thought she was going to experience this moment.

"Oh great, they're here too," mumbles Pace as Atmos and Skylus appear from around a corner. "If it's really them."

"It's really us, Pace," says Jewel, letting go of Aura.

"I think she's telling the truth." Hayze gives Jewel a quick hug. "When we ended the Games, they were sent here. There was nowhere else for their minds to go."

Skylus lifts from the floor and flies the final couple of yards, landing in front of them with a smug look while Atmos scurries to catch up.

"Tempo!" she says. "What are you doing here?"

"What are any of them doing here?" says Atmos, eyeing off Pace.

"Don't worry," says Pace. "I'm not exactly thrilled to see you either."

"They came to get me," says Tempo. "From the real world. Then we came back here because apparently I was about to die."

"You *were* about to die," says Aura. "You still might. Hopefully your mind is strong enough to help you cope when we get you out."

"Can you get us all out?" Atmos asks eagerly. "I really want to get home."

"I'm actually quite happy here," says Skylus, lifting from the floor again and doing a spin.

"Don't worry," says Hayze. "You'll still be able to do that when you get out."

"Well?" Atmos pushes. "Can you get us out?"

"Sure," says Aura, relieved that rescuing them has turned out to be so much easier than she thought it would be.

"Ah, no," says Pace. "It's not that simple."

"Typical." Atmos glares at his nemesis. "You just don't want to get us out."

"No, he's right," says Hayze. "Our real selves will be in the small room where we transitioned into this world before we came up here in the lift. You're back in a pod in your Quadrant somewhere. We have to get you out of there first before you can join us."

Aura groans, realizing he's right. She'd been so excited to see Jewel, she hadn't stopped to think it through.

"What's a lift?" Jewel asks.

"It's those small rooms that take us up and down levels," says Skylus, shaking her head as if Jewel is frustratingly stupid. "Honestly, everyone knows that."

"How did you know that?" Jewel cocks her brows.

"She looked at the sign," says Atmos.

"Your specialty," Pace chuckles, sending them all into fits.

Aura lets out a breath and slips her arm around Jewel, pleased to have any version of her friend back.

Her arm hovers in the air as she finds herself holding onto nothing but thin air.

"Where did she go?" Aura steps back, her jaw falling to see Jewel has disappeared.

"You mean *they*," says Hayze, pointing to where Atmos and Skylus were standing only moments ago.

"We have them now," comes a familiar voice that sends a shiver down Aura's spine.

"Rateen," she growls as she turns to see if she's right.

"Where are they?" Hayze asks, marching toward the old woman in the long black robes who's just emerged from the corridor.

"Careful, Hayze," Aura warns as Pace steps protectively in front of Tempo.

"I think we're pretty safe," Tempo says, confused. "She's about a hundred."

"Looks can be deceiving." Aura also steps in front of Tempo. The only way to fight Rateen is with their powers. And Tempo's are far too undeveloped right now to be of much use.

"Where are they?" Hayze asks again, holding his palms in front of his chest, ready to strike. "What did you do with Jewel, Skylus, and Atmos?"

"We have them now." Rateen smiles. "There's no point looking for them."

"We will always look for them," Hayze sneers, sending out a flame.

"Hayze!" Tempo gasps as the fireball hurtles toward Rateen.

But Rateen predicts exactly what Hayze was going to do. She leaps at the wall beside her, her feet running up the smooth surface like gravity's a concept that doesn't exist. She uses her momentum to throw herself backward, bending herself into a ball and executing a triple backflip, landing in a squat at Hayze's feet. Her bony hands dart out, swiping the floor and sending Hayze crashing down.

But Rateen isn't the only one to predict her opponent's move. Before she can pin him down, Hayze sends out an even bigger blast of fire that burns bright blue. The intensity of the heat sends Pace and Tempo scurrying backward while Aura marches forward, knowing fire can't possibly hurt her.

The flame clears, revealing Hayze on his knees, his hands outstretched and a pile of steaming ash in front of him. Aura throws herself at him, wrapping her arms around him as he holds her tight.

"What in the sweet world of Eterna was that?" Tempo gasps. "Did she just—"

"She did," says Pace. "But don't worry. She's not real."

"But *I* am," comes Rateen's voice as another version of the old woman walks out from the corridor.

Tempo lets out a shriek. "What the—"

"You're not real!" Hayze shouts, leaping to his feet.

Aura gets up and stands beside him, ready for whatever this virtual monster wants to throw at them.

Rateen opens her mouth to speak, but before she can get a single word out, both Aura and Hayze let fireballs loose. The hungry flames consume the old woman and she stumbles forward, reaching out to grab hold of them.

"Run!" shouts Pace. "Come on!"

Hayze and Aura link hands and run to the lift. Tempo and Pace are already inside and they reach out, hauling them inside.

Pace dives for the buttons and presses them frantically, trying to close the doors as the fireball that is Rateen continues to stumble toward them.

An alarm sounds and the panel of buttons lights up as they flash in turn.

"It's jammed!" cries Pace.

"*You* jammed it," huffs Tempo.

Aura and Hayze guard the door, ready to scorch Rateen again if needed. But it seems their powers won't be called on this time. Rateen crumples to the floor in front of them and the flames die down, leaving nothing but a pile of charred bones and cloth.

"That was lucky," says Aura, drawing in a deep breath as she tries to slow the racing of her heart.

"Not really," says Hayze, pointing.

Aura lifts her face to see something even worse than a new Rateen entering the room.

It's dozens of Rateens.

All of them running.

All of them furious.

And every single one of them deadly.

SEVEN

HAYZE

"Pace!" Hayze shouts, keeping his hands extended.

"I'm working on it!"

Hayze releases a blast as the wave of Rateens comes at them. The black-robed bodies divide, swarming up the walls like an army of ants. The fireball hits the opposite wall and is instantly absorbed.

The Rateens converge again, their duplicate faces twisted with the same fury. Even their black robes flutter in exactly the same way. It's like watching a refraction of the same violent rage approach. At speed.

"She's not real," Aura mutters beside Hayze.

Right before she unleashes a stream of fire. The roar of red arcs out, then across like a scythe intent on mowing the Rateens down. They divide once more, running over the walls and up to the ceiling, now far more like a swarm of spiders. Aura cuts off the flames with a cry of frustration and the Rateens tumble down, black robes flapping in disturbing synchronicity. They rush the lift, exposing their teeth in a snarl that's multiplied dozens of times over.

"Got it!" Pace cries.

A hand grabs Hayze by the back of his suit and hauls. He and Aura stumble backward as the doors slide shut. Hayze's breath of relief disintegrates as clawed fingers jam through the last inch, stopping them from closing completely. In a blink, more fingers wriggle through from multiple hands, clamping around the door.

"They'll open it again!" Aura gasps.

Pace jostles between her and Hayze. In one swift movement, he runs his hand down the twitching fingers. Each one turns black. Then white.

Then falls off.

The doors click shut and the lift drops. The collective screams that pierce the air screech over Hayze's nerves. He has to remind himself it's not real. There was no woman who could just lose her fingers to frostbite, let alone a hundred of them.

"You did that?" Tempo gasps.

Hayze turns around to find her leaning against the back wall, pale and wide eyed as she looks at Pace.

He hunches his shoulders. "They're not real. They can't die or feel pain."

Tempo shakes her head. "That's...impressive."

Hayze looks away as he suppresses a smile. Tempo is awed, not disgusted. And Pace just grew an inch.

Aura turns, preparing herself for when the lift stops. "The leaders aren't going to just let us go."

Hayze realizes she's right. They have no idea what will be waiting for them once they step out into Terra.

Apart from a capital none of them are familiar with.

Tempo groans, then starts sliding down the wall of the lift. Pace quickly slips under her arm and stops her from crumbling. She scowls at him, looks like she's going to push him away, but then sags, too weak to do much else. They reach the

Earth chamber and Pace supports her as they run past the monoliths and into the next doors. Cramming in, Hayze squeezes his eyes shut. White blinding light envelops the small space.

The doors open.

And Hayze unleashes a wall of fire.

The guards that were waiting for them cry out and retreat. "Come on," Hayze shouts, grabbing Aura's hand and running along the wall of the Sect.

Pace half carries, half drags Tempo behind them. Hayze keeps up the wall of fire between them and the guards as they run. They reach the first of the towering trees nearby and duck behind it.

"Hayze!" Aura cries, pointing.

He registers that the flames are leaping into the canopy above them. His eyes widen. Terra is built of these massive, twisted trees. He could've just started an inferno.

A targeted blast from Pace and the fledgling forest fire is extinguished. Tempo blinks as she leans against him, once again looking impressed.

"This way!" shout the guards.

"We have to keep moving!" Aura gasps, glancing one way then the other.

There's no time to decide whether there's a better direction to run, because an ominous whirring Hayze had hoped he'd never hear again fills the air.

"Drones!" Pace cries.

"Drones?" Tempo echoes incredulously.

The black machines swarm above, sending Hayze's heart shooting up his throat. This is real. The guards. The guns. The drones with their electric nets.

The possibility of being captured.

Or worse.

They collectively break into a run in the only direction that's possible—further into Terra. A drone swoops down, weaving through branches, its whirring coming closer and closer. Hayze spins to shoot it down but Pace beats him to it. A bolt of ice slices through the drone, sending a piece into an adjacent one. They both drop from the sky.

"Run!" Pace gasps.

Beside him, Tempo stumbles. "I...can't."

Wordlessly, Pace scoops her up and continues on. Hayze and Aura flank him, becoming their protection. Running blindly, they weave through the gnarled, twisted trunks that are as wide as the bunker Hayze grew up in. Some have roots that wind out and around, creating hollows, dividing into arches, even forming bridges between trees.

"If they don't yield, then shoot to kill!" shouts a guard.

The words send panic through Hayze's veins in the same way they shoot bile up his throat. Because if they die, then another batch of teens will be put through the Games in a never-ending search for Elemental powers.

They round a bend and discover a group of people, all wearing the brown strips of the Earth Quadrant. Eyes widen when they see Hayze and Aura in their red leather, and Pace and Tempo in their blue Water suits.

"Help!" Tempo cries weakly. "We need help!"

A gunshot ricochets off the trunk behind them, followed by the whirring of the drones. Screams erupt as people scatter. Mothers draw their children close and fathers shout in alarm. Hayze realizes the trunks are houses as the people of Terra disappear inside, slamming doors and pulling down thick, leafy vines over windows. No one is willing to help the strange-looking teens running for their lives.

"Keep moving," Hayze says through panting breaths, even

as he wonders where to. They have no idea where they are, let alone where the rebel tunnels could be.

He sees a narrow opening between two homes and takes a sharp left. The others follow, finding themselves in an alley of Terra. One that's a dead end. The trunk of what must be the biggest tree they've seen yet stretches out for several feet on either side, winding roots and thick vegetation framing it.

Hayze spins around, realizing he's taken them the wrong way, except a contingent of guards runs past the gap they just disappeared down. Aura yanks him back and the four teens move further in, seeking the safety of the shadows.

Pace is breathing hard as he leans against a root. "I...can... blast...them."

Hayze doesn't bother to glance down at his friend's hands. The ones busy holding Tempo. But he does glance at his own. The ones that can wield Fire. In Terra, they're deadly to every life within the capital's walls. He and Aura can't afford to use their powers. It's too dangerous.

"They must be down here!" a guard shouts.

The four teens tense, realizing they've been found. They're about to be surrounded by guards with guns and drones with nets.

They're trapped.

Hayze moves in front of Pace and Tempo even as he knows he won't use his powers. Killing in the Games is one thing. But risking homes and threatening the innocent isn't something he can do in real life.

Except he can fight. Maybe find a way for them to get away.

"We fight together," Aura says quietly, her voice hard as she stands beside him.

Hayze's gut tightens painfully. She knows what he was thinking. And she just made a promise to do exactly the same thing—escape.

Or die trying.

There's a creaking behind them and they spin, Hayze's hands instinctively rising. A woman scowls at them from a door that's opened in the large trunk. "Get inside. And hurry."

They hesitate for the briefest second. Long enough to consider this may be a trap, followed by the realization they have no other choice.

"Go," Hayze says, giving Pace a gentle shove. The woman steps back as he carries Tempo inside, Hayze and Aura right behind.

The door shuts with a click that Hayze feels in his bones. He spins to face the woman, taking in her intricate straps and a headdress of woven leaves and flowers. The cloth is more intricate than Jewel wore, which suggests this woman is wealthy. The question is, why has she helped them?

Pace is just lowering Tempo when the sounds of clattering boots have everyone stilling. They fill the area outside the tree home, followed by the faint whirring of drones. Hayze's pounding pulse jerks with each stomp and swoop.

Everyone inside the tree holds their breath.

"They can't get away!" a guard shouts. The boots retreat, leaving silence.

And the realization they're safe.

For now.

"Thank you," Hayze says to the woman, not quite letting himself unwind.

"Yes, thank you..." Aura says, looking at her questioningly.

"My name is Calla." She lifts her chin. "And I'm a trade master for Terra."

The tension is back with a flash of adrenaline. Pace scoops Tempo up again, ready to run.

"I know of the Elemental Games," Calla adds. "I know what you've been through. And I'm here to help."

Hayze and Pace glance at each other. Calla's suggesting she's like Tide. An unexpected ally. One stroke of luck is something he can believe. But two?

"Help how?" Aura asks, still tight with tension.

Calla glances at the door. "You need somewhere to hide." She glances at the interior of the tree they're in. "I have somewhere you can do that."

Hayze scans the room they're in for the first time. Large and domed, the floors are covered in mats woven from reeds, the single window has leafy vines over it. A large timber table is to his left with a platter of bread and fruit that has his stomach jolting. When was the last time he ate? Like, really ate, not the sustenance forced into them during the Games? A staircase extends up into the bowels of the trunk to his right, the steps shiny and worn. Everything is smooth wood, curved lines.

It could be a haven. Or a trap.

Calla walks to the table and picks up the platter. "You need food, water, rest." She moves to the staircase, then stops and turns, angling her head in a way that reminds Hayze of Avalan. "Follow me."

Hayze stills, knowing they have a choice to make.

Trust this woman, a trade master of Terra. Someone close to Avalan.

Or face the dangers of Terra.

EIGHT

Aura lies in the darkness, trying her best not to giggle.

"What's wrong?" Hayze asks in a whisper. He's pressed up against her so firmly she can barely tell where he starts and she ends. "Nothing's funny."

"I'm just happy." She puts a hand to her belly, full of bread and fruit that Calla had allowed them to devour. This is what convinced Aura that the Earth's trade master means them no harm. What would be the point in wasting food on someone right before you slaughter them? Besides, they have to stay. Now that Tempo's safe, Jewel is the next priority. And Calla will know where she's hidden. At first light, they'll start their search.

"You're happy?" Hayze's confusion only makes her want to giggle more.

"Yep," she says. "I'm happy. We've eaten. We've washed. We have a soft bed to sleep in and we're wearing clean clothes."

"Ah, you call these clothes?" Hayze shifts his bare leg against Aura's, sending a different kind of happiness pooling in her belly to mingle with the fruit. Calla had given them fresh strips of cloth to sleep in—the same sort worn by Jewel and Geo in the Games. Aura had gratefully accepted, relieved to take a break from her leather vest and trousers for a night.

"This bed is heaven," says Aura. "I wonder how Tempo and Pace are faring?"

Hayze suppresses a chuckle of his own. "I'm sure they're fine."

Calla took them up the narrow staircase and offered them two cubby holes behind doors made from woven reeds. With space enough only for a small bed made from soft ferns, Hayze and Aura were quick to claim a room for themselves. Tempo wasn't as keen on this sleeping arrangement but was too weak to complain, so allowed Pace to place her down on the bed where she immediately turned her back to him and fell into a deep slumber. Calla had retreated to the upper boughs of the treehouse, claiming she wanted to keep guard.

"Do you know what my favorite part of the Games was?" Aura asks.

"Getting out of them?" Hayze guesses.

"No." She puts a hand to his bare chest, enjoying the feel of his skin beneath her palm. "When we were in the Scorchlands, we went into the forest and for one moment we dreamed of being able to stay there forever, trapped in the Games but safe. Together."

"I remember that." He trails his fingertips lightly down her arm. "It feels a little like now."

"Except we're not in the Games." She bites down on her lip, desire swirling inside her. "Which means nobody can see us."

"I wish I could see you." He unties the strip of cloth covering her chest.

"You already know what I look like," she says.

"Not the new Aura," he replies, expertly undoing the cloth that's tied around her waist.

"And who's the new Aura?" she asks, shamelessly fishing for a compliment to further inflate the bubble of happiness she's floating in.

"She's stronger than the old one." Hayze squeezes her bicep teasingly. "More courageous. More powerful." Then he grasps the untied length of cloth at her waist and pulls it free. "Sexier, too."

Aura can't help the smile that spreads across her face. She's been with Hayze in this way before they turned eighteen. But that was two kids sneaking around behind their parents' backs. This time is different. Just like Aura is no longer the person she was before all of this started, neither is Hayze. He's gone from the boy she always loved, to the man she'll never let go of.

She reaches for his waistband and undoes his cloth, her throat dry with anticipation. Licking her lips, she turns to her side and brings her face to his.

"I love you," she whispers.

He answers with a kiss, pressing his mouth to hers and moaning as his lips part and he seeks out her warmth with his tongue.

Aura closes her eyes, finding it hard to believe this is really happening. If someone had told seventeen-year-old Aura that one day she'd be in Terra, naked on a bed, kissing Hayze, she'd have thought they lost their mind.

But here they are. And now she's the one losing her mind. With love. With desire. With pure and hungry lust.

She runs her hand over Hayze's shoulder, trailing her fingertips to his back, then down to her favorite part of him. His butt could win the Elemental Games as a competitor all of its own.

He moans, lighting a desperation inside her to feel more. To make *him* feel more. Her hand moves to his front and she decides his butt will have to settle for second place in her list of favorite parts of Hayze.

But clearly, Hayze has some favorite parts of Aura all of his own and his hands greedily seek out each and every curve as he murmurs his appreciation.

"Aura," he whispers between kisses. "Aura, I love you."

She knows it. She feels it. Everything he's ever done has proved it, including keeping information from her that he was certain would tear her apart.

Feeling a desperate need to take things further, Aura rolls to her back. "I want you."

Hayze moves on top of her in a way that was once familiar but is now deliciously foreign, it's been so long.

And there in the darkness of a treehouse in Terra, they become one.

Aura's happiness soars as every one of her cells lights with pleasure. She claws his back wanting him even closer. He presses down on her and she whimpers, feeling herself unraveling as she wraps her arms and legs around him.

He moves in the way he knows drives her wild until she's forced to press her mouth to his shoulder to muffle her cries. When she can hold it no longer, she lets go, her release spinning her into a tornado of bliss.

Hayze follows, joining her in the storm and together they travel through the sky and back again, riding the waves their passion has sparked. Afterward, they lie perfectly still, eyes closed and panting heavily as they revel in what just took place between them.

"Aura!" Hayze rolls off her so fast it almost hurts, not physically but because she's nowhere near ready to be separated from him. "There's smoke!"

Aura sits up, her eyes wide to see tiny sparks have ignited all over their mattress made from ferns. Hayze immediately throws out his hands, trying to draw out the heat before the sparks become flames and set the entire treehouse alight.

"There are too many," Aura breathes as she gets to work helping extinguish the sparks. But as soon as they manage to sort one out, three more pop up.

There's the thumping of frantic footsteps outside and Pace throws open their door, the dim lighting of the landing filtering in.

"I can smell smoke." Pace's eyes widen to see the mattress in flames and Aura and Hayze's naked state.

"Do something!" says Aura.

Pace's hands fly out, drenching the ferns, along with both Aura and Hayze.

It does the trick and sparks turn to smoke as Aura quickly picks up a loose frond and holds it in front of herself.

"Ah, thanks for that," says Hayze. "You were just in time."

Pace nods toward Hayze's groin and laughs. "Now I can see why Aura was so excited she lit the bed on fire."

Hayze grabs the nearest fern frond and presses it to his middle. "Cut it out, Pace."

"No, seriously," Pace laughs. "That's quite impressive. So was trying to burn down the house of the only person in this capital who's prepared to help us."

"That was me," says Hayze, taking the blame. "I got carried away."

"Yeah, I heard." Pace rolls his eyes. "Talk about rubbing salt in my wounds. Tempo hasn't turned around all night."

Aura feels heat rise to her cheeks to think of what Pace must've heard. And how it made him feel.

"Sorry, Pace," she says. "We're both responsible for what happened. We'll be more careful next time."

"What?" Pace shakes his head, still amused. "Next time you find yourself hiding out in a trade master's tree in a foreign Quadrant?"

Hayze removes his frond to smack Pace with it.

"I surrender!" Pace holds up his hands. "I know where that leaf's been. And the things it's seen. Please! No more."

"Then be serious," says Hayze, putting his frond back in place. "And besides, you're not exactly leaving much to the imagination in that get-up."

Pace looks down at his loin cloth and grins. "Except clearly, Calla didn't need to bother giving me as much fabric as she gave you."

Hayze removes the frond again, just as Calla appears in the doorway with her face scrunched up. With lightning reflexes, Hayze has the frond back in place.

"I smell smoke," says Calla. "What's going on here?"

"We're so sorry," says Aura. "It was an accident."

"An accident that could have cost me my home." Calla narrows her eyes. "And you didn't seem that sorry a moment ago. I heard you laughing."

"They weren't laughing at that," Pace says quickly. "They were laughing at me. They really are very sorry. Hayze had a nightmare and his fire powers sparked in real life. But I managed to put it out."

"So, it really is true." Calla looks at them all in turn. "You've harnessed your powers."

They nod and a feeling of unease winds through Aura's gut. Perhaps they were wrong to come here. The way Calla is looking at them makes her wonder if she's foe rather than friend. Was all the kindness she bestowed on them a ploy to keep them here long enough for the leaders to get here?

"Maybe we should leave?" Aura suggests. "It might be safer."

"Wait?" Pace frowns. "Why?"

But Calla nods. "Maybe you should. I'm not sure I want to risk you burning my house down. This tree has been in my family for generations."

Well, there goes the theory of keeping them here for as long as possible. Unless the leaders have already arrived...

"We need to find our friend," says Hayze. "Jewel. If you tell us where she is, we'll leave immediately."

"You'll leave when I tell you to." Calla crosses her arms. "You have no bargaining power in my home."

Aura bites her tongue, knowing this isn't true. They could set her house on fire, which appears to be Calla's greatest fear. But blackmailing the person who saved them from the guards, fed them and gave them a bed, wouldn't be right.

A banging on the front door echoes up the stairwell, and Aura makes a swipe for her leather trousers and vest. She dresses herself quickly, no longer caring if Pace sneaks a peek. If those are the leaders outside, they're going to need to run for their lives. And she sure as heckus isn't going to do that with nothing but a fern to cover herself.

"Stay here and keep quiet!" Calla scurries down the stairs.

"Get Tempo," Hayze whispers to Pace as he scoops up his own clothes. "And get dressed! Hurry!"

They dress quickly, pausing for the briefest of kisses that somehow still punches desire into Aura's gut. She pulls back, afraid of the consequences as they head out to the landing.

Calla is shouting something at her front door, but her words are too garbled to make out.

"Where's Tempo?" Aura mouths when Pace appears on the landing alone.

"I couldn't wake her," he whispers. "She needs more rest."

"We need to see who's down there," Hayze says in a low voice as he takes a step up the staircase, instead of descending.

"Where are you going?" Pace hisses.

"Calla's lookout," says Aura, having already figured out what Hayze's thinking. It will be the best place to assess what danger they're in before they have to face it. "Wait here."

Hayze is already halfway up the winding staircase, keeping his footsteps light. Aura hurries to catch up, not liking that they're separating from Pace and Tempo but not seeing they have much choice. A loud bang echoes through the staircase that sounds like it's coming from above instead of below, which can't be right. Aura shakes this thought away, telling herself she's just being paranoid.

They emerge through an open hatch onto a platform that stretches between the ancient branches of the tree. Aura looks around, realizing the noise had definitely come from below. There's nobody else out here apart from the bright stars sparkling in the night sky, casting shadows through the leaves. It makes her yearn for home where she'd sneak out of her bunker with Hayze when their parents were fast asleep. They'd lie on their backs in the burned remains of their forest watching for falling stars.

But there's no time for that now. She needs to be grateful for the moment of joy they managed to catch hold of earlier in the night. And hope that one day soon, another moment comes their way.

They crawl across the platform, past a crumpled blanket where Calla had been sleeping and make their way to the edge. Lying flat on their stomachs, they wriggle forward to peer down.

Aura stifles a gasp when she sees who's gathered in the streets.

"It's the Elemental Alliance," whispers Hayze.

And it seems they haven't just knocked on Calla's door.

69

They're knocking on every door they can find, shouting threats and shaking their fists.

"What are they doing?" Aura asks.

"It's Project Eterna," says Hayze, sitting up and shaking his head. "They realized they couldn't access the Sect from underneath, so they're trying a different way."

"What do we do?" Aura pulls herself to her knees, inching closer to Hayze.

He wraps an arm around her, his love her only constant in this ever-changing world.

"We stop them," he says. "Otherwise, we're all going to die."

NINE

HAYZE

"No," Aura breathes, echoing the single word that just detonated in Hayze's mind.

They move simultaneously, dashing back down the stairs. They pass Pace as he hovers beside an exhausted-looking Tempo, then Calla in the main room of the tree house, and burst out the door. They run down to the alley opening where the rebels are running past.

"Hayze!" gasps a voice that has his heart lurching.

He's encased in strong arms a moment later. "Thank blazes you're alright."

Hayze hugs his father back, then presses his cheek to his mother's head as she wraps her arms around both of them. He pulls away, conscious of the crowd that's closing in around them, even though they're all rebels. It seems the people of Terra have tucked themselves inside their homes.

"What are you doing here?"

"We got word you were being chased through Terra," his mother answers.

His father scowls. "It's the sign we've been waiting for. The leaders must be stopped."

Several people call out their agreement behind him, throwing their fists into the air. "No more!" a woman shouts.

"No more!" echoes the crowd.

"No!" Hayze says, then raises his voice. "It's not time!"

"What are you talking about?" his father hisses. "We're ready!"

Aura shakes her head. "We're not."

Hayze's mother glares at her. "You're not," she spits. "But the Alliance is."

"I'm part of the Alliance," Aura says, now also raising her voice. "And we're not ready."

Hayze's father inflates as his face turns a patchy red. "Now listen—"

"Aura ended the Elemental Games, Dad," Hayze says, making sure his voice carries over the crowd. "Right after she saved my life."

His father's mouth snaps shut. Hayze's mother glances between the two of them, clearly trying to understand what this means.

Hayze turns to the people of the Alliance. "It's not time," he calls out. "We need all of the Elements to win this."

"We have Fire!" someone else shouts back.

"And Water!" another calls out.

Pace steps up beside Aura, Tempo beside him. She lifts her chin, even though she's pale and no doubt still weak.

"But we need Earth and Air," Hayze says. "The Elements have never existed in isolation. We can't win this without them."

"Don't you see?" Aura adds, her voice strong with conviction. "Division was always the issue. We need to unite the Elements just as much as the people."

The crowd shifts as people glance at each other. Murmurs filter through. Frowns form on shadowy faces.

"We'll find the others from Earth and Air," Hayze tells them. "Then we end all of this!"

Aura punches her fist into the air. "No more!"

There's a pause.

Hayze's breath catches.

If a war were to start now...

"No more!" a man shouts.

"No more!" echo several others.

"No more!" cries the crowd.

Relief courses through Hayze, unwinding his coiled muscles. He's not sure what they would've done if the Alliance had been determined to attack the Sect tonight.

There's not much he could've done. Except to die alongside them.

"Go home," he tells them. "We'll send word when it's time."

Once they find Jewel. Then Atmos and Skylus...and convince them to think in terms of *we* instead of *me*.

The crowd expands as the rebels disperse, some looking relieved, most looking disappointed. Hayze understands why. The need for justice burns in their veins, just like it does his.

"Where are they going?" hisses a voice behind him.

Hayze turns to find Calla a few feet away, glaring at the rebels.

"They're leaving," he assures her. "There's nothing to worry about."

An indrawn breath has him spinning back to his parents. "She's a trade master!" his mother growls.

Hayze doesn't point out so is Tide, and none of them would be here without the risks and sacrifices Pace's father made. Not when that would mean exposing him. "Calla gave us somewhere to hide, Mom. And food, and a place to rest."

"You ate the food she gave you?" she asks in horror.

Hayze's stomach twists. They never stopped to consider it could be poisoned...

"You can't trust her," his father urges, stepping forward as if to put himself between Hayze and Calla. "She's Avalan's most loyal—"

A gunshot slices through the night air.

Someone screams. A man shouts.

The remaining rebels run, many covering their heads.

A guard appears to the left, his gun braced against his chest. A staccato of shots explodes from the tip and a woman cries out, dropping to the ground.

Hayze is about to run into the fray, conscious he can't use his Fire power without a deadly outcome when a bolt of blue shoots past his shoulder. It hits the guard, then expands out as a crackling sheet of ice. It grows up and out, trapping the guard in its frozen expanse as it reaches the trees on either side.

Creating an ice barrier.

Pace turns and shoots out more ice, forming glistening, opaque walls in both directions, cutting off the guards. Shots and shouts ring out as they instantly work at breaking through.

"Go!" Pace shouts to the rebels. "Disappear before they can find you!"

The rebels scatter, now silent as they blend with the night. Hayze hopes they'll reach their tunnels before any guards find them. The Alliance will lose before this even begins if the leaders discover the only way the rebels can navigate between the Quadrants.

And thank heckus the people of Terra have stayed inside.

The ice holding the first guard frozen cracks, fractures splitting around his body and out.

"We need to get out of here," Pace says, already turning toward Tempo. "Are you okay to—"

A louder, bigger crack fractures the night air.

"Help!" Calla screams. "They tried to burn my house down!"

Hayze spins around in shock, hating that his cheeks flame red. They did accidentally start a fire...after the passion with Aura set alight far more than his blood. "She's lying!" he shouts. "We would never—"

Calla cringes, raising her hands to her face. "Please don't hurt me."

"Step away from the trade master!" a guard shouts.

"Please, help!" Calla cries.

Hayze and Aura duck as the next volley of shots peppers the trees around them. Pace grabs Tempo's hand, just as ready to run, when Calla shoves past them and down the alley. She throws herself into her tree house and slams the door shut behind her.

Hayze doesn't have to try it to know it's locked.

Calla just betrayed them.

"Give us some time, Pace!" Hayze shouts.

Another blast of cold shoots past him before he finishes. A sheet of ice explodes in front of the guards coming from their right, then their left. This time, Pace blasts again and again, thickening and reinforcing it until the guards on the other side are barely visible.

"That should do it," Pace says, lowering his hands.

"Wow," Tempo murmurs, her gaze roaming over the glistening walls that reach up to the branches.

Pace ducks his head a little. "You can do it, too. You're Water, just like I am."

Tempo blinks, then looks down at her hands, biting her lip.

"Right now, we have to get out of here," Hayze grits out, still angry at Calla. They should never have trusted her so easily.

"But Jewel," Aura says, shaking her head. "Calla's the only one who knows where she is."

Somewhere in Terra, still in her pod, still trapped in virtual reality.

Shots hit the ice with frantic intensity, warning the teens they don't have much time. A faint crack slices across the surface, splitting like veins. Running is their best chance. If they stay, the only way to survive is to kill the guards then interrogate Calla.

But the Elements have to be united.

It's the only way to save every soul depending on them.

"Then we—"

The rumble that cuts Hayze off is subtle. Little more than a ripple beneath his feet. But he's felt that shaking before. The type that starts deep beneath you then rises and grows, moving everything from your body to the mountains with its immense power.

The next wave that pushes through the soil is bigger. More insistent.

"Earthquake!" Aura gasps.

"But they're not supposed to happen in the capitals," Tempo says, grabbing Pace's arm when she sways.

He steadies her, hesitates, and when she doesn't pull away, keeps hold of her hand. "The elements are closing in on the capitals and the Sect. It's why we hit lava digging up to it."

"It's why the leaders need us," Aura adds, her lips twisting.

It's why the leaders created the Games, and then killed dozens of others before them.

The next quake is bigger, more intense. The branches above

them shake, sending leaves tumbling down. Hayze is already turning back, realizing what will happen next.

The crack is louder than a gunshot.

The fractures that spear up the ice sheets are reminiscent of the jagged fissures that formed in the Quakelands when they were in the Games. They zig-zag up the glistening surface, cleaving it. Breaking it.

And sending blocks of ice crashing down.

The guards scream and run, but gravity is faster than they could ever be. Some cries become louder, some are cut off as the walls of ice collapse on them, the guards' black pieces of armor providing little protection against the weight and ferocity.

"We can't..." Aura doesn't bother to finish her sentence. She shoots out targeted balls of fire, hitting the largest ice pieces and instantly melting them.

Hayze raises his hands to do the same, hoping to save as many lives as they can, when another crack sounds.

"Pace!" Tempo screams.

Hayze sees her looking up and follows her line of sight. His heart plummets even as his pulse rockets. The crack wasn't the ice. A monstrous branch has snapped off Calla's tree and is plunging toward them.

Pace lifts his hands, although Hayze knows there's nothing his powers can do to stop its trajectory. The branch hits another, bigger one, then twists. Wood snaps as it continues its inevitable fall, now immediately above them.

Beside Hayze, Aura hasn't taken her gaze from the lives she's trying to save.

Which leaves him with no other choice.

He reaches up and unleashes everything he has. The roar of fire that arcs up is so hot it has Tempo crouching down and Pace wrapping himself around her. Hayze opens his arms and the fireball expands and elongates. It hits the branch. Swallows it. And incinerates the thick arm of wood.

It's a rain of ash that falls on Hayze and the others, pale and gray.

And harmless.

The leaves above them catch alight as the fireball rises into the sky.

Hayze tenses. "Pace—"

"I know, I know." A jet of water hits the burning branches and the flames die. Pace winks. "Got your back, brother."

Hayze nods, conscious that a bond was forged between them when the leaders swapped their memories. It's going to be an unintended consequence they're likely to regret.

"Retreat!"

Hayze turns to see a handful of guards get to their feet and splash through the puddles now coating the street. They run, disappearing amongst the shadowy trunks of Terra.

Aura lets out a breath and Hayze draws her to him, his own sigh deflating his chest.

There are bodies sprawled in the melted ice, dead. Too many. Although each one was the enemy, they're a casualty in this war. Collateral damage.

A loss that didn't need to happen.

"Come on," Hayze says, taking Aura's hand. "They'll be back with reinforcements as soon as they can."

"Not yet," Calla says, stepping around them.

Hayze and Aura tense, ready to fight. Pace also lifts his hands, Tempo mirroring him as she stands beside him.

Calla ignores them, focusing on Hayze and Aura. "You've harnessed your powers with impressive skill."

"Then you appreciate the danger you're in right now," Hayze growls.

Calla smiles. "You won't hurt an ally."

"You're no friend," Aura says, her voice steely. "Walk away or pay the price."

Hayze's parents were right. Calla betrayed them. She must've been the one who called the guards.

She arches a brow. "You wanted me to let them know I took you in?" she says archly. "I can't exactly help you when I'm dead, can I?"

Hayze frowns, not liking that she has a point. Tide has to lie about his association with them and the Alliance. It's the only way to protect himself so he could keep working from within.

"We can't trust you after what you did," Aura points out.

"You'll betray us the next chance you get," Pace adds.

"Except I know where Jewel is." Calla angles her head. "And I'm willing to tell you where her pod is."

"Where?" Aura demands. Hayze can hear her suspicion, but he can also feel her tension. Saving the Earth girl is more than just about the Elements. Jewel is her friend.

Calla turns and points to the horizon. A pale sun is just peeking over the whorls of leaves, lining them in gold.

"She's hidden in the upper branches of a great tree." She pulls out a piece of folded paper tucked in a pocket. "I've drawn you a map."

Hayze glances at it but doesn't move. Calla could be lying.

Or she could be holding the information they need.

Aura reaches out and grasps the piece of paper, watching the woman carefully. Calla smiles, then glances past them. "I don't think you need me to tell you time is of the essence."

They don't wait to see if there's anything there. The four teens break into a run, splashing through the water and stepping around the dead guards.

It's time to free Jewel.

It's time to unite the four Elements.

CHAPTER
TEN
AURA

Aura clutches the map like her life depends on it. Well, actually Jewel's life does, so it's not all that different. In the Games, they had one chance to make a mistake. Here, in real life, they don't have that luxury. If they fail Jewel even once, she won't be coming back.

And that is *not* going to happen. They're going to save her and then they're going to set Skylus and Atmos free.

"Which way?" Hayze asks, panting.

Aura draws to a stop so she can unfold the map and study it. Just as she's finding her bearings, Pace rips it out of her hands.

"What are you doing?" she screeches, trying to snatch it back. "We need that."

Pace holds it up higher than Aura can reach. The ground rumbles with another quake and Hayze tears the paper from Pace's hands while his focus is distracted. Thankfully it turns out to be an aftershock and the ground settles down without cleaving the earth in two.

"We can't trust that map," says Pace, not making a move to take it back. "Calla's not on our side."

Pelting rain begins to fall as if Eterna agrees with Pace.

Hayze quickly tucks the map in his suit to keep it dry. Perhaps also to keep it away from Pace...

Aura frowns as she shields her eyes so she can glare at Pace. "You think Calla had a bogus map in her pocket ready to go, just in case she got the chance to fool us?"

"She might have." Pace holds out his hands and creates a circle of dry space around them like he just punched a hole in the clouds.

"Impressive," says Hayze, immediately withdrawing the map from his suit.

Aura glances at Pace.

"I'm sorry," he mumbles. "It wasn't nice for me to take the map. I just really don't trust Calla."

"Interesting comment coming from the son of a trade master," says Tempo.

"I said I was sorry." Pace turns to Tempo and his face instantly softens.

"We need to follow the map, Pace," says Tempo, touching his elbow. "I had you to rescue me from my pod. Jewel has nobody to help her. Except us."

Pace looks at Tempo for a few tense moments, then nods. "Okay. But only because I'm outvoted."

Aura smiles, knowing that's not even close to being the reason he relented. Aura and Hayze's votes don't count for anything next to Tempo's. Especially given this is the only thing she's asked of Pace since she woke up—other than for him to get the heckus away from her.

Hayze hands Aura the map and she unfolds it, watching Pace from the corner of her eye in case he makes a grab for it again.

Sketched out on the paper is a diagram of the streets of Terra. Aura scans it for the only landmark familiar to her.

"There," she says, pointing. "Calla's house."

"And there's the Traders Market," says Pace, keeping his hands extended to ensure they stay dry while the rest of Terra is soaked with rain. "I used to go there with my father."

"After he stole my family's life savings," Tempo mutters under her breath.

Pace lets one hand drop and rain spatters the back of their legs. "Who told you that?"

"Nobody," says Tempo, even though it was Aura. "Are you denying it?"

Pace ignores her question, focusing instead on keeping them dry.

"Jewel needs us," Hayze reminds them, pointing at the map. "There'll be time to talk later."

"There's a guard!" Tempo hisses.

Aura squints through the rain and sees a familiar black suit in the distance.

They run to a clump of trees and squat down, Pace managing to keep them dry while increasing the intensity of the rain pelting the guard. Holding his hands above his head, the guard turns and walks the other way.

"Let's take that as a warning to be more careful," says Hayze, letting out a sigh.

"Are you okay?" Aura whispers to Tempo, concerned for her friend who only yesterday could barely walk.

Tempo nods. "The meal from Calla helped. And the sleep. I'm fine."

Pace studies her. "I can carry—"

"I said I'm fine," Tempo snaps, leaving Aura wondering why it was so much easier for her to forgive Pace's family's betrayal when she thought she was

Tempo. Perhaps the pain hadn't cut her as sharply because deep inside she knew it hadn't actually happened to her.

Before Tempo and Pace can get into another argument, Aura holds out the map, pointing to where she thinks they are. "Do we agree this is our current location?"

The other three lean over, then nod.

"Which means we need to head that way." Tempo points down a winding street lined with tall trees.

"That makes sense," says Hayze. "Calla said she was in the upper branches of a great tree."

"If she was telling the truth," Pace adds, then immediately winces. "Sorry. Couldn't help myself."

The ground rumbles again, reminding them they need to move quickly before another quake strikes.

"Come on." Aura stands and looks around for more guards, pleased not to see any. "It's stopped raining. Let's make the most of it before it starts again."

They head further down the street, passing a series of houses with doors carved into their trunks. Aura leads the way with the map, Hayze beside her. She's not sure if the residents of Terra are hiding from the storm or fear of the Alliance but they don't see a single soul.

They walk for several minutes before Aura hears the rustling of leaves to their right. She comes to an abrupt halt, squatting and holding up a hand to warn the others, who quickly follow suit.

But when a figure emerges from between two trees, it's not a guard.

It's something far worse...

A monkey.

Memories assault Aura of dozens of these small, furry creatures with sharp teeth, mercilessly attacking them with rocks in the Quakelands. She shrinks back, pressing herself closer to Hayze.

"That wasn't real," he whispers, his mouth held close to her ear.

She nods, remembering Jewel told them the monkeys she grew up surrounded by weren't a threat. But she's not the only one here who seems unwilling to stand up to find out if Jewel was right.

The monkey moves on, seeming oblivious to their presence. Another scampers out behind it, this one a little more aware of its surroundings. It stops and tilts its head at Aura to study her, sending her heart pounding. But it quickly decides she's no threat and hurries to catch up to the first monkey.

"I don't like monkeys," says Tempo. "I don't care what Jewel said."

Aura nods her agreement. "I can't believe I thought they were cute when I first saw one."

Pace chuckles. "You thought Hayze was cute when you first saw him, too."

"Hey!" Hayze laughs. "She still does."

"I suppose you do look a little like a monkey," Pace quips.

Aura shakes her head as she stands. "Stop it, you two."

Truthfully, she doesn't want them to stop. She loves the way these two have bonded. And Pace's humor has a way of breaking the tensest of moments. Surely even Tempo must appreciate that.

Aura turns to Tempo to see her adjusting the sleeve of her suit, seeming completely disinterested in anything Pace has to say. The next opportunity they get to talk alone, Aura needs to put in a good word for Pace. They would never have gotten this far without him on their side.

"Come on," Aura says, walking forward, her eyes now

peeled for both guards and monkeys. "The map says we're looking for a giant Douglas Fir. It should be just up ahead."

"I once met a boy called Douglas," says Pace.

"That's not even a name," says Tempo, with just the slightest hint of amusement. "You made that up."

Aura smiles. Maybe there's hope for these two yet.

There's another crackling of leaves and Aura drops into a squat. Just how many monkeys are in Terra? Jewel said they'd thrived, but this is ridiculous. They don't have the time to keep stopping every few seconds.

"It's a sign," comes a deep, familiar voice that has Aura's back straightening. "It's telling us to go this way."

"Atmos?" Aura stands up and scans the trees, her eyes wide. "Is that you?"

Atmos and Skylus step through the trees. Dressed in their purple robes, they'd look resplendent if they weren't soaking wet.

Aura blinks, then rubs her eyes, certain she's imagining them.

"What are you doing here?" Pace growls, absence not seeming to have made his heart grow any fonder.

"We could ask the same of you," says Skylus. "I mean, frankly, I'm shocked to see you here. I was certain you'd all have perished by now with your rudimentary powers."

"Who uses a word like *perish* in everyday conversation?" Pace mutters. "Or rudimen—what even *is* that word?"

"Basic," says Atmos. "It means basic. A concept you should be more than familiar with."

With that, Pace throws out his hands, sending a deluge of water from the treetops pouring down on Atmos. The boy from Air steps to the side only for the tiny rain cloud to follow him.

"Okay!" Atmos shouts. "You're a little above basic. Make it stop now."

"Not until you tell me I'm amazing," Pace teases.

Skylus flicks out her hand, sending out a sudden blast of wind that topples Pace over. The rain cloud swings away from Atmos and settles above Pace, drenching him until he regains his senses and makes it stop.

"Not so amazing now," scoffs Atmos, stepping a little closer to Skylus.

Hayze positions himself between Water and Air, which surprisingly are turning out to be the two Elements that have the most volatile outcome when combined.

"We're really glad to see you," says Hayze, smiling at Atmos and Skylus.

Aura nods her agreement. This is going to save them a whole lot of trouble heading into Aeris to release the Air teens from their pods. It might even save their lives.

"Who got you out?" Tempo asks.

"I did." Skylus rolls her eyes as if this was obvious. "I focused all my energy on my real self until I was able to return my mind to the pod. Then I disconnected myself, released Atmos, and locked the leaders in the room before we left to look for Jewel."

"Whoa." Pace holds up a hand, making Atmos wince. "You did *not* do all that."

"We did," says Atmos. "I'm not sure why you don't seem to be able to grasp just how advanced we are."

"We?" Pace lifts a brow.

Skylus waves a hand. "Well, it was me. But still, you get the point. Air has always been the most superior Quadrant, so it shouldn't be a surprise."

Aura glances at Hayze, wondering if he's regretting telling the Air teens how glad he was to see them.

"What were the leaders doing in Aeris?" Hayze asks.

Skylus shrugs. "I manipulate Air. I don't interrogate private thoughts and motives."

Aura wishes for once this girl could just speak plainly. They don't have time for this kind of talk. They need to get to Jewel before the leaders find their way out and are even angrier than they were before.

"Why did you come for Jewel first?" asks Tempo. "You didn't know I'd been set free."

"Why did *you* come for Jewel first?" Skylus counters.

Tempo shrugs. "Yeah, okay. Fair call. She always was the most likable."

Pace resists making a smart remark for once.

"Get down!" Hayze hisses. "Guards."

They all squat immediately, apart from Skylus who shoots into the treetops to hide in the canopy.

There are heavy footsteps as a dozen guards charge down the street directly toward them.

"There they are!" one guard shouts.

"Kill them!" the rest echo.

Aura shoots to her feet, resisting the urge to throw a fireball. If they set the trees on fire, Jewel will be in grave danger. Fire isn't the Element to save them now.

"Pace!" Hayze shouts, his desperation clear.

But Pace is already on it. He sends out a wall of ice just as Skylus hurtles a massive gust of wind. The wall barely has a chance to form before it cracks and shatters, unable to withstand Skylus's force and proving that Air and Water really don't mix.

"Work together!" Aura shouts as the guards surge forward. "We're a team!"

This time it's Tempo who's on it. She raises her hands and screws up her face.

"I am Water!" she shouts, sending out an icy blast. It's not quite as impressive as Pace's wall of ice, but it's enough to have the guards scuttling backward.

"I've got it!" Skylus shouts from above as the guards get to their feet and propel themselves forward.

But Pace isn't prepared to put his trust in the girl from Air. He throws out his hands, a new wall appearing in front of the guards in an instant. Skylus's burst of wind whistles through the air immediately afterwards, this time taking down the wall in one giant piece as it crashes down, crushing the guards underneath its weight.

If they hadn't arrived with threats to kill, Aura might feel guilty. Instead, she clutches her map, desperate to get to Jewel before it's too late. But there are so many trees and not enough time to study the map. How do they possibly find the right one?

"Skylus!" she calls out. "Find the tallest tree!"

Skylus flies high above the canopy, disappearing from sight, while Aura frantically scans the map.

"We can't wait for her," Pace pants. "And I trust her even less than Calla."

Atmos's eyes flare. "Hey—"

"This way," says Aura, certain they're not far. "Skylus will catch up."

They race down the street until they reach a clearing covered in dry pine needles, with an enormous tree growing right in the very center.

"This has to be it!" cries Aura, looking up at the tall trunk without a single branch low enough for them to climb. "This tree is huge! I can't even see the top."

"Calla could've told us we'd need a ladder," puffs an exhausted Tempo.

"Told you I don't trust her," says Pace.

"Look!" Atmos points to the top of the tree. "There's Skylus! She led us to exactly the right spot."

Aura's pretty sure she did that, but she bites her tongue as she watches Skylus circle the tree, then fly into its canopy.

Hayze slips his hand into Aura's as they peer up into the branches, waiting for Skylus to come down with a report. Hopefully one that says Jewel is safe and well. Now that they're so close, the anticipation is unbearable and Aura squeezes Hayze's hand like a lifeline.

Eventually, Skylus flies down, landing in front of them and shaking her head.

"What?" Aura gasps. "What happened? What did you see?"

"There's a structure hidden in the leaves," says Skylus, pulling her shoulders back.

"And?" Aura prompts, her heart lighting with hope. "Was Jewel in there?"

Skylus spins around, her gaze roaming over the wide trunk. "Her pod's right there next to Geo's empty one. Now, how are you *other* Elements going to get up there?"

ELEVEN

HAYZE

Hayze clenches his teeth. Then his hands. Then his frown. It's clear what Skylus was implying.

How are you *inferior* Elements going to get up there?

Even the sky seems angry as the rain starts up again. Hayze wipes at the water streaming over the corrugations of his brow. The rivulets resurrect themselves, pouring over his eyes and mouth. It's giving him flashbacks of when he was in Aqua searching for Tide. Except he's in Terra, so surely this deluge should stop soon?

Not that it matters.

They need to get to the top of this tree.

Hayze takes a step back, craning his neck as he tries to see the canopy through the gray curtain now soaking everything. "There has to be a way the leaders and their trade masters get up there."

How else are they overseeing Jewel tucked in her pod?

Aura steps forward. "Hayze is right. We just need to figure it out." She looks up, then squints as a storm of water hits her in the face. "It's getting heavier!"

A river is now pouring from the sky, unrelenting and darker gray by the second.

Suddenly, it clears. Hayze turns to see Pace standing in their center, his body ramrod straight as he gazes straight up. A few feet away, the rain continues to pour mercilessly, but the few feet surrounding them are dry. "It's a lot of water," he says, his voice tight.

Hayze and Aura quickly take the opportunity afforded to them, looking up and slowly turning. But even in the dry tunnel Pace has created around them, there's no obvious way to get to the first bough several feet above them, let alone any higher. A faint rumble ripples through the ground, reminding them there's more than one natural disaster they're facing right now.

"There's no sign of a ladder," Hayze says, his frustration rising along with his determination.

"So they're getting up another way," Tempo finishes.

"I have an idea." Aura steps out of their dry cocoon and into the rain. The deluge swallows her, instantly saturating her hair and clothes. Ignoring it, she starts running her hands over the rough bark of the trunk, a faint red glow surrounding her palm.

"You're going to burn it down?" Atmos gasps.

"Nothing is going to burn in this rain," Hayze responds, joining her. "And that would be far too risky for Jewel."

Behind them, Skylus gasps and Hayze suspects Pace has allowed the rain to continue unfettered, but he doesn't turn around to check. He's too busy trying to figure out what Aura's doing.

Then, he realizes.

"You're looking for a door?"

She nods, stepping to the side as she runs her hands high and low. They leave behind dark scorch marks that are quickly soaked by the ocean being unleashed from the sky. It's enough for the bark to shrivel and flake away, but not singe the trunk beneath.

"Frenius," Hayze says, his voice warm with admiration. He sparks a small flame in his own palm and copies Aura, reaching a little higher than she can.

Together, they sweep their hands over the trunk, looking for anomalies. There's little more than the thundering of the rain as they make their way around the tree, scorching shallow curves over its surface. They reach the back when their palms arc down and bump into the other. Hayze smiles as heat sparks and their flames merge for a moment, glowing brighter, a symbol of everything that's true when it comes to him and Aura.

They're stronger together.

His smile turns to a grin as he registers something else.

"A door!" Aura gasps, her own broad smile lighting up her face.

"Did you say a door?" Skylus calls out. She appears a moment later, blinking as she sees what Hayze and Aura have uncovered.

A hard, unyielding line is etched into the trunk. Some quick work by Hayze and Aura, and they reveal it's a rectangle a little wider and taller than they are. The sharp corners and straight lines are a startling mismatch to the natural curves and flowing contours Terra is built from.

A door.

Pace grins. "Nice one."

Atmos wipes away at the waterfall coursing over his face. "Now you have to open it."

Hayze rolls his eyes. They don't need pessimism or for the obvious to be stated. "Then let's open it." He lifts his hands to push when Pace speaks.

"This will be quicker," he says, moving forward.

Hayze steps back as his friend moves in, placing his palms on the door. White ice crackles outward, quickly engulfing the surface. Pace's arms bend as he pushes a little more and Hayze expects the door to swing in, but there's a deeper, louder crack. Then another. And another.

The door fractures as lines like lightning streak out and it crumbles.

Jagged, frozen pieces of metal fall to the ground, revealing a curved staircase carved inside the tree trunk.

"Nice one," Tempo says quietly, repeating Pace's words from earlier.

Pace flushes as he turns, finding her looking only at him. They gaze at each other in the rain and Hayze wonders what silent communication is passing. An understanding? A truce? Something more?

"Well then?" Skylus asks, her sodden robes flapping as she throws out her arms. Another small quake ripples through the soil, only emphasizing her words. "I thought finding Jewel was super urgent."

"Hence why we found the door and destroyed it," Hayze points out.

"Come on," Aura says, stepping inside and up the stairs.

Hayze is right behind, followed by Pace and Tempo, Skylus and Atmos.

"What else did you see up there, Skylus?" Hayze asks, peering into the bowels of the tree. The staircase spirals along the inner wall of the trunk, leaving a hollow center. Even now that the rain is just a thrum outside, it's too dark to see much. What are they about to walk into?

"Just the pods on a big platform. There were a lot of branches and leaves, so it was hard to tell from the brief peek."

"You didn't have a bit of a look around?" Pace asks. "You said Geo's pod was empty."

"I was excited to tell you the good news!" Skylus huffs indignantly. "And Geo's pod was closest."

Hayze doesn't comment, even though Pace is right. A little more information would've been good.

"If anyone else wanted to fly up and have a look, they were welcome to," Skylus mutters.

"The pods are outside?" Tempo asks, a frown in her voice. "Not in a room?"

Aura glances over her shoulder, her gaze connecting with Hayze as they realize she has a point. The pods are high-tech pieces of equipment. Does that mean they're out in this deluge? That Jewel's being soaked along with everything else?

Atmos tsks, the sound sharp in the hollowed trunk. "You guys aren't very good at being grateful, are you?"

There's no reply, and Hayze wonders if anyone is feeling guilty, just like Atmos wants them to. He certainly isn't. They've all fought and sacrificed to be here. They've all experienced how close to death each choice has brought them. Wanting to be prepared is understandable. Trying to make sense of what they're living through is only natural.

"I can see some light," Aura says in a low voice.

Hayze registers it, too. Muted and pale, it's little more than the soggy glow that manages to make it past the rain clouds that are now dominating the sky, but it's definitely light. They're almost at the top.

Everyone falls silent as they navigate the final curve along the inside of the trunk. An opening appears ahead, the sound and sight of the rain filling the space.

They've found Jewel.

"We need to be quick," Aura whispers, darting forward.

Hayze is right beside her, heat injecting through his muscles. They burst through the door, instantly saturated by an atmosphere that's more water than air. The rain pounds a large wooden platform framed by branches and leaves, encasing it completely. Although it wouldn't be visible from below, the rain still gets through, running over the timber floor in thick sheets. Faint ripples trip over the surface, hinting that the earth far below is far from still.

Hayze squints. Ahead, obscured by water, is the blurred outline of a pod. "She's here!"

"Jewel!" Aura cries, breaking into a run.

Hayze leaps to follow, then almost stumbles when a movement ahead sends his stomach to his feet. It looked like... He wipes his face, confirming it wasn't a trick of the water.

"Guards!" he shouts.

Black-bodied men materialize from between the branches and leaves, guns pointed. And shooting.

Hayze launches forward and slams into Aura. He twists as they tumble to the floor, rolling them over and over until they hit something hard. Pain jolts up his spine, but there's no chance to acknowledge it. They leap to their feet and duck behind a thick branch, trying to spot the others. All that's visible are guards and gray.

"We've been ambushed!" Pace roars.

"They must've been hiding!" Skylus cries.

Right now, all Hayze knows is if they're talking, they're alive. Somehow, they have to all stay that way.

"We have to get to Jewel," Aura says, her voice quiet but hard.

Hayze nods, acknowledging there are actually two goals. Don't die. And find Jewel.

Gunshots pepper the air, making them duck. Aura shoots out a fireball. Hayze quickly follows, conscious of every flammable leaf and twig around them. The blazing missiles hit a small group of guards now running at them. The flames explode out, forcing the guards to stop, then fizzle into nothing. Everything's too wet. Using Fire is no longer dangerous. It's going to have little impact now that Terra is turning into a giant puddle.

Another round of bullets shreds the leaves above their heads and Hayze and Aura press themselves behind the branch. The thick wood feels far too fragile to protect them from the relentless onslaught. It certainly can't protect them from the truth.

They're trapped.

Screams echo through the rain and Hayze peeks up to see the guards covering their heads as glittering shards fall from the sky. Behind them, Pace has his hands extended, water coursing over his stony expression.

He's turned the rain pummeling the guards to ice!

"Now!" Aura gasps, breaking into a run.

Hayze's heart shoots straight to the stratosphere as he leaps to catch up. They sprint to the pod, skidding to a stop beside it. Their ability to move is stolen from them in an instant.

"It can't be..." Aura breathes.

But it is.

The pod's empty.

A quick glance at the one adjacent reveals the same sight.

Empty.

"Where is she?" Hayze rasps out. How could Jewel not be tucked inside?

"Have you got her?" Tempo calls out.

"She's not here!" Hayze shouts back, still struggling to make sense of what he's seeing.

"How can she not be here?" Skylus screeches. She hovers a few feet above the ground, looking like she's about to shoot into the sky when she should be helping Pace subdue the guards. One gust and they'll realize exactly how high up they are.

Atmos is twisting one way, then the other, panic stamped on his face. "We have to get out of here!"

It's all the encouragement Skylus needs. She becomes a purple blur as she launches through the branches, disappearing from sight.

"Skylus!" Atmos squeals, now looking terrified.

Hayze mutters a different name he thinks is far more fitting, even as he looks around. The Air teens may be cowards, but they're right. They have to get out of here.

"This way!" Pace cries, clutching Tempo's hand as he runs straight ahead. He crashes through the railing surrounding the platform and launches them straight into the gray haze beyond.

"Pace!" Aura cries.

The rain engulfs him just as a fresh staccato of shots rips through the air. Hayze takes Aura's hand and breaks into a run, following their friends. "Come on, Atmos!"

"But we don't know—"

Hayze and Aura leap into exactly that—the unknown. They launch off the platform and watery gray swallows them. For the briefest millisecond, they're hovering, held by Mother Nature. Then rain and gravity draw them down.

Fast.

Almost immediately, they land on something hard and smooth. And cold. Hayze clutches Aura to him as they find themselves shooting forward and down. On a slide of ice!

Somewhere ahead, Pace whoops, clearly enjoying the escape he's crafted. Behind them, a weird keening sound is coming from Atmos, which at least means he got out alive.

Hayze and Aura hold on tight as they gain speed. Rain rushes down the slide, freezing as it goes, the slide building itself as the teens descend. It's cold and wet and completely out of control. Hayze braces himself for the moment they hit the ground. At this speed, it's going to hurt.

Except it's water they plow into. Aura is wrenched from Hayze's arms as he's thrown over its surface, tumbling several times before sinking below. He pushes his feet down, then powers up, discovering he's standing in knee-deep water. He spins one way, then the other, frantically searching the wet, gray world Terra has become. "Aura!"

"I'm here!" she calls, appearing to his left.

They splash through the water, allowing themselves a brief second to clasp tightly. Then, they turn, finding Pace and Tempo not far away. Atmos is spluttering a few feet to their right.

The first gunshot piercing the air is all they need.

"Run!" Hayze shouts.

CHAPTER
TWELVE
AURA

Rain. Wind. Lightning. Tremors.

Mother Nature is throwing everything she has at them, as if to prove she's the true master of all four Elements.

They run through the knee-deep water away from the guards, the tree, and Jewel's empty pod. Skylus flies above them, a purple blur in an angry, gray sky. A bullet skims past Aura's head, so close she feels it cut through the pelting rain. She gasps in fright but doesn't pause her steps until she sees Pace spin around. He waves his hands and a wall of ice shoots up behind them.

"Come on!" he shouts, breaking back into a run as more bullets slam into the ice.

"You're amazing, Pace!" Aura shouts, with no idea if he can hear her over the thunder rumbling in the angry sky.

"I know!" he calls back, keeping close to Tempo's side.

She doesn't need to see his face to know he's smiling.

Atmos mutters something Aura can't make out, but she can easily guess he wasn't agreeing with her assessment of Pace's abilities.

Hayze takes Aura's hand, urging her to run faster and she knows she won't tell him how close that bullet came to ending everything.

The earth shakes harder beneath their feet, sending branches crashing down, only narrowly missing them as the people of Terra scurry into their homes to take shelter. Large cracks open up in the ground ahead, and rivers of water run into them as the five teens crowd together at a safe distance with their hands over their heads.

Pace creates a circle around them where the rain ceases to fall, although this time it's not nearly as effective given the water level is past their knees and rising fast.

"Where do we go?" Tempo asks. "It's too dangerous to keep moving."

"And it's too dangerous not to," Aura says on a shudder, the memory of her close call with the bullet causing her heart to pound.

"Where's Skylus?" Atmos peers up into the dry tunnel Pace has created from the sky.

"Who cares where she is," snaps Pace. "She lied to us about Jewel."

"That wasn't a lie!" Atmos growls back. "All of us thought she was in that pod until we got close enough to look."

"That's true," says Hayze, putting an arm around Aura when she shivers. "But Skylus knows how to look after herself. We can't worry about her now."

"There's too much rain," says Tempo, pointing down at the water that's rushing past them, creating a raging river in what was once a peaceful valley filled with nothing but trees. "Terra's turning into Aqua."

Atmos rolls his eyes. "Then why don't you stop it, instead of making your boyfriend do all the hard work?"

"Nobody can stop all this water," says Hayze before Tempo

can react. Her powers aren't as honed as Pace's, just like Atmos has been nowhere near as successful as Skylus. "We need shelter."

"We could try Calla's house," says Aura, aware her desperation is clouding her common-sense.

"She betrayed us," says Pace. "Just like Skylus."

Atmos steps forward. "She did n—"

A tree branch crashes down, breaking their dry circle and sending them scattering.

"Watch out!" Tempo screams.

Aura spins to see a wall of water rushing down the street, straight for them. It's like one of the tsunamis Aura remembers from Tempo's childhood. It sweeps her from her feet, tearing her away from Hayze and drags her down the flooded road. With hands flailing, she manages to grab hold of a branch that's still attached to a tree, and comes to a stop, her feet above ground level, making it impossible to stand.

Looking around as she gasps for breath, she sees Hayze clinging to another branch several feet away. Pace, Tempo and Atmos are clumped together in another tree a little further down the street. Miraculously, they're all alive. It's hard to believe this was the same street they walked down to get to Jewel. It's more of a raging river now.

The ground rumbles as more tremors shake the earth, but Aura can barely hear them over the booming of the thunder and pelting of the rain.

There's a sharp scream and Aura looks up to see a flash of purple. She holds tighter to the branch as she realizes it's Skylus hurtling down with her arms flapping like an injured parrot. She lands with a splash and floats to the swirling surface of the water, face-down and completely still. She must've been hit by a bullet to fall from the sky like that.

"Skylus!" Aura calls, feeling more helpless than she ever

has. It's impossible to keep even just herself afloat in these conditions, let alone be able to get Skylus to safety.

If it's not already too late.

The water carries Skylus past Aura, then toward Hayze. He glances at Aura and she already knows he won't let go of his branch as that would sweep him away from her. He stretches out, straining as he tries to grab hold of Skylus. But she rushes past his fingertips and continues on toward the others, her robes billowing in the water like a purple cloud as the rain thrums at her back.

If they don't get to her soon, she's going to drown, which is an irony Aura doesn't want to contemplate. The girl from Air cannot possibly die from...lack of air!

Dragging in a breath, Aura lets go of her branch. The greedy river takes her, rushing her forward until she's dragged to a stop by a strong hand that pulls her to a firm chest.

"Hayze!" she pants, pressing herself to the familiar comfort of his body. "We have to help her!"

"Pace is going," Hayze says, holding her tightly. "Look."

Aura turns in his arms, grabbing hold of the branch to see Pace kicking out toward Skylus. Relief ripples beneath her freezing cold skin. Pace grew up surrounded by water. If anyone can do this, it's him.

Pace reaches Skylus in several strong strokes and flips her onto her back. Aura squints through the rain, looking for a sign of life in her pale face.

There's a flurry of movement as Skylus's hands flutter into the air, grabbing Pace around the shoulders as the two of them are dragged further away.

"She's alive!" Aura gasps.

"And she's going to kill Pace," says Hayze as they see their friend's head get pulled under the muddy water as Skylus struggles to keep herself above the surface.

"She doesn't know what she's doing," Aura whimpers. "She's panicking."

Hayze and Aura don't need to discuss what to do next. They can't possibly let their best friend drown in the very Element he's just learned to harness. They let go of the branch and allow the water to sweep them down the street past Atmos and Tempo.

Aura catches sight of Pace's hand shooting out of the water, and she knows he's trying to clear a safe bubble where he can breathe. But with Skylus thrashing about and holding him under as they move further away, it's impossible for him to save himself.

"We can't reach them!" Hayze shouts.

Aura is sucked under the water and her butt hits something hard.

She tumbles on solid ground, her elbows and knees hitting compacted earth as she comes to a stop that leaves her dazed and confused about where all the water just went. It's not even so much as raining anymore. And where the heckus has the river gone? There's nothing but a decimated road around her.

"Aura!" Hayze shouts, crawling up beside her and wrapping his arms around her as another tremor shakes the earth. "Are you okay?"

"No," she says. "Yes. I mean...where's Pace? What happened?"

Hayze drops a kiss on her damp forehead and they get to their feet, turning in a circle as they survey the obliterated landscape, scattered with leaves, branches and debris. There's no sign of any other people who must have locked themselves in their homes. Hopefully still alive.

"What the fractal," Hayze breathes. "Look at Tempo."

Aura follows his line of sight, finding Tempo standing a few yards away with Atmos crumpled at her feet. Both her hands are stretched out in front of her and she has her back to them. A wall of water is dammed just past her, building in height as it can't get past.

"She did it," says Aura, her eyes wide with amazement. "She used her powers to hold the water back."

"We need to get to Pace!" Hayze takes her hand and they run down the street, passing Skylus who's sitting up and coughing, clearly alive.

"I'm okay," she splutters, pointing. "Go to Pace."

"Get to higher ground," says Aura, pointing to a side street that goes uphill. It might be just high enough to keep them dry for a while. "We don't know how long Tempo can hold the water back."

Aura and Hayze rush to Pace who's lying in a heap, his long arms and legs a tangle and his head twisted at an awkward angle.

"Pace!" Aura cries as Hayze scoops him up and carries him to the side street. "Is he alive?"

"I'm not sure." Hayze sets Pace down as they reach the peak of the street and Aura squats beside them, no longer caring about the persistent rain. "Come on, Pace. Wake up!"

Pace turns his head, coughing up water and groaning. It's one of the most beautiful sounds Aura's ever heard.

There's a loud roar and the street is flooded with water once more as Tempo must lose hold of her dam. It sweeps forward, swallowing everything in its path and Aura can only hope Terra's residents were able to get to higher ground. The forest rumbles as if in protest, the tremors shaking the water and creating furious waves. Blankets and chairs float past along with bowls and baskets, leaving Aura wondering how many of Terra's residents had their homes destroyed.

Pace's coughs subside and he tries to sit up.

"Pace," Aura sobs as Hayze urges him to relax. "You scared us."

"He scared me too," says a voice behind them.

Aura turns to see Tempo with tears running down her face.

Hayze and Aura immediately vacate their positions to allow Tempo to get closer to Pace. She sits on the damp earth and cradles his head in her lap.

"You're so brave," she says. "And I was so stupid for not seeing it sooner."

Pace blinks up at Tempo like he's seeing a vision as she strokes his dark hair away from his face. He opens his mouth to say something, but she presses a finger to his blue lips.

"Don't talk," she says. "Just breathe. Just...be alive. Please."

He smiles and color instantly returns to his face as if Tempo was the elixir he needed.

She leans down to kiss his cheek and he turns his face, catching her lips with his own. It may not be their first kiss, but it's their first one built on truth instead of the false memories of the Games.

Aura threads her fingers through Hayze's, enjoying witnessing this moment she feared she'd never see. Amidst all this death and destruction, love is continuing to find a way.

Atmos comes up behind them and puts his hands on his hips. "Sorry to interrupt, but do you think we could get out of here?"

"Atmos," Aura interrupts. "Give them a moment."

Skylus limps up to Atmos, her purple robes stuck to her damp skin.

"What happened?" he asks her. "Why couldn't you fly?"

Aura turns her attention to the girl from Air, wondering the same thing. "Were you shot?"

Skylus throws Aura an unimpressed glare. "No, I wasn't

105

shot. I'm not actually sure what happened. One minute I was flying, the next I was falling."

"Can you fly now?" Atmos asks. "Have your great powers been healed?"

"Let me see." Skylus lifts two feet off the ground and comes down again. "Yes, I appear to be just as powerful as I was before."

Aura glances at Hayze, wondering if he's as puzzled as she is. Do the leaders have a way to turn their powers on and off at will? But surely, if that were the case, they'd all have lost their powers by now.

Permanently.

Hayze gives Aura a small shrug.

"We need to get out of here," says Atmos, motioning toward the valley that's a raging river once more. "Unless she can make it stop again."

Pace looks up at Tempo. "You did that?"

She smiles and nods. "It's amazing what you can do when someone you love is in danger."

"You love me?" Pace shoots up a brow as he tries to sit up.

Tempo nods. "Of course, I love you."

"She must've got knocked on the head," Atmos mutters as Pace sits up and kisses Tempo passionately.

"That's more like it," Hayze laughs, a rumble of thunder seeming to agree with him. "Although, I feel like I'm back in the Games seeing them do that."

"We need to find Jewel," says Pace as Tempo finishes kissing him and helps him to his feet.

"Which means we need to go back to Calla," says Hayze.

"Who's this Calla you keep mentioning?" Atmos asks, seeming annoyed.

"She's a trade master," Aura explains. "She's the one who told us where to find Jewel."

Pace grunts. "You mean, she's the one who led us straight into a trap."

Aura nods, unable to deny this. "But she's the best hope we have. Hayze is right. We have to go back to her."

A rumble rolls through the trees, shaking the earth and Tempo holds out her hands, trying her best to keep them dry.

They need Jewel, and not just because she's their friend.

She's also the missing Element, making her the only one who can stabilize the earth in this war against nature.

"If anyone has another idea for how to find Jewel, please speak up," says Aura, looking around at the blank faces.

"Right then," says Hayze, taking Aura's hand along with a step in the direction of Calla's house. "It's time to get some answers."

CHAPTER

THIRTEEN

HAYZE

The ground squelches beneath Hayze's feet as they trudge through the rain. This kind of deluge isn't something he would've thought they need to deal with in Terra, but holding desperately onto Aura as they were almost swept away is a moment he'll never forget.

Water is a powerful force. As dangerous as Fire.

Or any of the other Elements.

This is what he and his friends have been created to control. Is that even possible?

And is that what Hayze wants?

"Come on," he says, even though they're all moving. "We need to hurry."

Uniting the teens, the ones at the center of all of this, has never been more important. Hayze and Aura break into a run, the others behind them. Who knows how far away the guards are and if the rain doesn't stop, very soon there will be no higher ground.

"You're not going anywhere."

The half-shouted words have them all stopping as Calla materializes through the curtain of rain. Water slicks over her dark hair, her headdress replaced by a crown of leaves. More bodies appear, all wearing the strappy cloths of Terra.

All wearing the same expression as Calla—cold, hard fury.

"You sent us into a trap," Hayze growls, conscious his friends have fanned out on either side of him.

Calla curls her lip. "And yet here you are."

"Where's Jewel?" Aura demands.

Calla throws her head back, uncaring of the rain spattering her face as a grin graces her face. Her smile remains as she lowers her gaze back down. "I can guarantee you one thing— you'll never find Jewel."

"Like fractal we won't," Hayze spits.

"Is she even in Terra?" Aura demands, sounding like it just occurred to her.

Hayze realizes they've made an assumption, something that's been nothing but dangerous since they entered the Elemental Games. Aura's right. Jewel could be in a pod in any of the capitals. Possibly even the Quadrants.

Calla's only response is a tight, brittle smile. "Take them," she orders. "The guards will be here any moment."

The people the trade master brought move in, forming a circle that tightens like a noose. Some are holding spears. A few are carrying rocks.

Hayze lifts his hands, registering that Aura and the others do the same as they contract, their shoulders touching. "I wouldn't move if I were you," he warns.

The people hesitate, suggesting they're aware of what they're up against.

"See?" Calla calls out. "This is why they must be captured! No one will be safe!"

"What?" Tempo gasps.

Hayze glares at Calla while he keeps his senses on high alert. The thrumming roar of the rain batters the scene as no one moves. "We're not the threat here!"

Skylus hovers a couple of feet, making the people closest to her gasp and retreat. "Do you know who we are?" she roars.

"Of course we do!" shouts a woman. "You're the Solution!"

"The what?" Aura gasps.

Calla raises her arms. "The leaders have announced their plan to all the Quadrants," she shouts, even though her gaze is on the teens. "The way we will survive Mother Nature's war!"

Hayze shifts his weight, unease turning his skin cold. A war against Mother Nature?

"They've been planning the Elemental Solution all along!" Calla continues. "They've created the means for us to never be at the mercy of this again."

"They're crazy," Pace growls.

Hayze glances at Aura, seeing her face is as pale as he feels. Calla's talking like they're some sort of weapon. An ultimate one.

One that needs to be controlled.

"But the power has gone to their head," Calla continues. "The Solutions are trying to overthrow the very leaders who created them!"

"No!" Tempo cries out. "That's not what's happening!"

A man steps forward, lifting a spear. "Then why are you threatening to attack us?"

Hayze blinks at him, then frowns. "Have you heard of self-defense?"

"The leaders have lied to you," Pace shouts. "You can't trust them! They're cold, heartless bastards!"

"They're the liars," Calla screams, pointing at the teens. "They're the ones refusing to fight for your lives!"

"Please, listen," Hayze shouts. "We want to help—"

"Then why haven't you stopped this rain?" a woman shouts.

"We're drowning!" shouts someone else.

Hayze draws in a sharp breath, then clamps his mouth shut as the flood from above almost has him choking. These people think they can stop this? That's what the leaders have promised them?

A rumble rips through the ground beneath everyone's feet, sending ripples of water over Hayze's feet. The people of Terra surrounding them gasp and cry out. "You're our only hope," a woman whimpers.

"Hayze," Aura says quietly.

He nods, conscious of the layers injected into his name. They've been gifted with the ability to fight this, whether they like it or not.

It's who and how they fight that's the decision to be made.

"Attack!" Calla screeches. "Before they kill us all—"

An arm whips around her torso, while another jams a knife against her throat. "No one move!"

"Dad?" Hayze gasps.

His father is behind the now immobile Calla. Hayze's mother appears on her other side, several other Alliance members by her side.

The people of Terra retreat, their spears and rocks raised even higher. "Release our trade master!"

"They're making this worse," Skylus hisses.

"Not until you release these teens!" Hayze's father shouts back.

Aura does a slow turn as she drops her hands. "Please. No one needs to die here."

"We're all dying!" Hayze's mother shouts, stepping forward. "And it's no longer just those of us in the Quadrants."

"The leaders." Hayze's father jerks Calla harder against his chest, making her eyes bulge. "And their trade masters will only hasten that."

"Let her go!" a man shouts.

"You don't belong here!" a young woman screams.

Hayze's mother slices her hand through the air. "We all belong here, no matter where we were born! The walls dividing us need to come down."

Hayze is barely breathing. The Alliance is here, his parents leading them. But the guards will also be here any moment.

All while Mother Nature tries to wash them away.

Hayze's father pushes Calla forward and she stumbles to her knees, mud splashing up her arms. "How many died so you could be here in Terra?" he demands of the crowd. "Who stole, lied, killed so they could live in safety?"

Hayze can't help but think of Tide and Ondine. They wouldn't have been the only ones desperate enough to do what they did.

His father's only response is another rumble and rippling of ground, the branches high above shaking and creaking.

Hayze's mother steps up beside his father, two other Alliance members with her. "Only to find you're not safe at all?" she calls out.

The people of Terra glance between each other, even the heavy rain not hiding their troubled expressions. How many were born here? How many had to sacrifice to be here? And how many are realizing that not even the capitals can protect them anymore?

The next tremor is bigger. Longer. And Hayze isn't sure whether it's because Mother Nature is agreeing with the Alliance.

Or warning them.

"Don't move!"

The shouted command comes from somewhere behind Hayze, in the direction of the river they just escaped. He goes to spin around even as he knows the guards have arrived but freezes at the sound that quickly follows.

The crack of a gunshot.

The Alliance member beside his mother drops to the ground, dead.

"No, no, no," Hayze pleads under his breath.

The war they're trying to prevent is about to be unleashed. It won't just be water raining down on them.

It'll be blood.

Calla staggers to her feet, straightens, and draws her shoulders back as she glares at the teens standing in the center of it all. "Surrender or innocent lives will be lost."

The guards keep their guns high as they continue to run up the rise. Hayze's parents and the rebels run toward the teens, the determination to fight stamped on their faces.

"Sweet fractal," Aura whispers in horror.

Surrender is exactly what they need to do.

It looks like the leaders will have their Solution after all.

The next shudder beneath their feet sends Aura careening into Hayze. He grabs her as the rumbling grows in strength and volume. Skylus cries out and rises into the air. Tempo and Pace move closer together, their hands once more ready.

A woman screams and Hayze braces himself for another shot. Except it's thunder that rips through the air. Violent, destructive thunder.

Thunder that starts deep in the ground.

The guards who were running toward them drop from view, screaming. Gunshots pepper the air as they tumble and scramble, but they can't stop what's started. The earth shears away, dragged down by the monstrous weight of the water eroding it from within and above. Sodden and saturated, it plummets, taking the guards with it.

And Calla, along with several of her people.

She screams, scrabbling at the air, then the moving mud, then at nothing.

She disappears. A split-second later, her terrified cry abruptly ends.

Hayze and Aura rush forward, Pace and Tempo beside them yanking the panicked people trying to flee the landslide to safety. More ground cleaves away and Hayze leaps, grabbing a man's arm as he drops. The man screams in terror as he falls, the soil wrenched from beneath his feet. Hayze is yanked down, then dragged through the mud as the ground disappears, now becoming a sheer drop.

"Hayze!" Aura screams and two hands grab his calves.

He comes to a stop, his torso now hanging over the muddy cliff that's been carved into the hill. He grits his teeth as he keeps his hold of the man now dangling over a raging river.

The same one that's already taken Calla.

"Don't let go!" the man gasps, water running over his white face.

Hayze reaches down with his other arm. "Hold on!"

The man grabs him and their hands interlock. Cold explodes beneath Hayze, followed by the sound of crackling. He realizes Pace or Tempo just turned the ground beneath him to ice, fortifying it.

The sound of a tree crashing into the water echoes in the distance.

"Pull!" Aura shouts.

The hands on Hayze's legs tighten and he's dragged backward, his stomach, then chest sliding over frozen ground. It's freezing and jagged and absolutely welcome. Moving back means survival. For both him and the man whose face is covered in tears and rain.

Within seconds, Hayze is on cold, solid ground. Several more, and the man's also safely away from the edge. Hayze releases him and staggers to his feet. A gasp has him opening his arms as Aura clasps him tightly.

A woman runs over to the man, sobbing as she wraps herself around him. The man hugs her back, then shakily brings them both to their feet. "T-Thank you," he pants.

Hayze nods. "We were never your enemy."

Aura releases him. "Go to your homes," she tells the man, then the remaining Terrans still here. "Find safety in the highest boughs you can."

The people are already running, the man and woman with them. Rain slices over the empty scene, a raging river now only yards away. Hayze's parents and a few Alliance members are all who remain.

His mother rushes toward them, but Hayze takes a step backward. She comes to a stop, water coursing over her confused face. "Hayze?"

"You shouldn't be here."

His father slaps his fist into his hand, spraying water in every direction. "The leaders must be stopped! It's the only way!"

"Look what they did to you," his mother pleads. "To us."

"It was wrong." Hayze shakes his head. "But so is this."

His father looks like he's been struck. His mother's hand flutters to her mouth.

Hayze's gut is just as tumultuous as the wet world he's standing in. He never thought he'd defy his parents like this.

Not when the next step is as gray and murky as the horizon. He may have rejected their call to war, but he has no clue what the right thing to do is. They have no idea where Jewel is.

How can the Elements be the solution when they're as divided as the Quadrants?

A voice slices through the growing tension. "To end this, you need to go back to where the Elemental Games began."

A voice Hayze never expected to hear again.

CHAPTER
FOURTEEN
AURA

"Geo." Aura stares at the boy from Earth, barely able to believe this is possible. "You're alive."

He nods, rain running down his face, his dark eyes fixed on Aura.

A huge clap of thunder pierces the air and Hayze steps forward.

"We need to go somewhere to talk," he says as the rumbling subsides.

Geo nods, motioning for them to follow as he steps away. It seems he used up all his words when he appeared and told them that to end the Games they need to go back to where they began. But how do they do that when the true Sect holds nothing but despair and decay?

"Wait!" Sera grabs hold of Hayze's arm as he turns to follow Geo. "I refuse to lose you again."

"You're not losing me, Mom." Hayze embraces her quickly, then his father. "Last time they took me from you. This time you're letting me go."

117

"And he'll be back," Aura adds. "We all will be. Including Jewel. And when that happens, *then* we'll be ready to strike."

Hayze releases Ember to take Aura's hand as he nods at his parents. "We can't afford to get this wrong. Prepare the Alliance, regain your strength, and we'll come for you."

"I can't promise they'll wait," says Ember. "But we'll try."

"Hayze! Aura!" shouts Pace, several steps away now with Geo and the others. "Hurry up!"

Hayze gives his parents a smile that's filled with love and courage, and they return it with a look of pride in the man they raised.

Aura squeezes his hand, and they wade through the water in pursuit of Geo. Skylus flies ahead, just as sodden as the rest of them but at least she's not knee-deep in muddy water. Aura wouldn't mind some Air powers right about now.

The streets are chaotic and as Aura glances up, she can see people climbing high in their trees, seeking refuge until the storm passes. There's no sign of more guards to replace those swallowed by the hungry earth but that will only be a matter of time. Wherever Geo's taking them, Aura can only hope it's nearby.

Atmos slows, waiting for them to catch up.

"What's the matter?" Hayze asks him.

"Can we trust him?" Atmos tilts his head toward Geo. "This could be a trap."

Aura's eyes widen. It never occurred to her that Geo might be leading them into danger.

"He's one of us," says Hayze without hesitation. "Which means we can trust him."

"Pace is also one of us," Atmos grumbles.

"Exactly," says Aura, wondering if those two will ever see eye to eye. "Which is why you can trust him, too."

"The only way we can get through this is to stick together," says Hayze. "Geo coming back is the best lead we've had yet in finding Jewel."

Aura nods. "We need to hear what he has to say."

"Do you two ever disagree?" Atmos rolls his eyes, but he continues walking forward which means he's at least prepared to take their word for it and trust Geo for now.

"We've had disagreements," says Hayze. "Big time. But we also believe in forgiveness and second chances. You'd be wise to do the same. Pace is a good guy."

Atmos says nothing, just trudges forward.

"Hey," says Aura, thinking she realizes where they are, despite the streets having turned into rivers. At least it's only flowing at their ankles now, so is easier to move through. "That's Calla's tree."

Aura shudders as she recalls the gruesome way Calla died. Sure enough, Geo goes directly to Calla's enormous, ancient tree and pulls on the front door, which is thankfully just above the water level. He hauls it open and goes inside without so much as turning to see if the others are following.

"I suppose Calla doesn't need the tree now," says Hayze, his face riddled with guilt, even though they had nothing to do with her death.

"How did Geo know where she lived?" Aura asks. "He's from the Quakelands, not Terra."

"Let's find out," Hayze says, glancing around to check they haven't been followed by anyone.

Pace waits for Tempo to enter the tree house, then disappears into the darkness behind Geo. Atmos is just about to follow when Skylus drops down from above, landing with a splash and edging her way inside. Hayze puts a steadying hand on Aura's back, guiding her in.

It's such a relief to finally be out of the rain that Aura can't help but grin widely. It's like having a long drink of water after being lost in the desert. She lets go of Hayze's hand so she can wipe the rain from her face and shivers, realizing how cold she is. Hayze instantly lights a flame in his palm and everyone crowds around him as they rub their frozen hands together. Aura smiles, having forgotten for a moment that she never needs to feel cold again. She lights her own flame and Tempo and Pace flock to her for warmth.

"I suppose Fire can be useful at times," says Skylus, her purple robes turning a lighter shade as they dry.

Geo's the first to break away. He goes to one of Calla's shelves and retrieves a bowl of fruit that he sets on the table like he owns the place. Then he hands Hayze a large metal container with a few lumps of coal in it.

Hayze carefully transfers his flame to the coal and a warmth emanates across the room. Aura allows her own small fire to extinguish. There aren't enough seats for them all in this tiny kitchen, but Geo seems happy enough to stand, along with Skylus who's barely used her legs since she learned to fly. Aura slides onto Hayze's knee, grateful for the excuse to be close to him. It feels like an eternity ago that she spent the night with him in this very tree instead of the hours it was.

"You have some explaining to do, Geo," says Atmos, biting into a long, yellow piece of fruit and scowling as he realizes he needs to remove the peel.

Geo nods, seeming to be drawing up the courage to use the words he needs. He barely spoke during the Games, so this isn't likely to be easy for him.

"Take your time," Aura says gently.

"Well, I'm not dead," says Geo with the hint of a smile. "In case that's what you all thought."

"We kinda did," says Hayze. "I saw you die in the Sect. Until I found out that was virtual reality as well. Even then, I didn't think the leaders would let you get away."

"They didn't." Geo pulls back his narrow shoulders. "This time, I had the powers to fight them."

Aura tilts her head. "This time?"

"I've been in the Games before," he says.

Aura sits backward, almost crashing the back of her head into Hayze's nose. "What do you mean?"

Geo swallows. "This was my second time in the Games. Except last year I didn't get my powers. Nobody did. Nobody ever has. This time was different."

"Has anyone flown before?" Skylus asks, crossing her arms.

Geo shakes his head. "There wasn't so much as a single spark in any of the previous Games."

"Or a breath of wind," Skylus adds, forever trying to make her Element the most important.

"Everyone d-died," says Geo, his voice breaking. "Every year. Everyone died. Most during the Games. And those who survived were deemed as duds and killed on exit."

Atmos shifts uncomfortably in his seat, having had this particular word directed at him more than a few times since the Games began.

"Why didn't they kill you?" Tempo asks. "You said you didn't get your powers. Didn't that make you a dud?"

"The Earth boy who was turning eighteen this year had an accident," says Geo. "He fell from a safe zone during a quake and broke his neck. So, they decided to keep me alive and send me back in to take his place. They called it an experiment. They wondered if going in twice might be what made the difference."

"Was that the first time that happened?" asks Pace. "Surely someone else died before turning eighteen. Especially someone from the Quadrants."

"Why do you think they pay our parents when we're born?" Geo asks. "It's to make sure they have enough resources to keep us alive. And it's why they watch us so closely. Unless I'm mistaken, I believe I'm the first person to go in twice."

"Is that why Jewel didn't know you?" Tempo asks. "She said she'd never met you until the Games. You weren't the same age."

"I wasn't around over the past year," says Geo. "The leaders kept me in the Sect. Although, in fairness, I didn't remember Jewel either."

"Then why didn't you tell us what was happening?" Aura asks, feeling a little miffed. "You could have warned us that what was happening wasn't real."

"I wanted to," says Geo. "I wish you knew just how much I wanted to. But if I breathed a word, the leaders promised to kill me on the spot."

"Which is why you barely spoke," says Aura, a new understanding of the Earth boy sliding over her. The poor guy wasn't shy. He was terrified!

"As soon as I showed my powers, they removed me," says Geo. "They were worried if they kept me in, I'd say something."

"How did you escape your pod?" Atmos asks.

"I'm going to guess it was the same way you did," he replies. "I used my powers against the leaders. Seems they planned for everything, except that."

"That's because we're the Solution," says Pace with a great deal of sarcasm. "I can tell you already that I'm not solving anything for those ass—"

"Pace!" Tempo gasps.

"The leaders' problems are the same as our own," says Geo, seriously. "It's the way they're going about solving it that I have an issue with."

Everyone nods, unable to disagree with that. Each of them had been torn from their families and forced into a war they hadn't known existed. There's no fairness in that.

"Did Calla help you?" asks Skylus, leaning in for an answer. "How do you know her home so well? Was she working against the leaders and harboring you here?"

Geo shakes his head as he leans back on the counter. "Ever heard of hiding in plain sight?"

There are a few nods, so he continues.

"When I escaped, I stayed in the one place they'd never think to look for me," he says. "Right here in Terra. And then I went to the last place here that they'd expect to find me. Their beloved trade master's home. I've been hiding in the highest branches for weeks now, coming down for food whenever Calla leaves."

"Were you here last night?" asks Aura, remembering the noise she'd heard in the staircase that she'd been certain had come from above instead of below.

Geo nods. "You nearly found me on the platform when I fell off a branch. I only just managed to get into the shadows in time."

"Why didn't you talk to us then?" Hayze asks, his dark eyes wide with shock.

"There wasn't time," says Geo. "And I had to be certain Calla wouldn't see me. After being in the Games twice, I've become a little jumpy."

"We found a book of names," says Aura, needing to address something that's bugging her. "In the Sect. The *real* Sect. I don't remember seeing your name in it twice."

Geo shrugs. "How closely did you read it?"

"Not very." Aura remembers how she'd paid attention to the first years of the Games, the names blurring as she turned the pages until she got to the final Games where the names came into sharp focus. It's very possible Geo's name was in the forty-ninth Games and she hadn't noticed.

"I have a question for you," says Geo, tapping his long fingers on the worn table. "Why do you call it the *real* Sect?"

"Because that's what it is." Aura furrows her brow. "There was the virtual one, which was a total mirage, but we broke through a wall and found the real Sect in an old, falling down building. It's where we found the book of names."

"The leaders planted the book there," says Geo, shaking his head. "Trust me. You never find anything they don't want you to."

"What about Tempo?" Pace asks. "We found her there. Are you saying they wanted that, too?"

"You've got me there." Geo smiles. "*That* I don't think they wanted you to find. But they're not exactly going to keep the dead bodies where they spend most of their time, are they?"

"I wasn't dead," Tempo points out.

"But I'll bet you were almost dead," says Geo.

Tempo nods, unable to deny this.

"Then if that's not the real Sect, where is it?" Aura asks, trying to keep Geo on track before he clams up again like in the Games.

He grimaces. "I'm not sure."

"Great," mumbles Atmos. "That's helpful."

"I've been there though," says Geo. "It's where they kept me for almost a year. And let me tell you there was nothing old or falling down about it. It was the most high-tech facility I've ever seen."

"Do you have any idea at all where we start to look for it?" Hayze pulls Aura a little closer on his lap. "How did you get from there to here? What Quadrant do you think it's in? Was it hot, cold, windy, did you feel tremors?"

"I wish I knew." Geo shakes his head at the barrage of questions. "They kept me confined. And they drugged me when it was time to bring me out. All I know is if we can find it, we can end the Games properly. We need to make sure they never get the chance to run them again."

"First, we need to find Jewel," says Aura, never forgetting her friend.

"But we have all four Elements now," says Skylus, her voice bordering on a whine. "We don't really need Jewel if we have Geo."

"I need Jewel," says Aura.

"Me, too," says Tempo quickly.

"I want to find her," adds Pace. "Bet Hayze does, too."

"Of course." Hayze nods. "We can't leave her behind. And now Geo can tell us where to find her."

Geo crosses his arms, a sadness passing over his troubled face. "Yeah, there's a bit of a problem with that."

"Such as?" Aura prompts.

"When I woke up here in Terra, just before I escaped, there was only one pod," he says.

"What do you mean?" Aura asks. "How can there have only been one? The rest of us were all kept in pairs."

"No idea." Geo shrugs. "But I'm telling you, there was only one pod. I don't have a clue where Jewel is."

CHAPTER
FIFTEEN
HAYZE

They have no way of finding Jewel.

The words loop in Hayze's head, trying to filter through to understanding, but failing. Disbelief and denial have created an impenetrable barrier.

Aura frowns. "But..."

Seems she's experiencing the same thing.

How could there only be one pod?

How can there be no leads to find the final piece of their Elemental puzzle?

A deep rumbling echoes beyond Calla's tree, making Geo push off the counter. He frowns. "That sounded like another tree going down."

Hayze tightens his hands on Aura's waist. Suddenly, the thick wood keeping them dry doesn't feel so sturdy.

Pace rises to his feet. "I think it's time we see if Calla was right."

Tempo looks up at him, stilling. "To find out if we're the Solution?"

They want to see if they can stop this pounding rain? Stop the flooding?

Pace nods. "Time to test exactly how powerful we really are."

"Only one way to find out." Tempo pushes to her feet and slips her hands in his. "I say we recede the floodwaters while we're there."

Skylus shakes her head as the Water teens leave. "There's overconfidence and then there's overconfidence."

Hayze arches a brow. "Wouldn't want them getting too big for their robes—I mean, suits."

She narrows her eyes at him. "That could be disastrous."

Another rumble, this one closer, has Geo frowning. "So is what's happening outside."

"Let them try," Aura says quietly, her gaze on the gray wall of rain beyond the window. "We need to know what we're capable of."

Because apparently they're the Elemental Solution.

Whatever the fractal that means.

Skylus gets to her feet, for the first time looking as if her robes are dragging her down. "While they do that, I'm going to rest."

Atmos jumps up to join her. "I'm tired, too."

He leads Skylus away, as if he's also worked hard today as they battled the Elements. Hayze watches them, for the first time wondering what Atmos's failure to harness his Element is going to mean. Geo said anyone who failed the Games was killed.

Hayze sighs, the room feeling colder now that four fewer teens are in it. "We hadn't finished talking about what our next steps are going to be."

Aura smiles sadly as she weaves her fingers through his.

"They've reached the inevitable conclusion quicker than we have."

That there's no way to find Jewel.

That they have to give up the search. For now.

"That means..." Hayze chews on his lip, unsure if he wants to say it out loud.

Geo nods, not needing the words to be uttered. "There's only one way to move forward."

Aura stands, surprising Hayze as she tugs on his hand. "I can't believe I'm saying this, but I think Skylus has the right idea. Let's rest while we can. Decisions can be made in the morning."

Hayze is about to object, but he clamps his mouth shut. He finally acknowledges the exhaustion dragging at his muscles, making even getting up an effort. What's more, time alone with Aura is precious right now. It recharges his heart and mind, which are both struggling as much as his body.

Geo's gaze drifts to the window. "I'm going to stay here. Keep guard."

Hayze nods in gratitude, wondering what impact being in the Games twice has had on the Earth boy. Having to endure them the second time as he watches a fresh batch of teens have their worlds turned upside down would change a person.

Hayze would probably be on high alert at all times, too. Any assumption of safety has been stolen. Destroyed. And possibly never returned.

Aura leads them out of the kitchen and up into the small room they slept in. Was it really only less than twenty-four hours ago? Memories of their moments here, evidenced by the scorched ferns, have his blood heating. Yet as they sink into each other's arms, neither of them seeks more than the comforting touch they're giving and receiving.

Aura sighs as she snuggles in, her head on his shoulder and her arm around his chest. "This is just what I needed."

Hayze presses a kiss to the part in her hair. "Me too."

Blazing passion is one form of their love. One that burns away anything but the feel of Aura's skin, the scent of her, the taste of her.

So is simply holding the girl who touched his heart long before he can remember. This— feeling her heartbeat, hearing her breathe—is all that matters in his world. Hayze draws her even closer, smiling a little when Aura wraps a leg around his, twining their bodies together. There are too many moments where death almost separated them forever. Memories Hayze doesn't want to think about but will never forget because they're branded into his mind.

"I love you," he murmurs against her hair.

Aura sighs again, rubbing her cheek on his chest. "I'm glad. Because you're the reason my heart beats, Hayze."

She angles her head up and their mouths drift closer, lips brushing in a sweet caress as they seal their words as if they're a promise. A vow.

The reason they're fighting in a war they've never understood.

Aura settles back down, her blue eyes studying him. "I know it was hard to send your parents away."

He lets out a breath, turning to gaze at the rounded roof of their room as he tucks his other hand behind his head. Of course, Aura would focus on that. The guards, the flooding, the near-death punches that just keep coming are all on his mind.

But defying his parents pained him the most.

"They looked so hurt."

Aura's hand spreads over his chest, right above his heart. "You stood up for what you believed in. One day, they'll be proud of that."

"I hope so," Hayze says quietly. His father's been his role model and mentor his whole life. His mother the steady, loving foundation for them both. Fracturing their relationship was never something he'd want to do.

"And you were right," Aura adds.

Hayze glances at her, conscious there are layers to what she's trying to tell him.

"The leaders are wrong. But the war the Alliance wants is also wrong."

He gazes at Aura, seeing the soft conviction in her ocean eyes. He realizes that for the first time since they woke up in the Games, they're in agreement. United.

It's all Hayze has ever wanted.

In a twisted way, the Elemental Games gave him that.

He turns so they're facing each other, then threads his fingers through her hair. "The question is, what's the right thing to do?"

Aura's lashes flutter, all she needs to convey that she doesn't know the answer either. The people of the Quadrants are dying thanks to forced division and natural disasters. And Hayze, Aura and the others were created as a *solution*.

Aura stiffens. "Listen," she whispers, excitement and a hint of awe threading through the one word.

Hayze can't hear anything, but that's the point. The rain has stopped.

Pace and Tempo have subdued the deluge.

"They did it," Hayze breathes.

"Come on," Aura says, scrabbling over him and out of their little nook. "I want to see."

Finding himself grinning, Hayze follows as they make their way up through the tree to the upper boughs. There, they find Pace and Tempo standing at the edge of the platform. Hayze and Aura join them, his smile fading as they stop to take in the broad vista that opens out now that the rain isn't cloaking this twilight world in gray.

Terra is an ocean. A dark, expansive stretch of water punctuated by massive trees rising through in blooms of black. The streets have been swallowed by floodwater, creating a horizon that could be mistaken for Aqua.

Mother Nature is steadily blurring the lines between the Quadrants. Even she doesn't want the division. Except she's killing anyone who's not listening.

Pace drops an arm around Tempo's shoulder, sagging with exhaustion. "We stopped the rain," he says, stating the obvious. "Receding that much water is a far bigger task."

"The people of Terra are safe for now, which is what matters," Aura says, slipping her own arm around Hayze's waist. "The waters will recede on their own."

He pulls her close, his gaze still roaming over the sea that Terra has become. Could Pace and Tempo evaporate, absorb, control this much water? Even if they couldn't, if they'd started earlier, the flood never would've happened.

They've proven Calla right. They've proven the leaders right.

They're the Elemental Solution.

Hayze takes a step back, bringing Aura with him. "I think you should rest," he tells Pace and Tempo. "You've done more than enough."

Pace nods, his eyes heavy with more than just fatigue. They're heavy with understanding. Weighted by the knowledge of what's to come.

Tonight, they all rest.

Then at first light, they're going back to the Sect.

To the heart of where this all began.

To do what's right.

CHAPTER
SIXTEEN
AURA

The sun rises as it always does, bathing the world in light. But with light comes shadows, and with shadows comes trepidation. Aura snuggles closer to Hayze, fearful of what the day will bring.

They've had to accept they won't find Jewel. Not yet anyway. But they can still find what Geo described as the real Sect. Then they can bring all this to an end.

"What's the opposite of a Game?" Aura asks.

"That sounds like a riddle." Hayze drops a kiss on her forehead.

"No," she murmurs. "It's a serious question. Because Games aren't the solution to the world's problems. I'm just wondering what the opposite might be."

"I'm not sure," says Hayze, his voice croaky from sleep. "Reality?"

"Hmm, maybe." She runs a fingertip down his bare chest. "Just as long as it's not virtual."

He laughs. "Yeah, I've had enough of that to last a lifetime."

There's a knock at the door and Pace appears. He has dark

circles under his eyes and his hair is mussed. Aura's not sure if he's exhausted from bringing the relentless rain to an end or if he's been making up for lost time with Tempo overnight. She doesn't plan to ask.

"I thought I heard voices," he says. "Everyone else is downstairs. We're keen to make an early start before the guards come looking for us."

"Good thinking." Aura pulls the finely woven blanket a little higher. "We'll be down in a moment."

Pace leaves them and they get dressed in their Fire clothes. As much as her leathers feel like a second skin, Aura far preferred the closeness of being naked under the covers with Hayze.

"We need to be careful today." He pulls her into a hug. "I can't lose you. Promise me you'll be careful."

"I promise." She smiles up at him before he presses his lips to hers in a gentle kiss.

It's not until almost an hour later when they're crawling through the hole in the wall to the ancient Sect that the gravity of what Aura promised sinks in. How can she be careful when it's impossible to anticipate what could happen next? So much of what's been thrown at them has been out of their control.

The fact they'd made it through Terra and back to the wall without being seen seems too good to be true. Or maybe they just got lucky at last. Either way, they need to keep their wits about them.

"What is this place?" asks Skylus as she climbs through the wall, having lowered herself to their level—quite literally—to walk on her feet. "It's awful."

"I could think of something even more awful," Pace mutters, thankfully out of Skylus's earshot.

Tempo gives him a warning look then slips her hand into his. It warms Aura's heart to see these two falling in love again. It's a shame it took Pace almost dying for Tempo to come to her senses, but at least they're back on track.

"This is what we thought was the real Sect," Hayze explains as they blink up at the decrepit building stretching into the morning sky.

"Except it's not the real Sect," adds Geo.

Aura scans the surroundings. "And you think there's a good chance the real one can be found somewhere around here?"

Geo nods. "It makes sense. They couldn't have built it in one of the capitals. The leaders would never have agreed on which one. This land in the middle of all the Quadrants is the only neutral ground."

"Very true," Aura agrees. "That does make sense."

"Then let's have a look around," says Atmos, waiting for them to go first before he follows.

Aura can't blame him. With his powers still latent, he's the most at threat out of all of them. Even if he won't admit it.

Skylus moves ahead, hovering a few inches off the ground as if walking those few steps had worn out her feet. The rest of them follow, glancing around like they expect a guard to jump out from between one of the jagged cracks in the pavement.

When Skylus reaches the large double doors with the broken windows, she stops and screws up her face like they offended her.

Hayze moves ahead and pushes them open. The same musty stench as last time wafts out from the building.

"I might see what's up on the roof," Skylus announces. She shoots upward before anyone can open their mouth to protest.

"That might be useful, I suppose," says Aura, wishing the

Air girl would have at least stayed to discuss their options before disappearing again.

They step into the dark foyer and Aura and Hayze light torches in their hands, casting eerie shadows on the walls.

"Where do we start?" Tempo asks. "This place gives me the major creeps."

Geo points to the stairs. "Let's head up. I always felt like I was high above ground level when I was being kept in the Sect. I swear the building felt like it was swaying sometimes."

Atmos nods enthusiastically. "Skylus going to the roof was a good idea then."

"The Sect won't be on the roof." Pace rolls his eyes. "Unless it's invisible."

"Yeah, all right." Atmos follows Geo up a few stairs. "But she might find a clue that will help us."

"We need a system," says Hayze as the rest of them follow. "Why don't we start from the top of the building and work our way down?"

"Sounds good to me," says Aura as they pass the floor with the hospital wing and continue up. It feels strange to be climbing so high after spending her life living underground in a bunker. It's hard to know what's scarier. Falling from a height or being crushed under the earth.

She shakes her morbid thoughts away, wondering when and why she started thinking like that. Probably when she was taken from her home and forced to either harness her Elemental powers or die trying...

"You okay?" Hayze asks.

"I'm good." She does her best to smile, even if it has no hope of reaching her eyes. "You okay?"

"Never better." He winks, and surprisingly her smile doesn't just shoot to her eyes, it warms her heart. This boy from Fire makes everything better. "It's so dusty," says Tempo as they pass what seems to be another abandoned floor. "If the leaders were walking through any of these corridors, surely we'd see footsteps."

"Nothing's ever as it seems when it comes to the leaders," says Pace. "We'll still need to search everywhere."

With aching legs, they reach the top floor of the building where they found Tempo. The stairs open to the large space that looks like it contains nothing but dusty floors with cracked tiles and walls coated in peeling paint. The windows are boarded up and Aura and Hayze move their flames around, trying to get a better look at the room as they catch their breath after their climb.

"This is where we found you," Pace explains to Tempo. "Behind that fake wall."

Tempo frowns. "That wall is fake?"

Pace nods, just as Skylus bursts through a door at the rear of the room with a sign above it indicating it takes them up to the roof.

"Oh, there you are," she says, smoothing down her robes and smiling. "I thought it was going to be much harder than that to find you."

"I'm surprised you tried to find us at all," Pace says.

"Why do you all look so *exhausted?*" Skylus frowns at them. "Surely there weren't that many stairs."

"Next time, why don't you climb them and find out." Aura plants her hands on her hips.

"What's up there?" Hayze indicates the door to the roof.

"Nothing," Skylus says quickly. "Just a leaky roof. It's quite dangerous, actually. I wouldn't go up there. Unless you can fly, of course. *Like me.*"

"Oh, really?" Pace cocks a brow. "Can you fly? Why didn't you mention that earlier?"

"Are you blind?" Skylus reels back, clearly better at defying gravity than understanding sarcasm.

"Eterna didn't bless them with your powers," says Atmos, trying and failing to smooth over the situation. Skylus looks appeased, but Pace's face is turning as red as Tempo's hair as he holds back his next remark.

"Let's just have a quick look," says Hayze, marching to the door to the roof. "Then we can move on with the rest of the search."

Skylus steps in front of him. "I told you there was nothing to see up there. Don't you trust me, Hayze?"

He comes to a stop, his mouth flapping as he struggles to come up with an answer that isn't a lie.

"We're a team," says Aura, stepping up beside him and deflecting. "We're all working together."

"Yet some members are trusted more than others." Skylus pouts.

"We just need a quick look," says Geo.

"Fine," Skylus huffs, taking a step away from the door. "But I want a full apology when you see I'm telling the truth."

Hayze leads the way up a narrow, concrete staircase and opens a door at the top, letting in bright sunlight.

Aura allows the flame in her palm to go out, squinting as her eyes adjust.

They step out onto the roof, seeing that Skylus was indeed telling the truth. Both about there being nothing up here and it being dangerous. The surface of the roof is lined with sheets of rusted tin, the safety rails long since fallen apart, their remains lying on the edges of the vast space like ancient skeletons.

"Dammit," says Pace, his disappointment clear that Skylus was right. "Geo, does this look familiar?"

Geo shakes his head. "We're looking for a high-tech facility, not a rusted roof."

A large raven soars overhead, reminding Aura how high up they are. She feels like she's standing in Eterna's clouds. If only the Air Quadrant could put some of their pinwheels up here they'd get all kinds of information about the weather. If they didn't blow straight off the roof, back to the Stormsphere.

They're just about to return to the stairwell when the raven squawks.

Aura spins around, not trusting even the most innocent of animals after her time spent in the Games.

The raven swoops up into the sky and...

Disappears.

"Did you see that?" Hayze asks, his jaw dropping.

"It's like the fake wall we found Tempo behind," gasps Pace, his eyes glued to the sky.

Hayze points up as another bird flies overhead. "Look, that's the same bird we can see over there."

Sure enough, when Aura scans the sky, she finds not only are there two of the same bird, there's a replica of each and every cloud.

"It's like a mirror," says Tempo, taking a few cautious steps across the tin panels. "It's hiding something. A place the first bird flew into when it disappeared."

It seems Pace's earlier joke about the Sect being invisible may have been more accurate than any of them realized.

Tempo continues walking and Pace darts forward to follow her.

And just like the bird, after a few more steps, they both vanish.

"Pace!" Aura shouts. "Tempo!"

There's no response.

"Surely, they can still hear us," says Hayze, a puzzled look on his face. "Pace! What's over there?"

Again, nothing but silence bounces back in the breeze.

"How is that possible?" Geo practically runs forward, quickly disappearing into the nothingness.

"Great," says Atmos. "Now three are missing."

"Soon to be two more," says Hayze as he takes Aura's hand.

She nods. There's no way they can't go after their friends. Not when they might need their help. That's not even up for discussion.

"This day just keeps getting better," Atmos grumbles. "Fine then. I'll wait here."

"No." Skylus appears behind them at the top of the stairs, her face pale. "We should stay together. Come on, Atmos. We'll all go and take a look."

Atmos sighs deeply, then nods. The four of them walk forward. Well, three walk and one floats, which probably isn't a bad idea given how rusty this roof is.

There's a subtle change of light, and Aura blinks as her surroundings morph from a vast expanse of tin to a solid room with a roof and three walls.

"No!" she cries when she sees Tempo, Pace and Geo being held by guards with bags tied over their heads. "It's another ambush!"

Before Aura can raise her hands to wield her powers, a strong set of arms grip her around the waist and drag her down.

Then...

Darkness.

CHAPTER
SEVENTEEN
HAYZE

Hayze wakes up roaring and ready to fight.

Both instincts are cut off by electrifying pain arcing, slicing, razing down every nerve.

Screaming in agony, he jerks his body back. The one that had launched forward, prepared to attack, to defend Aura, only to hit a barrier.

One that electrocuted him.

Blinking, he twitches as his world comes into focus. A black net surrounds him, electricity flickering over the thick threads that are only inches from touching his skin. Above him, a drone hovers, the netting extending from its dark interior.

Just like the one above every other teen in the room.

"Hayze," Aura whispers, her face pained as if she felt everything alongside him.

A few feet to his right, she's also immobile, the electrified strands creating a bubble only a couple of feet on all sides, ensuring she can't go to him.

Just like he couldn't go to her the instant he woke up.

"Bastards," Pace growls from Hayze's other side.

He turns to see his friend, Tempo a little further down, followed by Skylus, Atmos, and Geo. They're being held in a line by drones above, a captive audience in the room they've found themselves in.

A room that holds seven pods.

And four leaders.

"Welcome," Avalan says with a smile. Hayze can't tell if it's gracious or smug. Likely a little of both.

His hands twitch at his sides, warmth pooling in his palms. Incinerating the electrified cage holding him is the next logical step.

"I wouldn't if I were you," Infernos says, his eyes flashing.

Cyclonis nods. "Did you really think we'd create you without a way to control you?"

Oceania's head snaps toward Pace, her eyes narrowing. "You may want to consider that water conducts electricity."

"Bastards," Pace snarls again, going still. Seems he was ready to do what it takes to escape, too.

"Fire doesn't," Hayze spits. He and Aura can render the net to ashes in a blink. And it's possible Geo could do something with his Earth powers. Maybe even take the floor out from under each of them.

Avalan inclines her head, challenge darkening her eyes. "The moment you try to use your powers, the net's programmed to close in around you."

Wrapping Hayze in a torture device.

Pace is right. The leaders are bastards.

"What's the Elemental Solution?" Aura asks, her voice slicing through the room.

Avalan turns her steady gaze to her. "Eterna's wish," she says, lifting her chin a fraction. "The only way humanity can survive."

Tempo gasps. "Eterna's real?"

"Of course she is," Skylus snaps.

"We tried to tell you," Atmos adds.

Hayze ignores the Air teens and their superiority. "What does that even mean?"

Cyclonis crosses his arms, his purple robes swallowing them. "Once you all have your powers, you'll understand."

Hayze doesn't need to glance at Atmos to know who the leaders are referring to. "Or you could just tell us."

"We deserve to know," Aura adds. "This is what you created us for, after all."

"Which you keep seeming to forget," Infernos snarls.

"We did create you." Oceania's lips thin. "You owe us everything."

"And we owe you nothing," Avalan finishes, her voice growing hard.

Hayze's response is just as flinty. "Yet you want our compliance." More than that, they want their loyalty.

Avalan draws in a sharp breath, the action flaring the anger in her gaze. "There's more than one way to ensure that."

Hayze half expects Skylus to pipe up saying the leaders already have her undying devotion, but she doesn't. It means tense silence stretches through the room. Registering it for the first time, Hayze sees it's exactly what Geo described—high-tech. The veined pods in the center are pristine white, the walls of the room filled with screens displaying more information than Hayze can process. Some have images of the old Sect, some of the virtual reality Sect, some of Terra and Aqua and Aeris and Ignis. Others simply have numbers scrolling over them in an endless stream. The space is clean in a way that's only ever existed in the fake world of virtual reality, practically perfect in its immaculate, blinding white. And the technology they're surrounded by is unfathomable to a boy who grew up in the Scorchlands.

Only a handful of people in the Quadrants or the capitals know this place exists. The majority of humanity lives in poverty, at the mercy of four Elements which are only becoming more powerful.

Hayze blinks. Then blinks again. "You want us to control the Elements," he breathes.

Although he has no doubt every teen trapped with him has already suspected this, saying it aloud has now made it real.

The Games, all fifty of them, were an attempt to create humans who can tame the Elements battering humanity.

And ultimately, control them.

"Eterna knows it's the only way," Avalan says.

"If she's real, then let her show herself," Pace demands. "She can outline this plan we were designed to enact."

Infernos glares at him. "No one demands to see Eterna."

Hayze reels back, then catches himself, conscious of the electrified netting behind. "You haven't met her, either."

Infernos curls his lip. "I don't answer to you."

"That's convenient," Tempo says quietly, although certainly loud enough for the leaders to hear.

The Fire leader's face twists with fury. His hand comes up, a small black rectangle within it. One angry jab of a finger and Tempo screams in pain.

Her net goes from a bubble to a second skin, electricity crackling and arcing as if it's furious too. She drops to her knees even as her back arches, her neck straining as the tortured sound explodes from her throat.

"No!" Pace yells, throwing himself against his own net, then leaping back as tiny bolts of lightning pepper him.

"Stop it!" Hayze roars.

"This is wrong!" Aura screams.

Hayze turns to the Water leader, the one person he's seen any hint of humanity in. Oceania looks pale yet doesn't move.

Seems any help she was willing to offer is gone now that the two Water teens have their powers.

Infernos jabs his control pad again and the net releases Tempo. She falls to her knees, her chest rising and falling in jagged breaths.

"Tempo, baby..." Pace says, agonized and helpless.

"I'll...be okay," she pants, her hair covering her face. A tear drops to the pristine floor, the only expression of her Element she can afford.

"Bastards!" This time, Pace screams the word, his hands impotent fists by his sides.

"You don't understand, do you?" Cyclonis says, shaking his head in disappointment.

"We understand, alright," Hayze snaps. "We understand you'll go to any length to see this through. Including killing dozens of people."

Infernos lifts his hand again and Hayze braces himself. The Fire leader has clearly found a way to unleash his frustration. But Oceania reaches out to press a hand to his arm. "They think they understand, but they don't." She turns back, her gaze roaming over the teens. "You've lived in the Quadrants. You've seen how many people are dying each and every day."

Hayze's gut clenches. Poverty is a given in the Quadrants. He just never thought to question why he and his parents were able to hover just above its clutches.

Because he was chosen, created, a *Solution*.

"If it continues, humanity will cease to exist," Cyclonis says. "As extinct as countless other species that are nothing but a memory."

Oceania nods. "Something must be done."

"By making us more powerful than Mother Nature herself," Aura concludes.

Avalan stills, and Hayze isn't sure whether it's in anger or something else. "We will never be at her mercy again. Not another life will be lost to her senseless violence."

Her words are said with such intensity that they hang in the air for long moments, refusing to fade.

Demanding to come to fruition.

"What do you want from us?" Geo asks, the first time he's spoken since they were captured.

Asking the question that now counts the most.

"You must return to the Elemental Games," Avalan says. Her dark gaze settles on Atmos. "To confirm whether you all have powers or not."

A chill trickles down Hayze's spine. Atmos must feel the same because his face goes pale. The unspoken threat is clear.

If Atmos doesn't prove he can harness Air, he'll suffer the same fate of every other teen who failed the Games.

Death.

"No." Hayze spits the word out, firing it like a bullet.

"This isn't the answer," Aura says with just as much force.

Avalan sighs. "You may want to recollect there's more than one way to ensure your compliance."

The drones above each teen hum in agreement and the nets crackle with anticipation.

"We need to do as they ask," Skylus says, her voice thready but sure.

"They're not asking us to do anything," Hayze growls. "They're forcing us to do this."

Tempo gets to her feet, her face almost as white as the walls. "We don't have a choice."

"That sounds like an assumption to me," Hayze growls.

"Hayze," Aura gasps. "No—"

But he's already moving. He lifts his arms, flaring a fireball in each palm. "You can't—"

The netting contracts, encasing him in pain. The only thing

that explodes is agony along every muscle fiber as electricity whips through like vicious lightning. Hayze roars, the sensation of every sinew and nerve being stretched and contracted simultaneously seizing his mind.

"Hayze!" Aura screams.

He cracks his eyes open, registering she's being herded forward by the netting, forced to move so it doesn't touch her. And he's being lifted, his body thrashing with the voltage being pumped through it. He's carried through the air in a crackling, twisting mess of pain.

"Don't fight it!" Pace shouts.

Except fighting this is the only thing Hayze has left.

No matter how useless it seems.

He tries to focus on his hands and the power that lies within them, but each attempt is cut off by jolt after jolt of agony, all coming at him in a relentless onslaught. His body is being consumed by the energy being unleashed without mercy.

Hayze is vaguely aware that something else touches his skin. The pain is gone as suddenly as it was inflicted, leaving him trembling and sweaty. He squints, trying to bring the world back into focus. Trying to unjumble what's left of his brain.

He registers white, veined walls closing around him. Beyond that, he catches a glance of the other pods slowly folding in, no doubt Aura and the others inside. The leaders haven't moved, satisfied smiles gracing their faces. The drone still hovers above Hayze, waiting to see if he'll be foolish enough to try and stop the inevitable.

Well, he sure as damnatus is—

The new world Hayze finds himself in wipes away any thought.

He executes a slow turn. He's been in the Games enough

times to know survival depends on his mind catching up with his surroundings. It still takes precious seconds for what he's seeing to make sense, though.

It's an...arena. One with towering walls that soar up to an open sky, creating a massive, impressive prison. Colored chairs line them, as if this is a spectator sport. One section is red, and the others blue, purple and green. Aura's several yards to Hayze's right, looking like she's fighting to understand this as much as he is. Pace is to his left, Tempo and the others spread out in a wide circle.

"It's the Elemental Games," Geo calls out. "This is where I was the first time."

This is where all of the other versions were held?

Hayze is about to tell the leaders exactly what he thinks when he registers the final piece of this sick puzzle.

In the center, high up on a floating platform, is a pale, terrified Atmos.

"Help me!" he screams. "Please!"

CHAPTER
EIGHTEEN
AURA

"Atmos!" Aura gasps, staring up at the floating platform where the Air boy is perched, his trembling obvious even from this distance.

They're standing in a large, circular pit on hard, brown soil. The empty space is ringed with colored seats that rise high into the sky. This place could seat tens of thousands of spectators, instead of the mere four they know are watching them now.

There's a movement on the other side of the arena and Aura realizes that there aren't seven of them here to compete in the Games.

There are eight.

"Jewel," she breathes, her fingertips fluttering to her mouth to see her friend running toward her.

Jewel throws herself at Aura, wrapping her arms around her neck and embracing her tightly.

"Aura!" she sobs. "I'm so happy to see you. I missed you so much."

"We've been trying to get you out," says Aura, hugging her

back before pulling away to look into her dark eyes. "We couldn't find your pod."

Jewel seems confused by this, but there's no time to explain. Not with Atmos's sobs growing louder by the second.

"Don't fear!" Skylus calls up to him. "I'll rescue you!"

She lifts from the ground and shoots high in the air as the others crowd around Jewel, staring at her like she's an apparition, which to be fair right now they all are.

Hayze puts an arm around Jewel. "It's so good to see you again."

She smiles at him, her eyes filling with tears, making Aura wonder what she's been put through since they saw her last.

Geo takes over from Hayze, giving Jewel a hug.

"Geo! I thought you were dead," says Jewel. "How are you alive?"

"Long story," he says.

"Which you're going to tell me later," she insists just as a loud bang shakes the arena. They immediately look up to see Skylus has flown into an invisible shield surrounding Atmos's platform. She propels herself forward with a determined look on her face, only to bang into the nothingness once more before being repelled back.

"Atmos!" she shouts, hovering at his level as she holds out her hands. "You need to jump across to me."

"No!" Pace calls out. "He'll bounce back like you did and fall."

Aura swallows. Falling from that height isn't survivable.

Except...

"You can't die!" Aura reminds Atmos. "There's no need to be scared."

Atmos nods, gets to his knees, then very slowly stands.

"I can't die!" he shouts, more to himself than any of them.

"Come to me," says Skylus, keeping her hands

outstretched. She's several feet away from him, which even without the invisible shield would make this task difficult. But still, it's possible.

"The shield might only work one way," says Tempo. "You can do it, Atmos!"

He steps back on the platform as far away from Skylus as possible, then takes two long strides, leaping into the air.

For two beats of Aura's heart, she thinks he's going to make it.

Until he slams into the shield, bounces back and with his hands grappling with the air, he hurtles to the ground, his blood-curdling scream echoing around the empty arena.

Aura winces, burying her face in Hayze's arm as Atmos connects with the solid earth.

"It's okay," says Hayze, wrapping his arm around her and squeezing. "He disappeared."

Aura turns her head to see the hard ground beneath the platform is completely bare without any sign of the tragedy she expected to see.

"Atmos?" says Jewel. "Where did he go?"

An awful sob filters down from above and they look up to see him clinging to the platform once more. Skylus hovers as close as she can, shaking her head at him with more disgust than relief.

"You need to learn to use your powers," she scolds. "Didn't you hear what the leaders said? It was quite simple. We all need to confirm we've harnessed our powers, then we can get out of here."

"They said that?" asks Jewel from beside Aura.

Aura nods. "Just before they put us back in."

"Hold on." Jewel lifts a palm. "You were all out? As in, everyone except me?"

"Like I said, we couldn't find your pod," Aura explains. "We looked everywhere we could think of in Terra."

"Thanks for trying." Jewel slips her hand into Aura's. "That must have been dangerous."

"Not really," Aura lies. "Where have they kept you? Your mind, I mean? Have you been in the Games this whole time?"

Jewel's eyes fill with tears as she looks away. "I've been in the darkness."

Now Aura knows why Jewel's so teary. She's been kept alone with nothing to do and nobody to talk to. That's the worst kind of prison there is. She must be ecstatic to be back in these torturous Games.

A huge gust of wind blasts them, and Aura lifts her hands to shield her face from the dust that's stirred up.

"It's Skylus!" Hayze shouts, pulling both Aura and Jewel to his chest. "She's trying to blow Atmos's platform over to her."

Aura squints as she looks up, seeing Skylus summoning the platform as Atmos desperately clings on with white knuckles, his purple robes and dark hair the only parts of him that defy gravity as they fly out in Skylus's direction.

The platform is blown toward Skylus, and Aura blinks rapidly, keeping her gaze on Atmos. He slams into the invisible wall as the platform tips vertically, sending him plummeting.

"No!" she gasps. "Not again."

The blast of wind stops, and the boy from Air rockets toward the ground, vanishing just as he makes contact.

Looking up again, Aura's not surprised this time to see the platform back in place with an exhausted Atmos perched on top of it.

A voice of indeterminate gender bounces around the arena. *"Skylus from Air passes the Elemental Games."*

Skylus shoots down and lands in front of them, smiling broadly. "Well?"

"Well, what?" Pace snaps back. "Don't expect our congratulations. Atmos is still up there."

"I'm the only one who's passed so far." Skylus rolls her eyes. "If you want to get out of here, you need to demonstrate you've harnessed your powers. I may not have helped Atmos just yet, but I've proven I can control Air."

"Skylus is right," says Geo. "You don't want to be a dud. They kill the duds."

"This is ridiculous," says Hayze. "We've already proven our powers in the Games."

"They weren't the real Games," says Geo. "That was just a warm-up. *This* is the real Games. This arena is where they've always been held."

Turning his back and stepping away, Geo raises his hands.

The earth rumbles and everyone drops to all fours, knowing what's about to come.

"No, Geo," gasps Tempo. "Atmos will fall again."

"He won't," says Jewel. "That platform's no different to a safe zone. He's the only one who won't feel the quake."

The energy in the earth builds, the tremor growing in size until a loud crash shatters the arena as a section of purple seats collapse in on themselves.

Geo drops his hands, and the quake subsides.

The mysterious voice returns, circling around the arena. *"Geo from Earth passes the Elemental Games."*

He walks back to them, seeming like a weight has lifted from his shoulders. Aura can't blame him given he's seen first hand what happens when these Games aren't passed. It's just a shame he couldn't have saved Atmos in the process.

"You still didn't help Atmos," says Jewel, seeming to have read Aura's mind. "Here, let me try. Stand back everyone."

They take a few steps and Jewel ushers them even further back.

"What's she doing?" Tempo asks as small rocks and particles of dirt begin to swirl in the arena, forming a small hill underneath the platform.

"She's being a frenius," says Pace, stealing Hayze's made-up word. "She's going to raise the earth to the platform."

More dirt swirls, and Aura literally feels the ground being taken from beneath her as the pit becomes deeper at the edges and the hill in the middle builds until its peak is only a few feet beneath the platform. It looks even higher than it did before now that they've sunk a few feet further into the ground.

"Atmos!" they all shout. "Jump!"

Atmos peers down from above, his eyes widening as he sees what Jewel's created. Dangling his feet from the edge of the platform he eases himself off the edge, and tumbles down.

"You did it, Jewel!" Aura cries out, her heart swelling with pride for her clever friend.

Atmos lands on the peak of the hill, except instead of tumbling down the side as they all expect, he sinks into the dirt, disappearing right into the very center.

"Atmos!" Jewel shrieks, waving her hands as she parts the hill, desperately trying to find him. Geo joins in, and together they comb through the tiny rocks and particles of dirt, watching the hill crumble as they search.

"He's going to suffocate," Aura whispers, finding herself holding her own breath. "Nobody can survive inside there."

"Which means he'll start again," says Hayze, pointing at the platform and groaning. "Look."

Aura follows his gaze, seeing Atmos back on the platform like he never left. He's visibly shivering now, the shock of having *died* three times in such a short period taking its toll.

The voice echoes around the arena once more. *"Jewel from Earth passes the Elemental Games."*

Jewel groans. "I'd rather have saved Atmos."

"Even *I* want to save Atmos," says Pace, shaking his head as he looks up at the platform.

"This is what he needs," says Skylus, pulling back her shoulders. "We all know Atmos hasn't been able to master his powers. He's the only one. Putting him in this situation is exactly what's required."

Aura winces at her harshness. "Nothing justifies terrifying someone like that."

"Over and over," Tempo adds. "It's barbaric."

"It's *necessary*," Skylus corrects before tilting her face upward. "Come on, Atmos, just fly already. I've already told you exactly how to do it."

"Maybe he can't," Pace whispers, feeling sorry for his nemesis at last. "Maybe he really is a dud."

"He just needs more time," says Jewel. "I'm sure he can do it."

Aura wishes she had her optimism. Surely, if he could do it, they'd have seen his feet lift from the ground by now.

"What if I fill the arena with water?" Pace suggests. "Then he could jump into the water and I'll slowly bring the level down."

"We had enough water already in Terra," Skylus groans.

"Don't you mean Aqua?" Jewel seems confused.

"No, sadly," says Aura. "There was a flood in Terra. Even the capitals are suffering now. Things are getting much worse out there."

Pace scowls at Skylus. "You can't stop us using our Element, just because you got a little damp recently."

"Then let's try another ice slide," Tempo suggests. "Like the one you made in Terra."

Pace's face lights up as he shakes his head in awe. "How did I not think of that?"

"We can work on it together," says Tempo, grinning.

As they all step back to give the Water couple some space, Hayze wraps his arm around Aura.

"Can you think of any way we can help if the slide doesn't work?" she asks.

"I really can't," he says. "We might just have to do what Geo did and prove our powers without helping Atmos."

Aura nods. "It's just that..."

He draws her closer to him. "It's just that what?"

She grimaces. "What will happen to Atmos? What if the leaders end the Games after everyone else has won? We're moving too fast. Maybe Atmos just needs more time, like Jewel said."

Hayze groans. "You promised me you were going to be careful. That's not being careful. That's putting yourself at risk for Atmos."

"It can't have been easy for him," says Jewel, listening in. "For Atmos, I mean. Watching all of us harnessing our powers while he remained stuck. I'd probably be rude too if that happened to me."

Aura can't imagine that for a moment, but she nods. As much as these Games have been difficult for everyone, they've indisputably been the worst of all for Atmos.

The sound of ice blasting drags their attention back to the arena as Tempo and Pace form a giant slide that stretches from the platform to the ground in a gentle slope.

"It looks like a frozen rainbow," says Hayze, clearly impressed.

"This has to work," says Jewel, nodding enthusiastically. "I can't see how it could go wrong."

Aura winces, wondering how Jewel can be so optimistic given everything she's recently endured.

"Atmos!" Pace shouts when the slide is complete. "Come on down!"

"You're not helping him," mutters Skylus. "What hope does he have of harnessing his powers when you're making it so easy for him?"

Atmos leans over the edge of the platform as he studies the Water couple's construction. He gives them a small smile, nodding at Pace with what can only be described as gratitude. Atmos may not have found his powers, but it seems he's found peace in the war he's been having with the boy from Water.

Atmos crawls to the top of the slide and positions himself on the ice. Using his hands, he propels himself forward, sliding several feet.

"It's working!" says Jewel. "Come on, Atmos."

He slides a few more feet then begins to slow, losing momentum when he should be gaining it. Then he grinds to a complete halt.

"What's going on?" Pace shouts.

"I'm stuck!" Atmos calls back. "The ice is too cold."

"It's freezing him to the slide," Aura gasps.

"Quick!" says Tempo, raising her hands. "We need to unstick him."

The sky opens up as the Water couple send rain falling from the sky in heavy droplets.

"Too much!" shouts Aura, blinking in the downpour.

Tempo and Pace wave their hands, undoing what they started. And while the rain instantly eases, it's too late for Atmos. The water melts the ice, the section he's sitting on caving in under his weight, sending him plummeting as it breaks away.

"Fly, Atmos!" shouts Skylus. "Fly!"

He flaps his arms more like a bird than a master of his Element.

Then crashes to the ground.

Vanishes.

And reappears on his platform.

A voice reverberates through the arena. *"Pace and Tempo from Water pass the Elemental Games."*

"Help me," sobs Atmos, his voice far weaker than the first time he'd cried out for help. "Please, help me."

A sick feeling punches Aura in the gut.

Everything they tried so far should've worked. And none of it did.

These Games are rigged. The leaders want Atmos to harness his powers, just like Skylus said.

Except, he can't.

Atmos is a dud.

Yet Aura refuses to watch him die.

CHAPTER
NINETEEN
HAYZE

"We can't use our powers," Hayze says, the realization making his gut clench painfully.

Aura drags her gaze from Atmos, the hard determined expression that had just molded it twisting with confusion. "We have to save him."

"Yes, we do," Hayze agrees. They can't leave Atmos to the mercy of the Elemental Games. "But we can't do it with our powers."

Understanding dawns over Aura's face, somehow tightening the determination even as it draws her shoulders in, as if she's nursing the now-fragile belief they can do this.

"You mean Atmos can't use his powers," Pace says, frowning.

Aura shakes her head. "No. Hayze and I can't."

Skylus huffs, crossing her arms. "Using our powers is the whole idea of the Elemental Games. The sooner you throw some Fire around, the sooner we can leave."

Aura looks up at Atmos. "If we do..."

"The Games will be over," Geo finishes.

Tempo's eyes widen. "And Atmos will be killed."

Geo nods, having lived under the same threat. Hayze can still remember the joy on Geo's face as he called the rocks to him when he stood on the ledge of the mountain. The victory. It would've been sweeter on so many levels.

Mostly because it meant he could live.

"Please help me," Atmos wails, now kneeling on his platform. "I can't keep doing this."

His voice cracks on the final word, as if the rest of him isn't far behind. Dying over and over in the Games won't kill Atmos, but being repeatedly pulled into a pit of hopelessness and helplessness will break his spirit. His body will inevitably follow.

"We'll get you down," Hayze calls up to him.

"Just hang on," Pace adds.

Atmos nods. "It's not like there's much else for me to do," he says, his lips twisting dryly. Then he scowls as his shoulders sag.

There's nothing else for Atmos to do because he's never harnessed Air.

He can't win these Games.

"We have to find a way to get him down," Hayze says, just as determined as Aura that losing doesn't have to mean dying.

"Without using Fire," she adds, narrowing her eyes as she scans the arena. All they're surrounded by are hundreds of staggered seats. She draws in a sharp breath, then spins back to Jewel and Geo. "What if we build him some stairs?"

"Yes!" Jewel exclaims.

Geo nods, already rubbing his palms together. "Those rows of seats are about to be rearranged."

"I don't think so."

Everyone spins toward Skylus, Pace's mouth open and no doubt ready to tell her what he thinks of her pessimism.

They all freeze simultaneously as they register what the Air girl has seen.

A monstrous column of ice is twisting and curling its way up to Atmos.

"Are you doing that?" Hayze calls out to Pace and Tempo.

"Not us," Tempo says. "It must be the leaders."

"Don't worry. We're on it!" Pace shouts. He and Tempo throw their hands forward, their faces intense and focused.

The white-blue pillar curls like a shimmering serpent, weaving its way relentlessly upward.

"Help!" Atmos screams as he watches it approach. "I can feel how cold it is!"

"It's not real," Hayze shouts. "Anything you feel is only in your mind."

Atmos nods, although he's becoming paler by the second. What will happen when the frozen, glittering column reaches him?

"We've got this," Pace grinds out. His fingers curl and the tendons on the back of his hands stretch taut as his whole body strains with focus.

"It's strong," Tempo gasps, her body trembling with effort.

The column slows its twisting growth. The exterior shimmers as its surface melts.

Then it roars up, faster and thicker than before.

It explodes outward as it reaches the platform, five ropes of ice shooting over the top. They crackle as they curve out like petals, then come together several feet up. Hayze draws in a sharp breath, more crackling fracturing the air as the strands solidify and thicken. Gnarled knuckles form, tendons and details become visible.

A frozen hand now holds Atmos captive on the platform.

Tempo drops her arms, panting. "It's no use."

Pace hesitates, then follows suit. "The leaders have ulti-mate control. If they don't want us melting the ice, we can't."

"The leaders want *us* to do this," Aura whispers.

Hayze yanks his gaze from the frozen fist to find her looking at him. It wasn't just her words that grabbed his atten-tion. It's their heaviness.

"They want Fire to melt it," she adds, frowning.

"Too fractal bad," Hayze growls.

"I was just thinking the same thing," Aura says, tensing as if she's preparing herself.

Hayze finds himself doing the same. The leaders laid down a gauntlet that he and Aura refuse to pick up. That won't go unpunished.

To Hayze's surprise, it's Skylus who moves next. She lifts a foot off the ground. "I'll see if I can at least weaken it."

She flies up toward the frozen fist holding Atmos before anyone can respond. Hayze doubts they had much to say. Even Skylus's arrogance has taken a beating. She's talking like she's not sure even her impressive powers can save her friend.

Atmos's face appears between two ice fingers, pale and shivering. "S-So c-c-c-old," he chatters.

Hayze is about to remind him this is virtual reality when Aura grabs his arm. "Unless the leaders are dropping his body temperature in real life," she says, her voice low as she knew exactly what he was going to say.

"They wouldn't..."

Even before Hayze has finished, he knows the leaders most certainly would.

They're trying to blur the lines between virtual and real. Which means blurring the line between Atmos believing he's dead.

And dying.

Skylus hovers in front of Atmos, bringing her arms out wide. Her robes flutter as she calls on her Air powers, but she suddenly stalls. "His lips are turning blue!"

Which could be fake.

Or a true representation of what's happening to Atmos's body.

"We have to get him out of here!" she cries, once more whipping up a storm.

A gust of wind blows through the arena, strong enough to buffet Jewel. Except it dies before she's knocked over.

Because Skylus is tumbling to the ground.

Limp and lifeless, her body falls like a rag.

"Skylus!" Tempo screams.

She's about to hit the hard soil when a thick tangle of vines shoots up and wrap around her. Skylus is quickly encased in twisting green, then gently lowered to the ground. White flowers bloom around her as the vines spread out, creating an eye-catching landing pad.

Hayze glances at Jewel and she shrugs, flushing a little. "No reason saving someone can't be pretty."

Aura rushes over and everyone quickly follows. She kneels down as Skylus sits up, her hand to her temple. "What happened?" Aura asks.

Skylus shakes her head. "I-I don't know. One minute I was up there, the next..."

She was being caught by pretty vines.

"My head..." Skylus murmurs, then falls back onto the bed of flowers. "I—" Her eyes flutter closed as she lets out a breath.

Aura quickly reaches out to check her. "She's fallen unconscious," she says, relieved.

Images of Skylus falling from the sky in Terra and landing in the floodwaters, so still they weren't sure she was alive, rise in Hayze's mind. This isn't the first time it's happened to Skylus.

"Ah, guys..." Pace has them all spinning back and registering he's looking back at Atmos's platform. "That's not me doing that."

Tempo joins him. "Or me."

Yet the frozen fist is melting. Hayze doesn't bother to glance at Aura, already knowing she's not the one doing this. Just like he isn't. Atmos's life depends on them not using their powers.

Aura steps forward, frowning. "The leaders must be doing it."

But why?

Atmos gets to his feet, his head, then torso rising above the melting ice. "Help!" he cries, waving his arms as if to remind them he's here. "Get me down!"

Tempo gasps as a giant finger snaps off, then another, and another. Yet nothing hits the ground. The digits disappear a split second before the rest of the hand. Within a blink, it's gone.

"They're going to try something else," Hayze says, keeping his voice low and senses alert. The leaders have a Plan B.

"Please?" Atmos shouts. "I'm getting thirsty."

"It's not real. You can't—" Aura cuts Hayze off again with a touch. He clamps his mouth shut, realizing she's right.

If the leaders can make Atmos cold, they can certainly stop any sustenance reaching his body. In fact, Hayze is thirsty himself. He realizes it's the first time he's ever felt that in the Games.

They're upping the stakes.

"Sweet fractal."

It's Pace who breathes the words. Tempo who gasps a second later.

Jewel and Geo are struck mute.

"Hayze," Aura gasps.

As he watches the next challenge unfold, he has no idea how to respond.

A roaring fire has come to life beneath the platform. Beneath Atmos.

It widens, the flames dancing with excitement as they expand and lengthen. In the space of a heartbeat, they leap up, flaring an unnatural, dark red. Hayze can feel the heat even from this distance and he has to remind himself it's not real.

"Help!" Atmos screams hysterically, his face a mottled mess of terrified white and flushed red. "Please, I can't..." He staggers backward as a wall of flames explode in front of him, then quickly catches himself as his heels reach the rear of the platform.

"Tempo," Pace calls, running forward a few feet only to be stopped by the wall of heat.

She joins him and they unleash waterfalls of water, throwing everything they have at the base of the flames.

They don't even vaporize. There's no hiss, no steam.

The rivers that should put the flames out are simply swallowed by the fire.

A scream rises from the platform. A curtain of flames surrounds Atmos, trapping him as surely as the frozen fist. He falls to his knees, his hands gripping his head as the wail grows in intensity. Both pain and terror fuel it as surely as the leaders are fueling the heat. The same inferno he can no longer tell himself isn't real.

It's only a matter of seconds before Atmos realizes leaping off the platform is preferable to this. And there's a chance he won't wake up as his mind gives up the fight.

Geo's shaking his head as if trying to deny what they're being forced to watch. "We have to do something."

"We need Fire," Jewel whimpers.

Aura's hand weaves through Hayze's, a silent communication they'll face this together. The leaders want them to put it out by using their powers. To prove what they've already proven.

They are Fire. They're the only ones who can extinguish the flames trying to devour Atmos.

Except, by doing so, they kill Atmos.

And that's not something Hayze wants to live with.

"I love you," he says, turning to look at Aura.

She glances back, frowning despite the words. She heard the hitch in them. The decision he's trying to tell her he's made.

"Hayze—"

He squeezes her hand, releases it, and breaks into a run. Atmos's endless scream becomes louder with every pounding step, the heat grows exponentially. Hayze uses both to fuel his desperate run, hoping to heckus that Aura doesn't follow him.

Hoping to heckus the assumption he's making is right.

"I can't die," he says over and over, the words now a mantra. "I can't—"

He leaps into the pyre beneath Atmos, instantly swallowed by the shades of scorched air. The heat is overwhelming in ways it hasn't been since he discovered his powers.

This is outside of him, not within.

The scream that's wrenched out of Hayze is involuntary. The pain rips at his throat, propelled by every cell being incinerated. He falls to his knees, his hands braced on the ground, registering the way his skin's already blackened and blistering.

It's not real.

"I can't die..." he whispers through numb lips.

Except his body is an inferno.

It's not real.

"I. Can't. Die."

The skin of his arms peels away like bark, the red flesh beneath instantly turning to charcoal.

This feels so real.

"I can't—"

Then nothing.

CHAPTER
TWENTY
AURA

Agony tears at Aura's soul.

Hayze is on fire.

The hungry flames are devouring him, sending the searing stench of burning flesh roaring around the arena.

"Hayze," she sobs as the guy she loves is reduced to nothing but ash. "Hayze."

She knows he's not dead. Not really. But the agony he felt was real, as is the grief tormenting her now. Because the leaders can't be trusted. The icy hand that grabbed Atmos was proof of that. There's no guarantee Hayze is coming back.

She crumples to the hard ground, burying her face in her hands. She can't watch this. She won't watch this. The leaders are sick. And Hayze is the most courageous person she's ever met.

There's a hand on her back and she spins around, her heart lighting with hope.

Except it's Pace.

He squats beside her and pulls her into a hug, reminding her of the comfort he'd provided when Hayze had first been

167

taken from the Games. She presses herself to her friend, needing his support just as much now. Perhaps even more.

"Hayze will be fine," he whispers, knowing exactly what words she needs to hear.

She nods, even though with every second that passes the hope in her heart extinguishes just a little. Atmos appeared immediately on the platform each time he died.

"Where is he then?" she chokes out. "Why isn't he back?"

"I'm here," comes the voice she needed to hear most. "I'm here, Aura. I'm fine."

Pace releases her and she springs to her feet to find Hayze standing before her. She throws herself at him and he hugs her, swinging her around so her feet leave the ground.

"We can't die," he says. "You should know that."

"And you should know rules don't exist out here," she scolds. "You may not have died, but you could have been pulled from the Games."

She doesn't need to add that would be a death in itself. Every moment they spend apart is one that doesn't feel worth living.

Hayze presses his cheek to the top of her head and she lifts her face. His lips are drawn to hers and she kisses him with everything she has. Because it's a kiss she hadn't counted on being able to have.

"I love you, Hayze," she murmurs.

"I love you, too."

"Umm, guys." Pace coughs beside them. "I hate to interrupt, but we have a situation unfolding here."

Aura and Hayze break apart, scanning the arena for what Pace is talking about. The fire has gone out. Everything is quiet.

Too quiet.

Atmos is lying down on his platform, almost completely out of sight, aside from an arm dangling over the edge. And the other four teens are sprawled on the ground, completely exhausted.

"The leaders aren't nourishing us," Tempo croaks, drinking some water she manifested.

Geo holds out his cupped hands and Tempo fills them, before doing the same for Jewel. Skylus opens her eyes and sits up, looking groggy. Tempo rushes to her and gives her some water too. They all know it's a useless effort. If their real bodies aren't being nourished, it doesn't matter how much they drink out here. They're still going to be thirsty. Although, it feels good in the moment, which is something.

"Save your energy," Aura says to Tempo. "Using your powers is tiring you out. You need to rest."

"We need *you* to use your powers." Skylus glares at Aura and Hayze, seeming to be gaining strength as the rest of them lose it. "The leaders won't feed us until we're out of here."

"It's true," says Geo. "They'll watch us die before they nourish us."

Aura looks up at the platform, her concern for Atmos growing. "Skylus, you need to check on him. He's very still up there."

"And fall out of the sky again?" Her eyes widen. "I don't think so. Besides, didn't you just say we need to conserve our strength by not using our powers?"

"I'll do it," says Jewel, getting to a stand and wobbling with the effort. "I can use the same vines I caught Skylus with to lift me up to Atmos."

"No, don't," says Aura on a sigh, realizing her earlier advice was right. "We should save our powers for when we really need them."

"I vote Hayze and Aura use their powers now." Skylus's hand shoots into the air. "Who else is with me?"

"We're doing a vote?" Pace cocks a brow. "I don't remember agreeing to that."

"You don't vote as to whether you're going to do a vote." Skylus rolls her eyes, keeping her hand raised. "Well? Who else votes for the Fire couple to use their powers? I'd really like to get out of here."

"At the expense of Atmos?" Pace narrows his eyes.

"Well, at the moment, we're all dying at the expense of him," she snaps back. "We've given him every chance. Now, who else is voting with me?"

Geo slowly raises his hand. "Skylus is right. We'll all die if these Games don't end soon. An hour in here can be a whole day in reality. We don't know how long our bodies have been without food or water."

"I vote no," says Aura, crossing her arms. "Atmos deserves a little longer."

"I vote no as well." Hayze nods firmly.

"Me, too," says Jewel. "That's three against two."

All eyes turn to Tempo and Pace, who have the deciding votes. Aura's relieved. If there's anyone they can count on, it's them.

Tempo lets out an agonized whimper and raises a shaking hand. "I'm so sorry, but I vote yes."

"What?" Aura blinks, certain she must have misheard. But there's no mistaking the hand Tempo's waving above her. Pace seems equally shocked.

"We couldn't control that hand made from ice." Tempo turns to Pace. "You felt how strong it was. The leaders are leveling up the longer we all take to pass. We don't know what they might throw at us next."

Pace puts an arm around Tempo, clearly struggling with his decision. The vote is now a tie, which means it all comes down to him.

"Please, babe," says Tempo, dropping her hand to wrap her

arms around his waist. "I can't bear to lose you when I only just found you."

Pace glances at Hayze, and Aura already knows they've lost.

He puts his hand in the air. "I'm so sorry. I have to keep Tempo safe."

"We win." Skylus grins at Hayze and Aura. "Off you go then. Make some fire."

"We will," says Hayze. "But not yet. We're giving Atmos a bit more of a chance. Nobody's dying just yet. We have time."

"But the whole point of the vote was that you had to use your powers," Skylus groans.

"Yeah, a vote we never agreed to," says Aura, sitting down beside Jewel as waves of exhaustion wash over her.

"Let me remind you that the Games will end soon," says Skylus. "And if you haven't used your powers, you'll be as dead as Atmos."

"That's our decision to make," Aura snaps back. "Don't worry. We won't risk your lives any more than we're prepared to risk Atmos's."

"Pace," says Hayze. "I thought I saw something in that row of seats. It's probably nothing, but would you come with me to take a look?"

"Sure," he replies, turning to see where Hayze is pointing.

Aura frowns at Hayze, a little miffed he'd asked Pace and not her. Then again, it shouldn't surprise her. He can see she needs a few minutes to rest—her protector at every step. Besides, it makes sense to take someone with him who can actually use their powers if needed. It's also likely he just wants to take Pace aside after he voted against them. She knows how important it is to Hayze that they all work as a team.

"Be careful," she tells him.

"I'll be right back." He gives her the smile she knows he reserves only for her, and she catches it with her heart.

Hayze and Pace walk across the arena and Aura rests her head on Jewel's lap, closing her eyes. Jewel strokes her hair away from her face.

"I missed you, Aura," she says.

"Me, too." Aura blinks up at her. These Games took so much from her but there's no doubt it also brought her some friendships she'd never have made otherwise.

"Why are they taking so long?" Tempo asks, coming to sit on Aura's other side.

"They've only been gone a couple of minutes," says Aura, straining her neck to see Hayze and Pace at the edge of the arena. They're deep in conversation as they walk, seeming more interested in that than whatever it was Hayze thought he saw, confirming Aura's suspicion that he only wanted to talk.

"Not them," says Tempo. "The leaders. Why haven't they made their next move?"

"This is their next move," says Geo. "They're giving us time to come to our senses."

"That's right," says Skylus. "They're hoping the two of you make more intelligent decisions next time. Otherwise maybe you deserve to—"

"Enough, Skylus!" Jewel glares at the Air girl. "Why don't you take this chance to have a rest, starting with your mouth?"

Skylus shuffles a few feet away and pouts, mumbling something about nobody appreciating her superior wisdom.

Aura closes her eyes again and Tempo and Jewel lie down beside her, doing the same. Except the moment of peace doesn't last long, quickly shattered by Pace shouting Aura's name.

Her eyes spring open and she's on her feet before she consciously decides to stand up.

Pace is waving his hands from the other side of the arena. But instead of Hayze standing beside him, all she sees is a white dome.

"Hayze!" Aura gasps, breaking into a run. Whatever the leaders have cooked up, this is all shades of unfair. Hayze has only just suffered a great trauma. Clearly, the leaders are getting desperate to force him into using Fire.

She stumbles forward, kicking up loose rocks from Jewel's earlier efforts. As she gets closer, the white dome reveals itself to be made from ice. Pace has his hands raised, desperately trying to melt it. But just like the icy tower that shot from the ground before morphing into a giant fist, Pace can't melt this one either.

When Aura reaches him, her worst fears are confirmed.

Hayze is locked inside the block of ice.

"I can't do it," Pace pants, breaking under the strain of his efforts. "We need to get him out. Now!"

Aura glances up at the platform seeing Atmos's motionless arm still hanging over the edge, then back to Hayze and his frozen expression of panic inside the dome of ice.

Atmos is never going to harness his powers, making him tragically doomed. But Hayze has so much to live for. She can't let it end for him now.

"Use your powers!" she screams at Hayze, knowing he can't possibly hear her through the thick ice. "Blast your way out!"

Then another thought occurs to her. If he uses his powers and she doesn't, the Games can continue, keeping Atmos safe a little longer. She's not sure how she didn't think of this earlier.

Tempo reaches Pace and raises her hands beside him. She manages to melt the ice a little. But it's not enough with the liquid immediately re-freezing.

Hayze is running out of time, if he hasn't already run out.

Panic grips Aura by the throat.

"Fine," she shouts, glancing at the sky, imagining the smug faces of the leaders as she grits her teeth. "You win!"

She blasts the dome with fire, coating it in heat and flames, then draws back, afraid of burning Hayze if she goes too far. Being devoured by fire once a day is more than enough for anyone.

Hayze bursts through the remaining thin layer of ice, heaving for breath as Pace pulls him out and lies him down on the ground. He's shivering badly, his skin as blue as the Water couple's suits.

Aura makes a small flame in her hands and crouches beside him, waving her hands up and down Hayze's body to warm him.

"Come on, Hayze," she urges, hoping he's not upset with her for using her powers to save him. "We're okay. The Games are still running."

A voice filters through the arena. *"Aura from Fire passes the Elemental Games."*

The color returns to Hayze's face as his temperature stabilizes. He reaches up to touch Aura's cheek and she lets her small flame extinguish.

"You used your powers," he whispers, his face filled with relief. "You passed. You're safe."

She draws back, a new realization dawning on her.

Hayze wanted this. He set this up. The leaders didn't trap him in a dome of ice.

Pace did.

That's why Tempo was able to melt it when she joined them, only for Pace to re-freeze it again. He wasn't trying to melt the dome. He made it!

Aura lifts her gaze to glare at Pace. "You tricked me."

Guilt slides over his face, confirming her suspicions. "I...I...

174

we...we wanted to keep you safe. We wanted to make sure if the leaders ended the Games that you'd survive."

"And what about Hayze?" she chokes out. "Because I don't want to survive without him."

Hayze sits up and takes Aura's hands. "Haven't you learned by now there's nothing I won't do to keep you safe?"

"But how do I keep *you* safe?" Her eyes prick with tears.

The leaders have their Solution for Fire now—Aura. They could argue they don't really need Hayze. Which means in all the dangerous situations he's been in, his life has never been more at risk.

"You need to use your powers," she chokes out, hoping Atmos would want the same thing. "Please Hayze. You need to do it now."

He shakes his head, as stubborn as he is protective.

She sinks to the ground.

The Games are far from over.

Whatever finale the leaders have planned, it's only just begun.

CHAPTER
TWENTY-ONE
HAYZE

Hayze kneels beside Aura. Her devastation is coming off her in waves. Guilt rips at his insides even as he knows he'd do it again.

Keeping her safe, keeping her alive, is all that matters.

"I'm sorry," he whispers.

Aura huffs. "No, you're not."

Hayze inclines his head, acknowledging the truth. "In some ways I am," he offers, his lips softening. "I didn't want to do it, if that counts for anything."

In one fluid motion, Aura launches herself at him. He catches her, surprised, but always willing to have her where she belongs—in his arms. She buries her face in his neck. "You need to use your powers, Hayze. Please."

His arms tighten. His heart constricts. "I can't," he whispers, pressing his nose into her hair. "Not yet." Atmos needs every second they can give him.

Aura sags in his arms, almost as if she expected that response. A shuddering breath wracks her body. "I can't lose you, Hayze."

If he held her any tighter, then oxygen could become an issue for the girl he loves. "Being able to do this for the rest of our long lives is the only outcome I'm willing to consider."

"Ah, guys..." Pace says the words in the same way he did not long ago. With growing alarm.

And sinking dread.

Hayze loosens his arms reluctantly. Never letting Aura go is second only to making sure she survives this hell. The smell registers before the sight. The sound comes from every direction.

Because so is the fire.

Skylus gasps, shooting closer to Hayze and Aura. "Sweet Terra, the stands!"

The rows of timber seats that line the monstrous arena are smoldering. Crackling. Turning the four sections, the four colors of the Elements to only one color—red.

"They're burning the whole thing down?" Tempo asks incredulously.

Pace's fists clench. "The leaders have proven over and over nothing is sacred in their search for a Solution," he spits.

Yet Hayze is struggling to come to terms with what he's seeing. Even as the flames go from glittering orange to intense red. Even as smoke darkens the sky.

Even as Atmos screams two words. "Save yourselves!"

Because it's not just him who's in danger of burning to death now. It's all of them.

Every set of eyes turn to Hayze, pinning him in place. The leaders are trying to force his hand. He clenches his jaw, grinding down on the knowledge he hates them for that.

Boom. An explosion erupts behind Hayze and he instinctively wraps himself around Aura. *Boom.* The next explosion is a little to the left of the last one. *Boom.* The next a bit further along. Section by section, the arena bursts into ferocious flames, each explosion bigger than the last as the heat feeds itself.

Boom.

Boom.

Boom.

A ring of fire is steadily being born.

By the time the explosions reach what's left of where they started, Jewel is crouching, her hands over her ears. Geo is paler than pale. Pace and Tempo are holding each other, eyes alive with fear. Even Skylus is looking nervous now that she's surrounded by flames. If she uses her powers to try and stop this, she'll only inflame the inferno.

The seats burn fast, no doubt thanks to the leaders' programming. Wood crashes, flames leap, fire devours. The heat is intense. All consuming. It scorches the very air, meaning every intake of breath is fire itself.

Hayze holds onto Aura, eyes stinging with smoke. This isn't a fire he intends on running into. He doubts that trick will work twice.

Which leaves...

His gaze rises to Atmos, finding him standing on his platform, his arm shielding his face. "It's always been inside you," Hayze calls out, wanting to give him one last chance. "Connect with the power you hold!"

Atmos drops his arms. He squares his shoulders, then angles his face up as he closes his eyes. His pleading voice carries over the roar of the fire. "Eterna, give me a sign."

"You've got to be freaking kidding me," Pace growls. He releases Tempo and strides a few feet away, his face flushed with heat. "I'll give him a sign."

He extends his hands and unleashes a torrent of water at the sea of flames directly ahead. The water hisses and vaporizes, but he doesn't stop. He becomes a conduit for his Element, an artery pumping water in a furious flow.

"Yes," Tempo hisses. She places her back against his and does the same, throwing a river of water in the opposite direction.

There's more hissing, more steam weaving through the acrid smoke.

But the flames continue to devour and grow, their promise of destruction as alive as they are.

Aura disentangles herself from Hayze, drawing his attention. "We'll try," she tells him, before stepping closer to Pace and Tempo. There she stands, her arms outstretched, slowly turning. Her eyes are clenched shut as she focuses.

Hayze watches, astounded as her exposed palms pass each section of flames and they shrink. She's not only subduing the flames, but she's giving Hayze more time.

She's giving Atmos more time.

Except the moment she moves on, the fires not only return, they double. Pace and Tempo follow, working hard to tame the flames, hoping they're weakened.

Yet the harder they work, the more the blaze grows. Cracks and snaps fill the air as the wood's incinerated,

"Geo," Jewel says, tugging him to their own patch of dirt not far from Aura. "We can do our bit."

He looks around, trying to understand how they can do that, when realization dawns. He joins Jewel, pressing his back to hers. "You might want to stand close to us," he tells Hayze.

Hayze steps in, but he doesn't get a chance to ask what they're planning.

"We are Earth!" Jewel and Geo cry simultaneously.

They sweep their arms down, then straight up, like they're scooping air. Except they gouge far more than weightless molecules. Hayze watches with eyes so wide they hurt as a monstrous wave of dirt rises from the floor of the arena. The particles move like sand, coming together, contracting, shearing away from the entire length of the expansive space. In a blink, Hayze and the others are standing on an island as the rest of the ground excavates up and out.

Forming a moving wall of shifting brown in every direction.

"Now!" Jewel cries.

The tsunami of soil powers outward, silent and hundreds of feet high, then crashes down on the blazing arena. The sheer weight collapses everything—the seats, the walls, any way of recognizing what this one was.

The roar batters Hayze's eardrums.

The plume of dust eclipses the smoke.

The aftermath is just as overwhelming.

Jewel and Geo lower their arms, their chests heaving. Jewel wavers and Geo quickly catches her, then lowers her to the ground. Aura goes to her, looking as stunned as the rest of the teens.

Hayze scans the devastation they're now surrounded by. They're on a small island a few feet higher than what's left of the arena. Any soil that once formed the floor is now gone.

It was used to pound the arena to shards.

All that remains is a moonscape of dirt, pockets of fire, all framed by a backdrop of smoke and dust.

It's the isolated mounds of wood and flames that hold Hayze's attention. The combined effort of Fire, Water and Earth has almost extinguished the blaze. But not completely.

That's all the leaders need to continue their 'unleash your Element or die' quest.

Hayze blinks as he registers what the flickering red and yellow threat is doing. "The flames..." he breathes.

Pace joins him, the same shock spreading across his face. "They're dying."

And fast.

The pockets of fire shrink and fade.

Then disappear.

Jewel sits up, frowning. "What does that mean?"

Aura moves to Hayze's side and he tucks her in, glad for her anchoring presence. Because he doesn't have an answer to Jewel's question. None of them do. The leaders have ended the round just like they did with the frozen fist.

Silence settles over the destruction. Over the teens. Over Atmos high on his platform. Hayze is picturing the leaders at their controls, already planning their next move.

Deciding to up the ante once more.

"You've made them angry now," Skylus huffs as she crosses her arms, confirming Hayze's suspicions.

Something big is coming. The leaders' patience must be running out.

Aura tightens her arm around Hayze's waist, just as tense as he is. Tempo and Pace hold hands as they scan the devastation that was once an arena. Everyone's ready. Waiting.

The blackness that engulfs them is so total that Hayze grips Aura hard, worried the virtual world has been wrenched away from them. But her familiar body remains in his arms, as still and silent as he is.

"What are the bastards up to now?" Pace growls.

"Don't let me go, Pace," Tempo whispers.

"Never."

Hayze blinks, then blinks again just to make sure his eyes are open. He's never seen blackness so absolute that it makes you question your existence. But he's standing in it. Holding onto Aura with everything he has just in case it swallows her, too.

"Is anyone there?" Atmos calls out, his voice trembling.

"We're here," Hayze assures him. "Just trying to figure out what this means."

An ambush in the dark?

A new scenario now that the arena's been destroyed?

Assembling an army of guards that they'll have to fight?

"I'll be here. Waiting." Although Atmos's words are an attempt at humor, the dejection in his voice weighs them down. They settle on Hayze's shoulders, then his chest.

Then his heart.

If they can't see Atmos, they can't rescue him.

"Fire is the only way out," Aura breathes. Hayze feels her look up at him, even though he's nothing but blackness. "It's the only Element that can defeat darkness."

Hayze is stunned by the simplicity of it. The corner he's been backed into is as absolute as the darkness.

If Aura lights a flame, the Games will continue. Who knows what will come at them next. The possibilities are endless in this virtual world.

But if Hayze sparks a light...

"What are we going to do?" Jewel asks, her voice small and vulnerable.

The real question is, what's Hayze going to do?

"This is a good time to point out we're all getting thirsty and hungry," Skylus says. "None of us can do this forever."

Hayze's teeth jam down so hard they grind. His empty stomach and dry mouth are traitors as they give Skylus's statements power.

Atmos's voice reaches them through the total midnight. "Save yourself." He sniffs and pauses. "Please, you have to go."

Hayze's eyes slam shut, finding the blackness is just as empty. Even with Atmos's blessing, he hesitates. Admitting defeat is also signing a death warrant.

"You need to do it," Aura whispers.

The words are said softly, but with a core of steel. She gave him and Atmos a chance when she tried to put out the fires, but it didn't matter. She's telling Hayze what has to happen next. Because she loves him.

Because he promised her he'd fight for their future.

Hayze's stomach curls. His heart painfully constricts. In the end, the decision is hard. Yet, surprisingly easy.

A flame flares to life in his palm. He lifts his hand, the one he can now see, so the decision he's made is the beacon he wishes it wasn't.

Although it's small, the light expands far beyond Aura's relieved face. Beyond Pace and Tempo, Jewel and Geo, and Skylus as she lets out a breath.

It bathes the arena in a soft glow.

The platform is now sitting on the ground, empty. Atmos is gone. Probably dead.

"Hayze from Fire has passed the Elemental Games."

Then, everything is gone.

CHAPTER
TWENTY-TWO

AURA

Aura wakes, keeping her eyes closed to delay having to accept a world where Hayze was forced to choose between saving one life or many.

He made the right choice. The *only* choice. Even Atmos had agreed. Because his one life was unable to be saved. No matter how long they waited, he was never going to harness his powers.

She opens her eyes, steeling herself for what she's about to see.

Except...it's Hayze. His beautiful sleeping face is only inches from hers. She shuffles forward and presses a hand to his chest, relieved to feel it rise and fall. He's alive. And some-how, they're together.

"I love you," she whispers, removing her hand and sitting up.

She looks around, knowing immediately where they are.

They're not in their pods.

They're not back in their real bodies.

They're in the virtual reality prison. The same one Hayze and Skylus had been trapped in earlier in the Games.

Nothingness envelops them. It's like they're floating in space. Nothing above them. Nothing below them. Nothing in the miles that stretch on every side. It's almost as terrifying as the darkness Jewel was trapped in for such a long time. Aura's not sure how she survived with her sanity intact. She wants out and she's only been awake for a minute.

The only tangible thing she can see are the four symbols of the Quadrants floating beneath them. Tempo and Pace are curled up asleep on the Water symbol. Jewel and Geo are lying side by side on the Earth symbol. And Skylus is sitting with her knees tucked up to her chest on the Air symbol—the only one of them to be alone in her Quadrant. Not that she appears unhappy about this given the coy smile playing on her lips.

Putting down her hands, Aura feels the hard surface of the floor she can't see. She stands and walks toward Skylus with her arms outstretched, not at all surprised when she walks into an invisible wall.

"At last, someone else is awake," says Skylus. "You all seem to need so much more rest than I do."

Aura doesn't point out that might be because of the energy they all expended trying to put out the fire and save Atmos. Not that it worked. But at least they know they gave him every chance.

"Do you think they've killed him already?" Aura asks.

"Of course," Skylus says, answering a beat too quickly for Aura's liking. "What would be the point in keeping him alive?"

Aura's eyes widen at the Air girl's callousness, even though she should know better by now.

"Atmos was as successful at harnessing his powers as the leaders have been," Aura points out.

"The leaders don't have powers," Skylus scoffs.

"Exactly." Aura sighs. "So, what's the point in keeping *them* alive?"

"We need the leaders." Skylus gets to her feet, standing eye to eye with Aura despite the invisible wall dividing them. "Without them, the world is doomed."

"Without *us* the world is doomed," Aura corrects. "And strangely, I'm feeling less inclined to help them after what they just put us through."

She doesn't need to hope the leaders are listening to her. She knows they are. She looks around, wondering which angle they're observing her from. Possibly every single one.

"They fed us," says Skylus, stretching out her arms. "Can you feel the difference? They're nourishing us. It's a reward for passing the Games."

Aura nods. "How very kind of them. Torturing us. Killing one of us. Then feeding whoever remains."

"We're the Solution," Skylus says firmly.

"And what was everyone else?" Aura returns Skylus's cold stare. "What were all the people who died in the previous forty-nine Games? Were they the Solution, too?"

Skylus shakes her head. "They were the sacrifice. Sometimes difficult choices must be made. Your boyfriend should know all about that."

Aura clenches her fists. "That's not the same thing."

"Yes, it is," says Hayze, coming up behind her and putting a hand on her shoulder. "I sacrificed Atmos so you could live."

"No!" Aura cries out, unable to bear the guilt embedded in Hayze's eyes. "You didn't kill him. That was the leaders."

"I ended the Games," Hayze says quietly.

Skylus flicks her long blonde hair back over her shoulders and gives Hayze a dazzling smile. "It's so nice we agree at long last, Hayze. We could make quite the team, you know. Air and Fire are a powerful combination."

Aura's brows shoot up. Is Skylus flirting with him?

"My team's full." Hayze slips his hand into Aura's, and she feels a familiar warmth spread up her arm and into her chest.

"Your loss." Skylus rolls her eyes.

"What happened to you?" Aura asks Skylus, wondering about the stretch of time they were separated when she first discovered her power of flight and left them in the maze. "What have the leaders promised you?"

"The same thing they promised the rest of you." Skylus crosses her arms and taps a foot. "A future. Except, it seems I'm the only one here intelligent enough to realize that. You've done nothing but work against yourselves since we woke up on those rafts."

"Aura!" Jewel calls from the corner where all four Quadrants intersect. Geo is beside her. Tempo and Pace are also with them on their side of the invisible walls.

Aura and Hayze go toward them. Skylus follows, wanting to be part of this even though she's made it clear she's set herself apart. Aura can't help but wish that if there was going to be a dud from Air, that it hadn't been Atmos.

She shakes away the uncharitable thought.

"I thought the Games had ended," says Pace, turning in a circle.

"They have," Skylus snaps. "This is where the leaders hold us when they're figuring out how we can best be of use."

"I'm not their puppet," growls Pace, looking up and shaking a fist. "Or their Solution. And nor is Tempo."

There's a flickering light around them and a huge image is projected into each Quadrant. Larger than life, it takes Aura a moment to make sense of what she's looking at.

"It's the Scorchlands," says Hayze, pointing to the image in their Quadrant.

Aura holds Hayze's hand a little tighter as she processes

the devastating scene. Fires are raging, tearing through the already decimated forest, fueled by strong winds. The ground has cracked open in multiple jagged scars, and lava is seeping out, running over the charred remains of countless people as it erases all trace of them ever existing.

"No," Aura whimpers, turning to look at the other Quadrants where similar scenes are playing out. People are freezing in the Deadwaters, with thick layers of ice coating their barges. Tornados are sweeping above the wild ocean, changing direction at random intervals and picking up the floating homes, reducing them into thousands of tiny pieces, never to be put back together again—much like the poor souls who were cowering inside.

In the Quakelands, hungry wildfires are devouring the forests, the earth shaking violently, felling trees and feeding them to the hungry flames. The screams of birds, monkeys and humans echo through the forest, making their way to the virtual prison, rattling Aura's eardrums as well as her heart.

She turns to the Stormsphere, which is faring no better with wild winds and hail the size of cannonballs pelting the earth, blasting holes in the sides of mountains and exterminating any living creature brave or desperate enough to be outside.

"It's end days," Aura breathes, her words lost in the noise of the four natural disasters playing out before their eyes. "Mother Nature has launched her war."

The projections vanish and silence echoes through the invisible walls.

All seven of them stand there. Devastated. Overwhelmed. Defeated.

Then Jewel begins to sob.

"That was terrible," she says between gasping breaths. "So many people were dead and dying."

Aura's heart aches and her hands automatically stretch out as she longs to take her friend in her arms and comfort her.

"Geo," she says. "Give her a hug for me. Please?"

Geo nods, putting an awkward arm around Jewel. She buries her face in his chest and lets out more heaving sobs.

"We don't know that was real," says Hayze, raising his voice so everyone can hear him. "This could all be fake! The leaders are trying to scare us."

"He's right," says Aura. "This is exactly how they want us to feel. We're playing right into their hands."

"But things were already getting worse out there," says Tempo. "Even in the capitals. That storm we fought off in Terra almost beat us. What we saw just now looked real to me."

"No, baby." Pace pulls Tempo to his side and kisses her. "That wasn't real. Hayze is right. They're just trying to scare us."

"They're manipulating us," says Aura. "They want us to agree to become their Solution. And they're going to keep us here indefinitely until we do."

A shiver runs down her spine at the thought. Keeping them here is even worse than being in the Games. Her only consolation is that at least she has Hayze locked in her cell with her.

Skylus huffs. "They don't need us to agree to anything. Honestly, I really do wonder sometimes if I'm the only one with any brain cells around here."

"She's right," says Geo. "Not about the brain cells, obviously. But they don't need us to agree to help. We have no choice. If what we saw was real, we have to. Otherwise, countless lives will be lost."

"And if it wasn't real?" Hayze asks.

"Then pretty soon it will be," says Tempo, those horrific images having sucked any remaining positivity directly from her soul. "We all know that's the way the world is heading."

"Finally." Skylus claps her hands together and smiles, like what just happened was a good thing. "You're starting to see sense. Just like we have no choice, neither do the leaders. They had to do something to save everyone."

"You don't get it, do you?" Hayze growls, stepping up to the invisible wall to face the girl from Air. "Yes, they had to do something. But killing people and tearing them away from their lives without consent should never have happened."

"Says the guy who killed Atmos," Skylus huffs.

Pace throws himself at Skylus so hard that Aura's sure the invisible wall shimmers as it launches him back. His face is purple as he rights himself and glares at Skylus with clenched fists. "Hayze didn't kill Atmos any more than the rest of us did. We all used our powers and passed the Games. It doesn't matter who went first or last."

Skylus tips back her head and laughs, feeling perfectly safe inside her unbreachable prison cell. "You're just mad because you didn't get to kill Atmos."

"He tried to save him," cries Tempo, jabbing her finger at the wall. "It didn't matter what passed between the two of them beforehand. Pace did everything he could to save Atmos."

"Somehow I feel like if it had been you on that platform, he'd have tried a little harder," says Skylus, not prepared to give an inch.

Tempo lets out a cry of frustration. "That's not—"

Blackness swallows her words.

Silence.

Flashes of white light blind Aura's vision.

And she wakes.

Looking around, her heart beats fast as she reaches out to touch thin veined skin. It glows and pulses as it cocoons her in warmth.

She's back in her pod. Two words echo through her mind. *What next?*

CHAPTER
TWENTY-THREE
HAYZE

Once more, Hayze wakes up roaring and ready to fight. But this time, he's smarter.

He leaps out of his pod, expecting the netting, and stops. It means the pain never starts, but his explosion of rage continues. It rips up his throat and out into the room, looking for a target to crush.

The leaders don't even flinch.

They wait until he runs out of steam. Until the air clears of his anger. Until he's standing there, contained by electrified rope, just like the six other teens in the room.

"Jewel," Aura gasps quietly.

The details of Hayze's surroundings finally sink in. Just as he expected, they're back in the high-tech room with the pods, contained by a drone hovering a couple of feet above. The leaders are here, the banks of screens with endless streams of data are here.

Except two things should be different.

Like Aura just pointed out, Jewel isn't here.

And Atmos is.

"Good to see you alive," Pace says, the words as genuine as his expression.

Relief that Hayze didn't kill the Air boy flows through him. Somehow, they're all here...except for one.

"Where's Jewel?" Aura demands, her hands tight fists by her sides.

"And don't you dare kill Atmos!" Pace shouts. Tempo nods beside him, while Skylus is the only one who remains silent.

Avalan's voice whips through the room as she lifts her chin. "If you could direct that fury to helping humanity for a change, we'd all be saved."

"Did you not see what we're to become?" Cyclonis asks, his voice climbing with each word.

Hayze was right. The leaders are running out of patience.

"It wasn't real," Hayze snaps back, even though he's guessing. He wants the truth for a change.

"It will be," Infernos growls. He waves an arm to indicate the screens lining the walls. "Sooner than we expect."

"You don't know that," Tempo snaps, scowling.

"Yes, we do," Avalan says, her steady gaze scanning each of the seven teens they're holding prisoner. "Eterna's predictions are never wrong."

She lifts a hand and the data on the screens starts shifting. The lines on graphs climb steeply. The flow of information accelerates.

"She knows what's coming," Oceania says, her face drawn in tight, sad lines.

Avalan flicks her fingers and the screens fill with the images they were shown in the virtual reality prison. The Scorchlands burning. The Deadwaters freezing. The Quakelands shaking and breaking. The typhoon-filled Stormsphere. But the lines have become blurred. Winds in the Scorchlands fan the deadly flames. Parts of the Quakelands are burning, others flooding. The gales in the Deadwaters are far fiercer than anything they've seen in the Stormsphere.

There's one thing every Quadrant has in common. One consistent, sickening sight.

Dead bodies.

Aura draws in a sharp breath, drawing Hayze's attention. She's scanning the screens, the technology, the leaders. "Eterna's a computer?" she asks, the three words fueled by disbelief.

Yet injected with the realization they're true.

"An extremely advanced one," Avalan responds. "How else could the Games be created?"

"We've been collecting information for a long time," Cyclonis explains, his arms crossed inside his robes. He lifts his chin. "Very accurate information using thousands of data points in the Stormsphere."

Hayze frowns, wishing his mind would hurry and catch up with this latest revelation. Eterna, the great spiritual leader of the Stormsphere, is a machine. An *extremely advanced* one. That's who the Air people have been praying to. Seeking signs from.

"The pinwheels were part of a...computer?" Atmos asks, his face ashen.

Hayze's eyes widen. Those thousands of small, metallic flowers perpetually spinning everywhere they looked were collecting information? No wonder the people of the Stormsphere could predict the weather so accurately! And that information was fed to them through Cyclonis, so his trade masters could trade with the other Quadrants.

If it wasn't another devastating lie that their entire world has been based on, it would be genius.

"The pinwheels are essential to collecting the data Eterna uses," Avalan responds, faint lines appearing on her brow as if she's getting tired of the questions. "It's how we know what's coming."

"And that something must be done," Oceania finishes, her eyes pools of anguish.

Hayze glances at the electric net holding him captive, just like the others. "Like this? This is your Solution?"

"All you need to do is swear loyalty to us," Avalan says, her face settling into hard lines.

"You're asking us to trust you?" Hayze asks, hoping he sounds as incredulous as he feels.

"When you don't trust us," Aura finishes.

"You've based everything we know on lies." Hayze indicates the computers. "Long before you forced us into the Games."

"Sometimes sacrifices are necessary," Oceania says, sounding like even she found them hard.

Cyclonis points at Atmos. "Which you've proven you're willing to make yourself," he snarls, looking straight at Hayze.

The guilt that stabbed like a white-hot knife the moment the flame in his palm came to life returns. Hayze glares back at Cyclonis, the one who put someone from his own Quadrant, someone who he's supposed to protect, in the Games in the first place. Then at Infernos. Oceania. Avalan.

Even the Water leader stares back at him, unblinking. Unapologetic.

"Just pointing out I'm not dead," Atmos says. "And that I asked Hayze to do it."

"And you never even considered asking us about any of this," Tempo spits.

"Enough!" Avalan roars, the power in her voice leaving no doubt she's the leader of Earth. "Each of you has the ability to wield an Element. Our world is dying. You are the Solution. Do you swear allegiance to us?"

The room falls silent. The only movement is the prophetic images still playing on the screens. Prophecies of devastation and destruction and death.

"What else haven't you told us?" Hayze grinds out.

"Where's Jewel?" Aura demands.

"What's going to happen to Atmos?" Pace spits.

"You trust us and we'll trust you," Tempo finishes.

Avalan's shoulders sink. Oceania's head drops. Cyclonis ages a decade.

"You think there aren't more of you?" Infernos snarls. "That we're not willing to do this as many times as necessary until we create a Solution?"

The words are a clear threat.

One they have every intention of seeing through.

"What?" Skylus shrieks. "I swear my allegiance! I swear my allegiance!"

Pace glares at her, disgusted by the clear betrayal, but not surprised.

"Then you will be spared," Cyclonis says gravely, holding up a small black controller. "For now."

Doesn't Skylus realize the leaders will only keep her alive for as long as she's loyal? A puppet?

A weapon.

One Hayze intends on tapping into.

He moves fast, twisting his wrist and flicking his fingers as he shoots fire from his palms.

But the drone is faster.

It spits white foam, neutralizing his attack. Then unleashes one of its own.

The netting contracts, becoming a second skin as it wraps around Hayze. Electrocuting every inch of his skin. He tries not to scream as current flows through sinew, muscles, and bone.

He jams his jaw shut. He arches his spine until he's bowed backward.

And the agony still gains voice as it's wrenched from his throat.

"Hayze!" Aura cries.

He's vaguely aware of her moving, of a flash of red that's quickly extinguished by thick white. Then she's screaming too.

"Bastards!" Pace shouts.

Ice crackles across the floor, but it never reaches the leaders. Pace's own scream joins the symphony of pain, then Tempo's.

Hayze drops to his knees, then all fours as he drags air into his seizing lungs. The ground ripples beneath him and he realizes Geo is trying too. His cries are louder, far more uncontrolled.

There's no Fire.

No Water.

No Earth moving beneath them so they can escape.

Just pain.

"Stop!" Hayze shouts hoarsely. "Stop!"

The net releases and as he collapses to the floor, he sees the others are also sprawled and panting. His fingers twitch as he wants to reach out to Aura. To brush the strands of hair from her face. To try and bring some color back into her pale skin.

But he's trapped. Immobile.

And even his Elemental powers can't set him free.

They lie on their sides, gazing at each other over the short distance between them. Hayze blinks, even that motion slow and painful. Everything feels desiccated and fragile, like his skin could crack at any moment. He licks his lips, only to find his tongue as dry as the rest of him. It's like every shred of moisture has been destroyed. It's probably a good thing because tears are clogging his throat like sand. What was he going to say, anyway? I love you.

I'm sorry.

Aura's eyes shimmer with emotion. "Near... Far..."

"Wherever you are," he whispers, finishing their saying.

Pledging their hearts like they have countless times before.

"Touching," Avalan says, her voice flinty. "But as useful as your powers right now."

Hayze moves his head, but not to look at her or the leaders. He sees Pace try to push up to all fours, then collapse. Tempo whispers something to him. Geo looks unconscious but is breathing. The only two left standing are Skylus and Atmos. One because she's a traitor. The other because he's of no use to the leaders. They're not hell bent on breaking him to their will.

Although he's still about to die with them.

"Do you have no heart?" Hayze chokes, glaring at Skylus.

"Because I want to live? Because I want to save the people I love?" She arches a brow. "From where I'm standing, that makes me smart."

Hayze clenches his teeth, hating that she's struck a chord. Is refusing to break worth dying for?

Worse, is it worth losing Aura for?

And ultimately, are they fighting the inevitable? Were they always destined to be the Solution?

But the alternative is to swear loyalty to their captors...

The chance to live, to be free, now depends on each one of them becoming a prisoner of everything they've fought.

"I will never be loyal to you," Atmos growls, tearing at the sleeves of his purple robes. "This time, I don't need a sign to know what's right."

Alarmed, Hayze watches as he rips and shreds until his arms are exposed, yanking away the trappings that have defined him.

And found him wanting.

"Atmos," Aura gasps. "You don't need—"

He leaps, proving her right. He doesn't need the power of Air to reach the underside of the drone. He doesn't need Elemental powers, period, to jam a wadded piece of purple robe into its underside.

And instantly disable the netting.

The drone whirrs, chokes, then falls. Atmos strikes it and it smashes into the floor at his feet. He disentangles himself from the mesh that's now hanging on him lifelessly.

Then he runs.

"You did nothing but lie to me!" he screams, his body an arrow aimed straight for Cyclonis. "To us!"

He leaps, fists raised, proving that the leaders may have contained the power of the Elements.

But not the power of the heart.

TWENTY-FOUR

AURA

Cyclonis braces himself, clearly anticipating Atmos's attack. The Air leader isn't afraid of a skinny, young man with no powers. What he's not expecting is the weapon clutched in Atmos's hand.

Aura gasps even though she saw Atmos break the propellor off the drone before he smashed it to the floor. He slams the sharp metal blade into Cyclonis's chest.

The old man stumbles back, blood staining his purple robes, a dark circle expanding out from where the blade has pierced him. Shock, betrayal and agony streak across his face.

Aura doesn't dare move from her position on the floor in case she sets off the electrified netting again. She's not in the Games now and has no idea how much more torture her body can take. Hayze and the others are doing the same. Although now that Atmos has shown them how to disable the drones holding them captive, all they need is to regain enough energy to make their effort count. There won't be any second attempts if they get this wrong.

Infernos dashes forward, grabbing Atmos's arms and

twisting them behind his back before he can retrieve his blade and inflict more damage. Atmos squirms, trying to get away but his fighting skills are only marginally more developed than his Elemental powers.

Yet they were enough to bring Cyclonis down.

The Air leader collapses to the floor and lets out a moan as he clutches his chest. Avalan and Oceania rush to him. Avalan pulls a wide ribbon from her hair and uses it as a bandage, while Oceania tears a strip of cloth from the bottom of Cyclonis's robes.

"We need to pull it out," says Oceania, wadding the cloth and wrapping it around the blade.

"No," Avalan cautions. "He'll lose too much blood. Leave it where it is."

Aura looks across at Hayze who's regaining strength. He sits up, his muscles tense as he readies himself to pounce. This distraction could be exactly what they need to take the three uninjured leaders by surprise.

"Can you jump high enough to reach the drone?" Hayze whispers to Aura.

Aura nods. Tempo, Pace and Geo are also regaining strength and have managed to sit up. Skylus remains standing perfectly compliant within her net.

"Why did you do it, Atmos?" Skylus asks calmly as she shakes her head.

"They're going to kill me," Atmos sobs, wincing as Infernos grips him tighter. "There was nothing I could do in the Games. But here—"

"There's still nothing you can do," Skylus snarls before switching her attention to Infernos. "I'd like to put myself forward."

"For what?" Infernos asks with a sly smile.

"For the role as leader of the Air Quadrant, of course."

Skylus pulls back her shoulders, despite the netting draped around her. "Imagine what we could achieve with a leader who has powers as advanced as mine."

Aura's jaw falls at her audacity.

"I can help you in ways you can't even imagine," Skylus continues. "Making me the leader of Air is the ultimate Solution."

"Cyclonis isn't dead yet," Avalan growls from the floor beside the bleeding Air leader. "And even if he was, that would never happen."

"Why not?" Skylus asks. "I would be the best leader the world has ever seen."

Avalan glances at Oceania and something passes between them that looks like fear. If Skylus were to become the Air leader, the other three leaders would have a giant target on their backs. They created Aura and the others to become their puppets, not their masters.

Infernos pulls at Atmos's arms, making him yelp. "Did Skylus put you up to this? Did she ask you to attack Cyclonis so she could gain power?"

"I would never!" Skylus gasps, her skin turning a shade paler. "I was simply trying to help you out by offering my superior services in a time of great need."

"I wouldn't do anything she asked me to," Atmos spits out. "I can make my own decisions."

Infernos glares at Hayze and Aura. "Don't you two get any ideas. Should anything happen to me there's a clear succession plan in place. And it has nothing to do with either of you."

"We don't want your job," says Hayze, keeping his fists clenched, no doubt to stop himself from accidentally releasing a burst of fire and electrocuting himself. "All we want is our freedom."

Infernos laughs. "That will never happen."

Atmos slams his heel into Infernos's shin, taking him by surprise and eliciting a groan. But it backfires and the Fire leader doubles down on his hold of Atmos, twisting his arms so forcefully Aura's sure one of them pops out of its socket.

"Stop!" Atmos yelps. "Please! No."

Refusing his pleas for mercy, Infernos turns his attention to Cyclonis. "What do you want me to do with this dud?"

Cyclonis winces, propping himself up on his elbows despite Avalan's protests to stay still. His jaw works as he tries to form a response.

"Kill him," he says, before collapsing again.

That's all Aura and Hayze need to hear to launch into action.

Aura tears the leather band from her vest and leaps into the air, jamming it into the drone above her, sending it tumbling to the floor where it shatters and whirrs. As she untangles herself from the disabled netting, she glances around to see Hayze, Geo, Tempo and Pace doing the same.

Hayze runs forward and throws himself at Atmos, breaking him free from Infernos's grasp. They crash to the tiled floor and Aura positions herself in front of Infernos. She raises her hands, ready to incinerate him if he dares to even think about carrying out Cyclonis's instructions.

The Fire leader freezes, a flash of uncertainty betraying just how aware he is of the power Aura holds in her raised hands. He may rule their Quadrant, but she's the one who rules the Element they worship.

Pace, Tempo and Geo surround Avalan and Oceania who are still crouched at Cyclonis's side, while Skylus remains standing looking more like a block of ice than a girl from Air.

"Don't move," Aura growls when Infernos's hand twitches. "You're outnumbered."

"Four against six is hardly outnumbered," Infernos says calmly, his leather suit creaking as he sits up.

Aura frowns, having trouble with his math.

"There are seven of us." Aura glances at Skylus, hoping if it came down to it, she'd stand with them, especially after having her leadership aspirations snuffed out so brutally.

"Oh, I wasn't excluding Skylus." Infernos grins. "I was talking about him."

Aura gasps as she follows Infernos's gaze and sees a pool of blood running onto the white tiles beneath Hayze. "Hayze! No!"

Except, as Hayze rolls off Atmos, Aura quickly realizes the blood isn't his.

It belongs to Atmos.

The boy from Air has a propeller blade sticking out of the left side of his chest and is slumped on the floor, his dark eyes wide open yet completely vacant. Hayze gently moves Atmos's face, moaning when he realizes he's too late to save him.

With her own heart aching with loss, Aura looks back to Cyclonis, who's clutching his chest wound with fresh blood flowing down his purple robes.

"You pulled it out," Aura says, trying to make sense of what just happened. "You threw it at him."

"That's right," Cyclonis pants weakly. "And I have far better aim than he did. At least I know where to find a heart."

"Surprising for someone who doesn't seem to have one himself," says Aura as Hayze comes to stand beside her, helping her keep guard over Infernos.

"You're going to regret what you did." Tempo leans over Cyclonis with her palms facing out. "You forget who you're dealing with."

Cyclonis looks Tempo directly in the eye. "I'd tell you to kill me, but you don't have it in you."

"That's not true," says Tempo as her hands begin to shake, proving his point.

"But I do," says Pace, sending a torrent of hailstones pouring from the ceiling that pelt Cyclonis until he's forced to remove a hand from his chest to shield his eyes.

"Enough!" cries Avalan. "You're attacking an injured man."

"He killed our friend," growls Pace, bringing the hailstorm to an end.

"Atmos wasn't your friend," Oceania laughs. "You hated the guy."

"We had our differences," says Pace. "Differences that we resolved when you put him on that platform, knowing he'd never harness his powers."

He sends down more hailstones on top of Cyclonis who curls into a ball, clutching his chest as he turns his face to the floor.

"Stop. Please stop!" Tempo touches Pace on the arm. "You're better than they are."

"She's right," says Hayze. "Don't do it."

Pace sighs, letting his hands fall as he grants Cyclonis a reprieve. This whole time they've been trying to tell the leaders there's a better way to do things. A *kinder* way. Killing Cyclonis only lowers them to the leaders' level.

There's the sound of whirring and Aura spins around to see Skylus shove a piece of her robe in her drone's underbelly. Delicately stepping out of the net, she levitates an inch off the ground as if using her feet is a major inconvenience.

"Good to see you join us at last," mumbles Pace.

"And now the numbers are even." Skylus smiles. "Five against five."

"What?" Aura crinkles her brow, shocked that Skylus is counting herself with the leaders. "After the way they just rejected you? You're one of us!"

"I'll never be one of you," says Skylus. "I'm far too powerful for that."

"Forget the numbers," Hayze growls. "There could be one hundred of them and we'd still win. Let her join the losing side."

"I'm a born leader," says Skylus, Hayze's words bouncing off her with zero impact. "These fools just need time to see that. And a little incentive."

A gentle breeze enters the room, picking up intensity with each second that passes.

"No!" shouts Hayze. "We have enough to deal with already. Don't do this."

"I am Air," Skylus calls as the wind sweeps the discarded netting and broken drones to the other side of the room, sending them crashing against the walls. "I am Skylus! And I am the leader of Air!"

Aura plants her feet on the floor, determined not to be swept away as it becomes increasingly difficult to stay in one place.

There's a loud rumble and Aura instinctively glues herself to Hayze's side as he wraps a strong arm around her.

"I am Earth!" Geo calls.

The tiles on the floor crack, forcing them to step aside as he squats, then runs at Skylus with a large piece of the flooring in his hand.

Nobody warns her.

Not Aura or Hayze.

Not Tempo or Pace.

And not a single one of the leaders she's so desperate to join.

Geo reaches Skylus and leaps into the air, swinging the piece of granite in his hand and bringing it down hard on the back of Skylus's head.

She crashes to the floor and the sound of rushing wind is replaced by Skylus's moans. She closes her eyes as she slips into unconsciousness and silence rings in their ears.

"Someone had to do it," says Geo, dropping the tile and returning to his position guarding the leaders.

"It's the quiet ones you have to watch," says Infernos, still seeming to be enjoying himself.

"You think this is funny?" Aura asks, having had enough of his attitude. "Is this what you were doing while we were in the Games? Laughing and having a great time while we were fighting for our lives."

"You weren't in any real danger," says Infernos, shaking his head. "The fact that Atmos was the first of you to die is proof of that. The rest of you are all perfectly fine. Including Skylus, unfortunately."

"Fine?" Aura throws out her hands, sending sparks flying. "You call this fine? Physically we might have survived, but what about the trauma you put us through? Does that count for nothing?"

"It was a necessary experience to help you learn," says Avalan, her dark eyes steely. "Not all lessons in life are easy."

"That's right," says Oceania. "Without experiencing the Games first hand, you'd never have developed in the way we needed you to."

Cyclonis moans, which seems to be all he's capable of contributing to the discussion.

"I have an idea," says Tempo, standing with her back straight.

"What is it?" Pace jiggles with eagerness.

"Oceania just said it." Tempo smiles. "Without experiencing the Games first hand, we'd never have developed in the way they needed us to."

"And?" Hayze prompts when she doesn't elaborate.

"Well, there are things we need the leaders to develop." Tempo runs a hand through her red hair. "Like compassion. Empathy. Humanity."

"Frenius," says Pace, glancing at the empty pods. "We put them in the Games."

"No!" Infernos booms. "I forbid it."

Aura allows a small flame to burn in her palms. "I'm not sure you're in a position to forbid anything."

Hayze puts a hand on Aura's back. "You like this idea?"

"I'm not sure," she answers honestly, still trying to turn the implications over in her mind.

"You said you're better than us," Avalan reminds them. "Putting us in the Games makes you just like us."

"That depends on how we treat you while you're in there," Tempo points out.

"I told you," croaks Cyclonis. "She doesn't have it in her. Don't worry."

Tempo's hand immediately shoots into the air. "I vote we do it."

Pace follows. "Me, too."

"And me." Geo raises his hand.

"You people do love a vote," says Infernos, shaking his head. "Except the two from Fire will never agree to this."

"What makes you so sure?" Hayze asks.

"It goes against your moral compass," says Infernos. "Which the Games have proven has quite an unusually high threshold."

Aura swallows, hating that Infernos knows Hayze so well. He may be strong and handsome and smart, but above all, he's a good person.

Kind. Forgiving. And Fair.

Aura would never have given her heart to anyone less.

"Three is a consensus," says Pace.

"Except you don't work like that," Avalan points out. "Such a big decision needs full agreement."

"Then I agree," says Aura, raising her hand. "Put them in the Games."

Hayze's eyes flare with surprise.

"You heard what Tempo said." She turns to him. "We don't have to treat them like they treated us. Think of it as a way to hold them while we figure out what to do next."

"That sounds like a prison," says Infernos. "You sure you're cut out to be a prison guard? I'm not sure it suits you, Hayze."

Hayze slowly raises his hand, disgust written all over his face. "It suits me just fine."

"We all agree," says Tempo, letting her hand fall as she nods.

"How are you going to get us in there?" Infernos asks, nodding toward the pods. "Got a plan for that, too?"

"It's pretty simple," says Pace. "You get into the pods, or we kill you."

"None of us believe that," says Oceania, her dry tone a contrast to the Quadrant she leads.

Infernos snorts his agreement. "The only thing any of you would be worse at than being a prison guard is a hitman."

"Your smugness is getting annoying," says Pace. "You're starting to remind me of someone. Someone who's currently having a lovely little sleep, thanks to Geo."

Infernos holds up his palms. "I'm glad you mentioned Skylus. Because I have a proposal for you."

"Here we go," Hayze mutters. "Let's hear it."

"No," says Pace. "Save your breath, Infernos. We don't want to hear it."

"You do," Infernos insists. "Because it means we'll go willingly to the pods and allow you to put us in the Games. No need for a fight. Or any casualties." He glances at Atmos's body.

Avalan and Oceania stand, leaving the badly injured Cyclonis at their feet.

"What does your plan have to do with Skylus?" Aura asks, not trusting any of these leaders for a second.

"She's the proposal," says Infernos. "Put her in the Games with us. Do that and we'll go in willingly."

Aura reels back. She hadn't expected a straight answer.

"Why?" Hayze asks, stealing the question from her lips. "You think she'll help you after the way you rejected her?"

"I know she will," says Infernos.

"We agree to your proposal," says Geo.

"What?" Pace raises a brow as he looks at the boy from Earth. "You barely speak and now you've decided to do it on behalf of all of us?"

"Skylus is a problem," says Geo. "We need time to figure out what to do about her as well."

A few reluctant nods spread across the room.

"We can't." Aura shakes her head. "That's putting someone in the Games who doesn't want to be in there. That's exactly what we've been fighting against this whole time."

"We don't want to be in there either," Avalan points out.

"That's different," says Aura. "You have blood on your hands. Skylus's behavior is only a reaction to the trauma you put her through. She's trying to take back the power you stripped her of."

"Insightful," says Infernos. "You always were a wise one, Aura. Must be the Quadrant you were raised in."

Aura rolls her eyes. "Where's Jewel?" she asks, realizing this could be her best chance yet to find out where her friend is. "You never told us where she is."

"She's still in the Games," says Infernos, slowly getting to his feet with his hands raised above his head. "Would you like us to pass on your regards?"

"I meant her body," says Aura. "Where's her pod? Why is she being kept separate from us?"

"We agree to go willingly," says Avalan, before Infernos gets a chance to answer. "With or without Skylus. There's been enough violence today already."

Infernos clenches his fists. "Avalan—"

"Do *you* know where Jewel is?" Aura asks, directing her question at the Earth leader this time.

Avalan nods. "She's in the Games."

Pace steps forward. "They're not going to tell us. But don't worry, we'll find her."

"We won't rest until we do," Hayze adds.

"It's touching how much you all love her," says Avalan, her words missing Infernos's earlier sarcasm. "But you'll never find her."

"Get in the pods," Pace growls, his hands poised, ready to unleash his powers. "Enough talking. Move. Now!"

"We didn't agree to this!" Infernos protests.

Avalan goes to him, hissing some whispered words at him. Whatever she said, she seems to find her mark as he follows her and Oceania to the pods and they climb in.

Hayze goes to Cyclonis and scoops him up like he weighs nothing at all, carrying him to a vacant pod.

"Will he live?" Aura asks.

Hayze shrugs. "We'll patch him up after we hook him into the Games."

Cyclonis doesn't speak, lapsing in and out of consciousness as the blood loss takes its toll. Hayze lowers him far more gently than he deserves into the pod, while Geo busies himself getting the equipment set up.

Geo nods and steps back as the skin of the four pods closes around the leaders, the eerie veins pulsing with light.

"They're going in," says Geo.

A sickness lodges in Aura's stomach as she's unable to deny something doesn't feel right. Why had the leaders resisted going into the Games, then agreed so willingly? And why would they have wanted Skylus with them?

None of it makes sense.

Which means that while the five of them have the upper hand.

There's still so much they don't know.

CHAPTER
TWENTY-FIVE

HAYZE

Hayze wrenches his gaze from the pods to the screens, his breath trapped in his too-tight chest. Uneasiness clamped around his torso the moment the decision was made to send the leaders into the Games and has done nothing but tighten its noose with each passing minute.

The leaders refuse to see what they've done is wrong. They're steadfast in their belief they're justified in sacrificing innocent lives for their ultimate plan.

Whatever the fractal that is.

But is this the answer? Will having a taste of their own twisted medicine show them they need to consider another way?

"I say we start the Games with water," Pace growls, slamming his fist into his hand.

"A lot of water," Tempo agrees.

Geo strides to one of the control panels. "We just have to figure out how to initiate the scenarios."

"Scenarios?" Aura asks, her brow furrowing.

Geo nods as he scans the array of buttons in front of him.

213

Some flash, some are yellow or green or red, some are lifeless, waiting to be pressed. "Each Games they pre-program a series of tests. They call them scenarios. A few presses of the buttons and then they sit back and watch the show."

The bitterness in the Earth boy's voice is unmistakable, and Hayze can't blame him. Geo's suffered far more than any of them at the hands of the leaders.

Which is probably why he's so determined to make them pay.

Hayze looks back to the screens, registering that they're blank. Then, his gaze falls on the Air leader's pod. "We need to make sure Cyclonis is okay first."

"Let him die," Pace growls. "Collateral damage like any of the other teens have been."

Like Atmos.

Hayze walks to the Air boy and kneels beside him. "I refuse for their wrongs to become our rights," he says, his voice shaking with both grief and conviction. "There is no collateral damage for us."

Aura joins him, squatting to gently close Atmos's eyes. "What is right isn't subjective."

Silence hangs in the room as the others digest this. The screens are black, waiting for a *scenario*. Skylus is still unconscious, for which Hayze is glad.

And the leaders are in limbo, a little like the teens as they decide what to do next.

"Here," Geo says, taking a few steps to the side. He presses a button and a drawer slides open, then he withdraws a folded length of material. "They keep these for the ones who don't make it."

Aura walks over and takes it, unfolding it as she returns to Hayze. He registers it's a sheet. One to wrap dead bodies in. His stomach clenches painfully. The leaders are prepared for death.

For collateral damage.

"They deserve everything coming to them," Pace snarls, stalking over to Geo and surveying the buttons.

Hayze and Aura glance at each other, the question of what they want to stand for hanging between them. Silently, they wrap Atmos in the sheet. The coppery scent of blood is strong as sticky red coats the floor, then the sheet. When they're done, they sit back. Their stained hands instinctively reach for the other, clasping tightly as their shared pain weighs them down.

Atmos is another life lost to the Games.

Geo shifts his weight. "There's a cremation room," he says, his voice subdued. "It's where they take the contestants who don't make it."

All the dozens of teens before them.

"How do you know this, Geo?" Aura asks softly, as if she already suspects the answer and knows it's a hard one.

"I woke up as they put me in there, assuming I'd died like all the others." Geo's lips twitch in his pale face. "Gave them quite the scare."

"It needs to stop," Tempo says, her voice whipping through the room with vehemence.

"The leaders need to be stopped," Pace adds with just as much conviction.

That Hayze can agree with.

"Another reason to keep Cyclonis alive," Aura says. "So he can be held accountable."

Pace's lips twist. He looks like he doesn't like the taste of the words but is willing to swallow them.

Tempo nods. "Aura's right. Cyclonis needs to answer to this just like the other leaders."

Geo sighs, then turns back to the control panel. "The pod can stabilize him. Just like it feeds and rests anyone inside, it can aid in healing." He frowns. "It's figuring out how to do it that's the next step."

"I want to help."

Everyone spins toward Skylus, surprised.

She sits up, gripping the back of her head as she scowls at Geo. "Cyclonis is my leader, after all."

"The one you offered to succeed without bothering to check whether he was alive," Hayze points out.

"I'm trying to do what's best for the people of the Quadrants," she hisses. She stands, steadies herself, then lifts her chin. "I've been gifted with immeasurable power. Power I've harnessed. I will not throw that gift away because I'm determined to buck the system."

Hayze clenches his jaw. "That's not what—"

Skylus shoots past him, her feet hovering a few inches above the floor, then lands beside Geo. "The Quadrants need the leaders. There will be chaos without them." She slides a glance at the others. "Don't hate me just because I'm strong enough to be one of them."

Hayze can practically hear Aura roll her eyes.

Tempo walks over to the control panel, Pace sticking close to her side. "These buttons have the cross symbol the healers' barges had in the Deadwaters."

Geo joins her. "Yes, we also had them in the Quakelands."

Skylus jostles in. "Let me have a look. Cyclonis is my leader, after all."

Pace scowls but manages to keep his mouth shut. The four of them scan the control panel, their brows pulled low. Tempo pushes a button and small screens just above come to life, lines beating rhythmically across them. "This one is Cyclonis's," she says, pointing to the one slower than the others.

"I was just about to say that," Skylus snaps.

Hayze turns away, not wanting to watch Skylus try to hold onto what little power she believes she has. "We'll find the cremation room," he says, tightening his grip on Aura's hand.

"So Atmos can have a proper goodbye," she adds quietly.

They leave the room as the others try to figure out how to help Cyclonis. Once they've done that, they'll have to do the same to start the Games. Hayze doubts it's just a matter of pressing a couple of buttons.

He and Aura slip through the door, then stop as it closes behind them.

"Wow," Aura murmurs.

"Yeah, wow," Hayze seconds.

The room they left feels archaic compared to the one they just stepped into. There are no screens. No control panels. Yet the sheer volume of information is overwhelming.

They're in the *true* Sect.

They're finally seeing the technology that's made the Games possible.

The walls themselves are filled with images and data. Opaque glass glows with numbers and lines and graphs, lining the room from floor to ceiling. Everything is white and sterile and stark.

Aura takes a cautious step forward. "This is the heart of the Sect."

Hayze joins her, unwilling to be more than a few inches apart in this strange new environment. "In the heart of the computer."

They glance at each other, speaking simultaneously. "In the heart of Eterna."

"Not quite," says a voice that has Hayze lifting his hands and ready to attack.

Rateen's image appears on a wall panel straight ahead,

217

smiling. "This is the data bank that drives every decision the leaders make."

Hayze wants to drag his gaze away from the image of the woman who's tried to kill him more than once to try and process his surroundings, but he doesn't. He hasn't come this far just to be killed by curiosity.

"Who are you?" he growls.

"And don't give us that NPC explanation again," Aura adds. "You're clearly more than some character with little control or say in all of this."

Rateen inclines her head. "The answer has always been in my name."

Hayze frowns. Then scowls. Rateen has always been an unusual name, but apart from referencing rodents, he's not sure what it's hinting at.

"Eterna," Aura breathes. She turns to Hayze. "Rateen and Eterna are anagrams. Words created using the same letters."

If Hayze wasn't holding Aura's hand, he'd take a step back as shock ricochets through him. "Eterna?"

She inclines her head. "I've been monitoring the Quadrants, collating the data. Predicting the outcomes with a high level of precision and reliability."

Avalan's words echo in Hayze's mind.

A very advanced computer.

Hayze strides forward, anger injecting through his muscles. "You're the reason the leaders have justified everything they've done!"

Aura appears by his side. "Do you know what that's meant?"

Lies.

Secrets.

Heartbreak and pain and loss.

Eterna's face disappears from one section of the wall and appears on another several panels down. "I've calculated the probability of every possible outcome. This was the only way."

One by one, the panels clear, surrounding Hayze and Aura in milky glass, faint reflections of themselves staring back.

"This is what would happen if we were to do nothing," Rateen says—Eterna, Hayze reminds himself—her voice omnipresent in the way Skylus and Atmos always believed she was.

The screens fill with color and Hayze braces himself, even stepping in front of Aura as if he can protect her from this.

Every panel comes alive, creating a circular picture around them. One they can't escape, no matter where they turn. This world is pale and ashen. Deserted and drab. Dusty and devoid of...anything. There are no longer any Quadrants. It's just one continuous horizon of destruction and devastation. There are no signs of life. No shred of evidence that humanity ever existed.

Hayze and Aura execute a slow turn. They don't blink, don't breathe as they realize they're surrounded by a prophecy of not just death but extinction.

"This is what would happen if we were to take down the walls and allow people into the capitals," Eterna says.

Hayze waits, already predicting starvation and desolation.

But nothing changes.

A world of death remains on every panel. He and Aura are surrounded by the same outcome.

"This is what would happen if the Alliance were to over-throw the leaders and take control."

Hayze and Aura move closer until their arms are touching. Their fingers twitch, tugging in tighter and harder around each other's.

They already know the gut-wrenching images aren't going anywhere.

"Or we could neutralize the threat," Eterna says, her voice holding just a hint of we-tried-to-tell-you.

One by one, the screens finally change.

One by one, they reveal the future the leaders have killed for.

And it's strangely underwhelming.

Hayze and Aura step forward, eyes roaming over the images straight ahead. It's the Scorchlands, their home, and it looks very much like the place of their childhood. Scarred by fire and desolate, the floor to ceiling panels show a bunkered village that could be any of the ones scattered throughout their Quadrant.

"There's no wall," Aura says, moving closer.

Following her, Hayze realizes she's right. There isn't a protective barrier surrounding the village, although the blackened trees beyond are the same.

"There's no need for one," Eterna says. "Fire's been controlled."

By Hayze and Aura...

Aura tugs his hand and takes him to the next panels. These are the forests of the Quakelands, once more, similar to those they visited in the Games. "No safezones," Aura points out.

Hayze looks a little closer, again registering Aura's keen observation is correct. There are no hovering platforms scattered throughout the Quadrant.

Because Geo and Jewel have stabilized it.

The next quarter of the wall is alive with the Deadwaters. This difference is far more obvious. "More barges," Hayze comments, pointing at the boats dotting the oceans.

Aura frowns. "There's still ice."

Hayze nods, having thought the same. He and Aura each carry Pace and Tempo's memories. They know mining icebergs is how the people of the Water Quadrant have something to trade. And that it's deadly, either by the creeping toll of frostbite, or the sudden death of being crushed by tons of frozen water.

"The people of Water will no longer be in danger when they mine," Eterna explains. "They'll be able to melt the ice, rather than chip away at it."

Thanks to Pace and Tempo.

The Stormsphere has even Aura stumped for long seconds. The mountains still stretch over the land, looking craggy and windswept as always.

"There's more...purple," Aura says thoughtfully. She reaches out and brushes her fingers over the fluttering robes of the small figure high on a mountain top.

"Yes," Eterna says, her face appearing on the screen beside it and making them take an instinctive step back. "People are able to move more freely because there aren't constant storms trapping them deep within the mountains."

Thanks to Skylus.

"The capitals?" Hayze asks, noticing they're not part of the imagery surrounding them.

Eterna inclines her head. "Will remain a safe haven for those who are able to enter. Which will steadily increase as people are able to harvest and trade more."

So much would be different.

Yet so much would be the same.

Hayze registers the capitals aren't visible, but he doesn't need to be an advanced computer to already picture that if the Quadrants are faring better, that the ripple effect in the capitals would be even greater.

"People are still segregated," Hayze says, slowly turning as the realization settles in his heart. "The lucky live in the capitals, the rest scratch out an existence."

"Yet people can live without the threat of natural disasters," Eterna says. "Humanity will survive."

"And you're suggesting controlling Mother Nature herself so this future can become a reality," Aura says, her hand coming to rest on her chest as if the words are a strike she's protecting herself from.

The images disappear as Eterna's face fills each screen, multiplied over and over, until dozens of her now surround Hayze and Aura. "You've seen the alternative. What would you choose?"

The alternative is extinction, not just for them, but for most species.

But the prediction leaves a bitter taste in Hayze's mouth. This is what they were created to do? Control the very force that is the definition of power?

Subdue Mother Nature herself?

"What if you're wrong?" Hayze demands, unwilling to accept those are his options. "There's no way you can measure and predict every little nuance."

"I know a storm is coming to the Quakelands today," Eterna says calmly. "And fire to the Scorchlands."

"I could've predicted that," Hayze spits. Those are regular occurrences in both Quadrants.

"Except the storm is a hurricane. And the fire will be at catastrophic level. Many lives will be lost."

Three screens on the left change.

Three more on the right.

The left fills with the forests of the Quakelands, a safezone in the center, dozens of people sitting on it as the trees tremble and shake. But the earthquake isn't what has Hayze moving closer to Aura, conscious they're about to watch something painful. The storm battering the trees and people is far more ferocious. The rain is an ocean being unleashed from the sky, the winds are a force of fury. The people on the platform are drenched and terrified. They cling to each other and the edges in panicked desperation.

"Hayze," Aura whispers.

There's a twisting typhoon of rage coming in at terrifying speed. It tears up trees as if they're twigs. It picks up the safe-zone and hurls it into the trees as if it's a sheet of metal. Hayze looks away before he can see the aftermath, bile searing the back of his throat.

Except his gaze falls on the images of the Scorchlands and the bile burns his tongue, bitter and acrid. The village in the scene is alive with fire in ways that he's never seen before. That he could never have imagined. It's even worse than the images the leaders showed them when they were trapped in the virtual prison.

"Hayze!" This time his name is a gasp of horror. Aura's hand in his is instantly as cold as ice.

The same frozen fear spears through him.

They're looking at their own village. The one they grew up in.

The one their parents live in.

The fire is burning the bunkers themselves, hot and hungry enough to devour cement and metal.

And the people within.

"Mom, Dad," Aura gasps.

"No," Hayze moans.

Within minutes, the village will be nothing but ash.

Suddenly, the screens go blank. There's no prediction of death and loss. No Eterna. One of the panels swings in and Pace appears. He blinks as he looks around the space, then shakes his head before returning his focus to Hayze and Aura.

"Come on." He opens the door a little wider. "We've figured out how to start the Games."

Hayze swallows, although it doesn't help his desiccated mouth.

They just watched a prophecy unfold in blazing color.

One where he and Aura lose everything that's dear to them.

TWENTY-SIX

AURA

Aura and Hayze follow Pace back to the room where the leaders are hooked into the pods. She pauses at Atmos's body, which has been moved into a corner. At least he's covered now, which feels more respectful. They'll continue their search for the crematorium as soon as they can and give him the send-off he deserves.

Aura's mother told her once that you can never fully judge someone until their final breath has been drawn. And while Atmos was a somewhat difficult person to live with during the Games, in the end his true colors shone through. He was courageous, strong, and loyal.

And he didn't deserve to die.

Even Pace came to agree with that, which is saying something.

Aura joins the others at the control panel. They crowd around, staring at the rainbow of buttons, their faces a kaleidoscope of expressions.

Geo is determined.

Pace is excited.

Tempo is resigned.

Skylus is priggish.

Hayze is apprehensive.

And Aura...well, she's still in shock over what Rateen just showed them. Or should she call the old woman Eterna now? Whatever her name, her message was the same.

They have two choices. Work with the leaders to build a world that's marginally better than the one they were born into. Or refuse and watch everything and everyone they love torn apart.

"There has to be a third option," she whispers to Hayze.

He pulls her close to his side. "Which is why we need to do this."

She nods, knowing he's trying to convince himself as much as her.

The third option is to build a life that's more than just a little bit improved. They need a bountiful world where people can thrive. One that has no walls between the haves and have-nots. One that doesn't even have walls between the Quadrants. Aura wants to visit Tempo and Pace and see their children grow up. She wants to spend time with Jewel, learning more about the Earth through her eyes. She wants to understand Geo and all the hurts he's experienced. She even wants to see where Skylus lives and meet her family.

None of that is possible in either of the options Eterna presented them with. Which means neither option is viable. They need to open the leaders' minds to see the world in a way they never considered before.

And the Elemental Games is just the place to do that.

"The screens are still blank," says Pace. "I hope they're enjoying the darkness."

"I hated the darkness," Tempo whispers.

Aura shivers, knowing Jewel is trapped inside that right

now. Which is even more reason to get this started. Although, how Jewel's going to feel when she wakes up with the four leaders for company is impossible to predict. Hopefully she gives them a piece of her mind in the same way Atmos did. Because the leaders can't hurt her in the Games, let alone kill her. They're about to find out what it feels like to hold no power over the direction of their lives. Which hopefully means they never do this to anyone else, ever again.

"What did you figure out, Geo?" Hayze asks.

Geo presses a few buttons. "We have a few options. We can play a pre-set automated scenario. Or we can freestyle it."

"Freestyle," says Aura, firmly. "The only reason I voted yes to this was because we agreed we weren't going to treat the leaders in the same way they treated us."

"For the record, I didn't agree to it at all," says Skylus. "In fact, we could get the leaders out of the pods right now."

"We've come too far for that," says Pace. "So, do we all agree to freestyling the Games? Like, make it up as we go?"

Geo shakes his head. "The problem with that option is I don't really know how to drive this thing. We could end up treating the leaders even worse than they treated us."

Aura gasps, horrified at that idea. They're trying to teach the leaders a lesson, not destroy them.

Hayze slips his hand into Aura's and squeezes it. "Could we run a pre-set scenario, then alter conditions as they occur to make the environment less harsh?"

"That would be a much safer option." Geo scratches his chin.

Hayze looks at Tempo and Pace. "What do you think?"

"Don't worry," says Skylus, answering for them. "I'm not going anywhere. I'll be here to offer my advice at every step of the way."

Hayze smiles at Skylus in an insincere way he's never

smiled at Aura before. "If we need your advice about *Air*, you'll be the first person we turn to."

"I'm well informed on the other Elements, too," she snaps back. "You really should make use of my knowledge. It's to your own detriment that you're so determined to hold me back."

It seems the bump to her head may have knocked her out, but it did nothing to diminish her over-inflated ego.

Pace makes no effort to hide his disdain for the Air girl as he physically turns from her to focus on Geo. "We should go with the most recent scenario. While it's fresh in our minds."

Geo nods his approval. "The arena might be easier to control given it's a contained environment. I like that idea."

Aura remembers Jewel telling her in the Games that Geo wasn't the shy boy they thought he was once you got to know him. It seems she was right. Now that they're all depending on him, he's really stepping into the role.

"And you're sure we can alter the worst bits, right?" Aura asks.

Geo points to the panel of buttons. "These red buttons control the Fire aspects of the scenario. The blue is for Water, purple for Air, and green for Earth."

"What are the yellow ones?" Tempo asks.

"They trigger the pre-set scenarios," says Geo. "If I press this one—"

"Wait!" Aura shouts. "Not yet."

Geo holds up a hand. "I'm not starting it. I'm just showing you an overview of what's in it." He pushes down the button and a screen on the panel lights up with a list of text. "You can click on a line of text to find out more about each step or alter the code to change what happens within each of them."

Aura leans in to read the overview on the screen.

Water Quadrant: Deadwaters
Each Solution on a raft in isolation
Initiate dolphins
Initiate jellyfish
Initiate frozen world

"That's the first scenario we woke up in." Hayze shakes his head at the memory.

"And the one we repeated," says Tempo. "Are we sure we don't want to put the leaders in that one? I'd love to see Infernos attacked by a dolphin."

"Let's stick with what we decided," says Skylus. "Try another button, Geo."

Geo moves his finger down the row of yellow buttons, pressing them at random to check the overviews of each scenario until he finds the one he's looking for.

"This is it," he says. "It starts in the arena with the floating platform."

"Yes," says Pace, bouncing on the balls of his feet. "That one. Let's see how they like it."

"How do we start it?" Hayze asks.

"Ahh." Geo shrugs. "I'm still working on that bit. I can't find a start button."

Hayze's brow furrows. "Oh, Pace said you'd figured that out."

Pace throws out his hands. "I thought he had. Well, I thought he would have by the time we got back here."

"It's okay," says Aura, biting down on her lip. "I think I know. Do you remember when we thought we were ending the Games in the virtual Sect?"

Pace and Hayze nod, while the others who weren't there stare at her blankly.

"It was when we were trying to find Tempo," Aura explains.

"We found ourselves in this strange room with colored walls and buttons. We each had to press a corresponding button on a different wall at the same time."

"That's right," says Hayze. "It was a check mechanism to make sure all four Quadrants were in agreement to end the Games. It must be the same to begin them."

"There's a black square in each corner of the control panel," says Aura, pointing to the one closest to her. "Could they be sensors, like we've seen at access points in the capitals?"

As the only one of them to have grown up in a capital, Pace leans in.

"She's right," he breathes. "How did I not see this? They're sensors."

"We need to scan our tattoos," says Hayze, his face lighting up. "One from each Quadrant."

Aura nods. "Now it makes sense why the leaders wanted Skylus to go in the Games with them."

"They did?" Skylus shoots up a brow. "I mean, of course, they did. Is that why Geo knocked me out? He was jealous!"

"I knocked you out because you were trying to blow us all into oblivion," Geo says. "The leaders wanted you in a pod so we couldn't use your tattoo to start the Games."

Pace lets out a long sigh. "I hate to admit it, but with Atmos no longer around, it was a clever plan."

"You don't know that was the reason they asked for me," Skylus snaps. "I'm sure they wanted my expertise inside the Games."

Aura grinds her teeth, not pointing out that if they'd agreed to Infernos's request, the Games would never have started for her to be able to help them.

"Are we ready?" Geo asks, turning his hand and holding his Earth tattoo over the sensor closest to the green buttons.

It makes a beeping sound and lights up with an emerald glow.

"It works," says Aura, her eyes wide.

Hayze kisses her on the forehead. "Always said you were a frenius."

"Air next," says Geo, looking at Skylus.

She crosses her arms. "As I said before, I never agreed—"

"Just do it!" Pace growls.

"I don't take commands from you," she sneers back.

"Just think how powerful you'll be," says Tempo quickly. "You'll be able to control all the leaders in a way you never have before. You might even be able to convince Cyclonis to cede power to you."

"Do you think?" Skylus's face light up. "I suppose... Well, it would make them listen to me. I could finally make them see just how powerful I really am."

"That's right," says Tempo, manipulating the girl from Air with the same expertise she's learned to wield Water.

Skylus puts out her hand and scans her Air tattoo over the sensor near the purple buttons. She smiles proudly when it beeps, as if she'd thought of this idea herself.

"Water next," says Geo, as a purple glow pulses into the room from Skylus's sensor.

"You do it," Tempo tells Pace, who needs no further encouragement. He leans in and waves his Water tattoo over the sensor, lighting it up in blue.

Aura nudges Hayze, wanting to give him the satisfaction of representing Fire, but he shakes his head firmly.

"It was your idea," he says. "You should do it."

"Okay." Aura holds out her trembling hand, studying the tattoo she's had all her life yet rarely had an opportunity to use. With ink mixed with precious edrian the Water people risk their lives to mine, she'd often thought of these markings as a taunt for the people in the outer Quadrants. Applied to their skin when young and useful only in the capitals, these tattoos were nothing more than an empty promise, giving the people false hope that one day they might be needed.

Except now Aura needs hers.

For a purpose the leaders could never have dreamed up.

"Come on, Aura," Tempo prompts. "It's time."

Aura puts out her hand, holding it over the sensor closest to the red buttons and gasps as it beeps then lights up with an eerie crimson glow.

The beeping of the four sensors falls quiet, and they withdraw their hands.

The large screens on the wall in front of them light up and Aura blinks as she makes sense of what she's seeing.

"It's the arena," says Geo, his voice filled with awe. "Let the Games begin."

CHAPTER
TWENTY-SEVEN

JEWEL

Blackness falls away and Jewel wakes.

She's in the arena.

She hates the arena.

But it's better than being trapped in an endless night.

She sits up and looks for Aura, her heart lighting with hope that she might see her again. Except she's all alone, surrounded by nothing but blue sky and a wide circle of hard, brown earth.

Earth.

Her Quadrant and the Element she learned to harness. Yet it's brought her nothing but loneliness and pain.

"Why are you doing this to me?" she cries out, hoping the leaders can hear her from wherever they're watching. She's never been in the arena alone, which makes her heart pound as a desperate feeling builds inside her.

She doesn't want to be trapped in here. She has a life to get back to.

Pace isn't the only one whose mother needs him. Jewel's

just needs her for other reasons. She's older than most mothers. And she's all alone.

She tilts her face to the sky, noticing four platforms are floating above her in a circle, spaced out at intervals.

"Aura?" Anticipation joins the fear beating in her chest as she gets to her feet. "Are you there? Aura!"

Squinting, she thinks she can see purple cloth hanging over the edge of the platform to her left.

"Skylus?" she calls out. "Atmos?"

She'd rather have the Air teens for company than be out here alone, which is saying something.

"Jewel!" A familiar voice rings out across the arena. "Jewel, I'm up here!"

She spins around and follows the voice, shocked to see Avalan sitting on one of the platforms. Infernos sits up on the one beside her and Oceania on her other side. The purple robes Jewel saw on the remaining platform must belong to Cyclonis.

Which. Makes. No. Sense.

When she wished for company, this wasn't what she had in mind.

She turns in a circle with no idea what to do next. Aura would know. She always knows. She's the smartest person Jewel's ever met. But Aura isn't here. The leaders are. And Jewel doesn't trust them one little bit.

"Jewel!" Avalan calls again. "We need your help."

"I can't help you," she says, barely managing to raise her voice.

"We need to get down," Infernos shouts, leaning over the edge of the platform, his white knuckles gripping the edge.

Jewel sits down, deciding to conserve her energy in the hot sun. "Nothing we did worked to get Atmos down. It's no use."

"Atmos survived the Games," says Oceania. "He woke safely in his pod."

Jewel narrows her eyes, not sure if she believes this. "Then why are you here? Where are my friends? Why didn't I wake safely in my pod?"

"They're not your friends," says Avalan, dodging her questions.

Jewel pulls her knees to her chest and rests her forehead on them, closing her eyes. They *are* her friends. Especially Aura. Even if Jewel wishes she were so much more.

Not that it matters. Aura's heart belongs to Hayze. Which means Jewel is alone.

Again.

It's a story that's quickly becoming the theme of her life. The more Jewel loves a person, the more out of reach they become.

First her mother, who abandoned her when she was only a week old.

Then her father, who died when she was so young her fragmented memories of him are made up of feelings rather than images.

Then her mother again, who returned to her only for Jewel to be taken away on her eighteenth birthday.

Then Aura.

The girl who for one fleeting moment Jewel had believed might love her in the way she yearns.

"Jewel!" Avalan calls again. "If you won't help us, then help Cyclonis. He's hurt."

Jewel lifts her head, unsure if this is a trick. "He can't die, remember?"

"His body's injured," says Avalan, her voice floating down like gentle rain. "If his body dies, then so will he."

"Which means I can't help him," says Jewel. "Honestly, for someone who created these Games, you really don't seem to know a lot about them."

"A strong mind is vital to a strong body," Infernos says, his deep voice echoing around the arena. "His injured body may be in the real world, but his mind is here. You must help him."

"How do I know it's really you?" Jewel asks. "We met Cyclonis in the Games and it turns out he was nothing more than a simulation. It was the same when Aura and Hayze met their parents."

"It's us," says Avalan. "Your friends put us here."

"Oh, so they're my friends now, are they?" Jewel remains seated on the hard ground, not feeling the slightest bit motivated to move. If the leaders are nothing more than simulations, they don't need her help. And if they are real, well...that makes her want to come to their aid even less.

"Please." Oceania leans out over the edge of her platform, her face as pale as moonlight. "We're very high up. I was born for the ocean, not the sky."

Jewel gets to her feet, wondering what she was born for.

She thought she was meant to live out her days in the Quakelands, but it's obvious now the leaders have other plans for her. Different plans to those they have for the seven other teens caught up in this nightmare. Because all of them have returned to their bodies between Games. Everyone except Jewel. She's spent her whole life feeling like she wasn't the same as everyone else. This experience has only confirmed that.

"I can't help you," she repeats. "If I reach you, the forcefield will bounce me back. If you jump, you'll regenerate on top of the platform. If I build a mountain beneath you, you'll fall inside it, and start again. It's the way you set up the Games. Nothing will work. And you only have yourselves to blame."

She walks toward the stand that rings the arena, ignoring the protests of the leaders as they call her back. Drawn to the red section of seats, she pushes down hope that she might find

Aura. It's a good thing she's not here. It means she's out in the real world somewhere with the others. Maybe what Avalan said is true and they overpowered the leaders and have taken control. Except part of her doesn't want to believe that. Because if it's true, why hasn't Aura released Jewel from the Games?

Jewel steps into the shade and approaches the red seats, no longer able to hear the leaders' cries. She walks up several rows, before sitting down. She looks out across the vast arena, her heart constricted with pain.

For the first time in her life, she wishes for everything to end. Or not quite everything.

Just her.

A single tear trails down her cheek. She doesn't bother to brush it away as another one joins it and splashes to the ground at her feet. She's tired of running. Of fighting. Of reaching out, only to grasp thin air.

But she can no more end herself than she can find a new way to begin. She could throw herself from the highest point in the arena only to wake again, her mind still shattered but her body perfectly intact.

It's hopeless.

She's hopeless.

All she can do is sit here and wait for whoever's controlling this reality to make their next move.

Curling herself into a ball on the hard seat, Jewel closes her eyes. Seconds pass that spin into minutes then twist into hours that could be years or days or the blink of an eye. Time has even less meaning here than her life itself.

"Jewel," a voice whispers. "Jewel, wake up."

"Aura?" Jewel sits up, disappointed to find she's still alone.

Her mind is playing tricks on her. Everything here is exactly as it was before, including the platforms floating in the distance. The only difference is that all four leaders are now lying down, perishing in the relentless sun.

"Jewel," comes the voice again. "Can you hear me?"

"Aura?" Jewel looks around, still seeing nothing.

"I'm not in the Games," says Aura. "It's only my voice you can hear."

"Can they hear you?" Jewel points at the platforms.

"No," says Aura. "Only you. Geo figured out how to speak to you."

Jewel shifts on the hard plastic seat. "You're with Geo?"

"I'm with everyone," she says, her words filling Jewel's empty heart with unbearable loneliness. "Except you. And Atmos."

"What happened to Atmos?" Jewel asks.

"They k-killed him." Aura's voice breaks.

Jewel shoots to her feet. "They told me he woke safely in his pod."

"Which is true," says Aura. "Then they killed him."

"Bastards." Jewel stalks up the aisle, passing rows of empty seats. "I knew I couldn't trust them."

"We need to know where your pod is," says Aura, speaking quickly. "We haven't been able to find you."

So that's why Aura hasn't released her from this hell. It's not because she didn't want to. She doesn't know how to. Another feeling seeps into Jewel's heart, displacing some of the loneliness.

Hope.

"I don't know where it is," says Jewel. "I have no memory of the pod. Does Geo know?"

"No," comes Geo's deep voice. "When I woke in my pod, I was alone."

Jewel slumps back down on a seat. "Why are they doing this to me? Why am I different to the rest of you?"

"We don't know," says Aura. "But we're doing our best to find out.

"We won't give up on you," Hayze adds. "Not ever."

Jewel nods, clearly able to picture Hayze clutching Aura's hand as he speaks. But now's not the time for jealousy to cloud her thinking. She's glad Aura isn't alone.

"Is it really the leaders who are here with me?" Jewel asks.

"It is," says Aura. "We put them in the Games while we figure out how to handle this. We needed somewhere to keep them."

"And we thought they could use a taste of their own medicine," Pace grumbles in the background.

Jewel finds herself nodding.

"They asked me to join them," Skylus says, her voice as smug as ever. "Unfortunately, I was unable to, which is a shame for them. And you, of course."

Jewel wonders how she could possibly have thought having Skylus with her would be better than being alone.

"Such a shame," she says. "Whose idea was it to put them all on platforms?"

"Nobody's," says Aura. "It seems the programming for this scenario puts anyone without powers on a platform."

"Can you make them disappear?" Jewel looks across at the arena as she bites down on her lip. "The platforms, I mean. Not the leaders."

"We could," says Geo. "But the leaders would fall and..."

"Regenerate on the ground," Jewel finishes. "Can you do that? Please."

"We agreed to treat them better than they treated us," says Aura firmly. "Falling to your death is terrifying. We can't do that. Not to anyone."

Jewel raises her brows and looks around, hoping Aura can

see her face. "And letting them die from dehydration on a floating platform is so much kinder?"

"We're hydrating their real bodies," says Hayze.

"Which means they'll die on the platform in the most awful way, only to regenerate up there and do it all again." Jewel stands again and walks down to the barrier of the arena.

"Yeah, about that," says Aura. "That already happened while you were asleep."

"Twice," Pace adds.

Jewel swallows, finding herself unable to feel sorry for leaders and the pain they're suffering.

"Why do you want them down there with you?" Tempo asks.

Jewel draws in a deep breath. "I want them to feel the terror of falling. Only then will they understand."

She receives silence as her reply and wonders if Aura's severed the connection after finding out what darkness Jewel's been hiding in her heart.

"Please, Aura," she begs, trying to find the words she knows will get Aura across the line. "That's all I ask. Make the platforms disappear. It's far kinder than letting them dehydrate over and over. That's an awful death."

There's another long pause.

"Okay," Aura replies.

Jewel can hear in that one word just how difficult that decision was for her. It's just one of the reasons she fell in love with this girl from Fire. In a world tarnished by hate and betrayal, Aura's heart is pure.

"Epic!" says Pace, before letting out a whoop. "Let's do this. Actually, maybe we can tilt the platforms first, then they can disappear?"

"Pace!" Tempo scolds, making Jewel smile.

"Go to the center of the arena," Geo instructs Jewel. "We're turning off the comms link now, okay? I need to figure this out."

"Bye," Jewel whispers, talking to everyone, but really speaking to the one person who holds her heart.

She walks into the arena, keeping her head held high as she moves. What she told Aura was true. She does want the leaders to experience some of the fear they inflicted on everyone else. But she also wants to meet them eye to eye. Some questions can't be asked at a distance. And it's way past time for Jewel to get some answers.

When she reaches the center, she plants her hands on her hips and turns in a slow circle, waiting for something to happen.

"Jewel," Avalan croaks, leaning out from her platform. A feather from her headdress comes loose and floats down, sweeping to the earth in graceful movements that she can't hope to replicate. "Jewel, help me."

"Sit up!" Jewel commands, wanting the leaders to be awake for what they're about to experience. "All of you."

Infernos's face appears at the edge of his platform, then Oceania looks down.

"It's a shame Cyclonis never learned to fly," Jewel says. "Because you're about to get your first lesson."

"No!" cries Oceania. "Don't do this!"

Jewel crosses her arms. "You did it to yourselves."

Pace must have gotten his wish as the platforms begin to tip. The leaders grapple to stay on top by clutching the highest edge.

Still unconscious, Cyclonis is the first to slide off. His body leaves the platform and he tumbles, his purple robes flying out, reminding Jewel of the hot air balloon they used to escape the Stormsphere. Except, unlike the balloon, he doesn't float.

He plummets.

Just before he hits the ground, his body glitches and vanishes.

"Cyclonis?" Jewel blinks, having expected him to reappear at her feet.

Looking up, she sees him back on his platform which is now at a forty-five degree angle as it continues to tip. Unable to hold on, he immediately rolls off and falls again.

"Cyclonis!" shouts Oceania, still clutching to her platform as the Air leader disappears just before hitting the ground.

Infernos has somehow managed to get to the very top of his platform and has straddled it, while Avalan has looped a strip of her clothing over one of the top corners of her platform and is using it as a hand-hold.

The platforms continue to tip, Cyclonis falling and regenerating five more times before they're completely vertical. Jewel knows Aura would never have agreed to this if she could have foreseen what would happen. But in a way Cyclonis is having the best experience out of all four leaders given he doesn't know what's happening to him. Besides, Atmos fell multiple times and he felt every single one of them.

"I can't hold on," Oceania puffs, her knuckles white and her cheeks pink.

"I can sit here all day," Infernos brags.

"You're kinder than this, Jewel!" says Avalan. "We didn't do this to you!"

"No, you didn't," says Jewel as Cyclonis careens to the ground, vanishes, and reforms on the side of the vertical platform with no hope of staying there. "You did far worse."

The platforms glitch and disappear and all four leaders grapple with the air as they begin their descent.

Oceania's scream is blood curdling.

Avalan's is more of a groan.

Infernos's cry is built of fury rather than fear.

And Cyclonis remains silent.

As for Jewel...She puts her hands to her mouth, forcing herself to witness the horror she willingly chose to inflict. Maybe now these four so-called leaders will listen to what she has to say instead of shouting down orders like they still control the world.

The leaders vanish before hitting the ground, then regenerate, sprawled on the earth as they pant for breath.

"Don't worry," Jewel says, not bothering to keep the sarcasm from her voice. "It's not real."

Avalan is the first to get to her feet. She straightens her headdress and smoothes down her white robes as she walks to Jewel with her hands outstretched.

"Don't touch me," Jewel snaps, taking a step back. "Don't ever touch me."

Infernos and Oceania stand, seeming more concerned with themselves than Cyclonis, who's breathing but yet to wake up.

"I'm so sorry," says Avalan, openly crying as she continues to hold out her hands.

Jewel narrows her eyes at this sudden change in attitude. Getting the leaders to see things their way was easier than she expected. Which is more suspicious than reassuring.

Oceania goes to Avalan and pushes down her hands, stepping slightly in front of her as she takes charge.

"What do you want from us?" the Water leader asks, looking around the arena rather than at Jewel.

"I want answers," says Jewel, forcing Oceania's attention back to her. "Starting with where my pod is."

Infernos and Oceania both turn to Avalan, who shakes her head.

"If you let us out, I'll tell you everything," the Earth leader says.

"Tell me everything and we'll let you out," Jewel snaps back.

Infernos puts his hands on his hips, making him even more intimidating in size. "You don't have the authority to make that deal."

Jewel sighs, knowing he's right. It's not up to her when these Games end. It's up to her friends at the controls. They didn't put the leaders in here to get answers about Jewel. They want something else far more complicated.

They want a better world.

Cyclonis groans as he rolls to his back and Infernos rushes to him, gently slapping his face as he crouches down.

"Wake up," he hisses. "You must wake up. Cyclonis, we need you!"

Cyclonis lapses back into the oblivion he'd just broken free from, and Infernos grunts in frustration.

"Why do you need him?" Jewel asks. "What use is he to you in here?"

"Do people need to be useful to be needed?" Infernos stands and puffs out his chest.

"Don't talk in riddles," Jewel snaps. These leaders have no power over her in here. She's stronger than all of them put together.

"We want to form an alliance," says Oceania. "With you. And your friends."

"Why?" Jewel tilts her head.

"Because we get it now." A sea of emotion flows from Oceania's sapphire eyes. She almost looks human, instead of the sleek, bald Water leader Jewel has always known her to be. "The danger in here may not be real, but all the feelings are."

Avalan nods. "I was terrified on that platform. We all were."

"Speak for yourself," Infernos mutters, reminding Jewel

that the four Quadrants are far from aligned. "But yes, an alliance makes sense."

"We already have an alliance," says Jewel. "With the people. We don't need you."

"You have a handful of people from the outer Quadrants," Infernos points out. "We have the respect of all the people, far and wide. Who do you think they'll listen to? Their four esteemed leaders? Or seven teenagers barely old enough to understand the world, let alone rule it?"

"Seven teenagers?" Jewel steps up closer to Infernos, knowing she's caught him out. "Who aren't you counting in that?"

"Well, you're in here now," he says. "So that's seven."

"I don't think it's me you were excluding," she pushes. "Who was it?"

Infernos flaps his jaw, struggling to find his words.

"Atmos woke safely in his pod," says Oceania, stepping in. "Infernos left you out because you're here."

"And what happened to Atmos after he woke safely in his pod?" Jewel asks. "If we're going to form an alliance, don't we need honesty first?"

"Cyclonis killed him," says Avalan.

"It was self-defense," Oceania quickly adds.

"Was it?" Jewel directs her question at Avalan who seems the only one tempted to tell the truth.

"Atmos attacked Cyclonis," she says, straightening a feather in her headdress. "And Cyclonis retaliated."

"But why did Atmos attack him?" Jewel asks.

Avalan opens her mouth to speak but Infernos talks over her.

"It's no secret that we've had our differences," he says. "What's important now is to focus on the future." He turns in a wide circle, addressing those he knows are watching him. "Let us go free and we'll put an end to the Games. Permanently. We'll work with you to not just find *a* Solution, we'll find *the* Solution."

"A better world for everyone is possible," says Oceania. "By putting us in here, we understand you better. But not only that, now you understand us better."

"How do you figure that?" Jewel asks, not at all convinced.

"Because you see now how hard it is to make the decisions," Oceania says. "When you let us fall from the platforms, you knew it was going to cause us pain. But you did it anyway. You were prepared to inflict suffering on us for the greater good."

Jewel's eyes open a little wider, unable to deny the truth in this.

"We're as bad as you," Jewel whispers as a shadow of shame washes over her.

"Or perhaps you're as good as us," Avalan says, her eyes spilling over with kindness. "We want the same thing, Jewel. Work with us."

Jewel looks to the sky, wishing Aura was still talking in her ear.

"What do we do?" she asks, the weight of the decision feeling too much for one person.

Darkness descends on the arena.

The Games have been suspended.

Once again, Jewel has no control over her life.

And once again, she's alone.

CHAPTER
TWENTY-EIGHT
HAYZE

"Why did you turn it off?" Pace demands, rounding on Hayze.

He crosses his arms. "This is wrong," he states emphatically, blocking the line of sight between the others and the button that ends the Games.

It had been hard to watch the leaders on their platforms, stubbornly refusing to yield no matter how dehydrated or hungry they became. Oceania had been the first to die, and Hayze had to remind himself it was nothing but a *game*. But the others followed, only Cyclonis lucky enough to be gifted with unconsciousness.

One press of the button from Geo and they'd reappeared, disorientated for a second, but still as stubborn. That's what Hayze hadn't counted on—their single-minded refusal to bend. They'd died again while Jewel slept, their faces as unyielding as they have been since this began.

When Jewel woke and asked that they be dropped, Hayze had refused. So had Aura. But there was something about the Earth girl. Something about watching her have to endure this from within the Games that had moved them both. Aura had been the first to capitulate, tempted by the promise of a quick virtual death for the leaders, rather than watch them slowly desiccate all over again. Hayze had grudgingly agreed, conscious something needed to shift the balance of power.

Especially after seeing what failure could mean. The images Eterna showed him will be forever scorched into his mind.

Still, his stomach had plummeted each time Cyclonis fell. Even as he told himself the Air leader was unconscious so couldn't feel a thing. Pace had grunted with satisfaction as the other leaders hit the ground. With each press of Geo's finger to resurrect the dead leaders, Hayze had known this wasn't the answer.

This wasn't the Solution.

Pace scowls. "This is only a drop compared to what they put us through."

Oceania's words echo through Hayze's mind.

You see now how hard it is to make the decisions. When you let us fall from the platforms, you knew it was going to cause us pain. But you did it anyway. You were prepared to inflict suffering on us for the greater good.

Avalan's words are blazing right behind.

Perhaps you're as good as us. We want the same thing, Jewel. Work with us.

Is Hayze far more like the leaders than he thought?

Have they been right all along?

Aura wraps a hand around his arm, her gaze steady on Pace. "We need to stop for a moment. Decide what our next step is."

Put the leaders back in the Games to torture them some more.

Or form an alliance with them.

Both options have Hayze's gut rebelling. Then his mind. Followed by his heart.

Pace huffs. "They're already offering a truce," he angrily points out. "We give them another dose of their own medicine and they'll be ready to acknowledge who holds all the power."

It's Skylus's turn to cross her arms. "You heard Infernos. Who's going to listen to us? The leaders are the ones the people follow. They're the ones they trust."

"They won't when they learn what they've been doing," Tempo says. "When the façade of benevolent, caring leaders is torn away."

Skylus tilts her chin up. "You think the Alliance is going to do right by everyone? They want anarchy. That's the last thing our people need."

"They want equality," Pace snaps, his hands now clenched into fists.

The images of what was left of the world if the Quadrants were abolished rise in Hayze's mind, just as devastating as the first time.

No one will survive.

Everyone will face the same outcome—death.

That's not an equality he's willing to fight for.

Tempo glances at the smaller screens above the control panel. "Cyclonis is stabilizing. He may wake soon."

Which means all four leaders will endure whatever comes next.

"I won't do it." Skylus takes a step back for emphasis. "I won't restart the Games."

Hayze glances at Atmos's body, wrapped and still in the corner. Without an Air member, they won't be able to press the four buttons that will start another simulation.

In fact, they won't be able to do it if Fire isn't in the room with them.

He strides over to Atmos and scoops up his limp, sheet-wrapped form. "I'm going to give him a proper goodbye."

Aura's already moving toward the door. "We all need time to think."

Hayze joins her, ignoring the way Atmos feels cool and a little stiff. And the way it makes his stomach clench. "We'll be back shortly."

They exit before anyone can say something, Aura closing the door behind them. Hayze stops, holding Atmos a little tighter. "Thanks," he says, closing his eyes for a moment. He needed to get out of there. Away from the weight of the decisions hanging heavy in the air.

Aura's hand brushes his own. "I needed the break just as much as you."

Opening his eyes, he gazes down at her. "That wasn't easy to watch."

The leaders may be wrong, but no one deserves to be put in the Games.

"It hasn't been since the moment we woke up on the rafts."

He nods, acknowledging the truth in her statement. If Aura hadn't been there with him, he's not sure he'd be standing here. Someone else would likely have him wrapped in a white sheet.

A quick scan registers the data is still pouring over the glass walls, but there's no Eterna. Hayze gets moving, not particularly interested in having another chat with the *very advanced computer*. "If the panel we just came through is a door, then any of the others could be too."

"Smart," Aura says, looking around pensively as she walks beside him. "Which one leads to the cremation room is the question."

Hayze shakes his head. "I don't care where it is. Atmos isn't going there." He deserves more than anonymously disappearing from the world. "We're taking him to the roof."

Moving faster, Aura walks ahead. "This door is the exit," she says with confidence. "It's the only one with information that isn't changing or moving."

Hayze glances around, realizing she's right. Aura's eye for detail for the win once again. She presses the edge of the panel and it depresses, then pops out. Pulling it open, she reveals a large white room like the one containing the pods. Except all that dominates this one is a wide set of stairs ascending into a bright light.

Yep. Aura's eye for detail for the win.

"You're amazing," Hayze says, wishing he could press a kiss to her head.

Especially when carrying the dead body of his friend is the reason he can't.

Aura slides him a soft glance. "I love you, too."

Together, they walk toward the stairs, which are wide enough for them to ascend side by side. This is where the guards would've carried the unconscious teens the moment they stepped through the veil hiding the true Sect. Straight down to the pod room so the leaders could continue their single-minded mission.

Bend eight Element-wielding teens to their will.

Hayze finds himself squinting as they ascend. Aura raises her arm to shield her eyes as the light grows brighter and brighter, blinding them to whatever they're walking up to. Yet neither of them slow. Maybe they're fed up with being scared.

Maybe they're tired and foolish.

Maybe they've simply had enough of feeling manipulated.

Either way, they walk through the light, their feet leaving white steps and landing on rusted tin. Hayze and Aura stop as they realize they're on the roof of the Sect. A faint breeze caresses their face, feeling far more real than the world they've left at the bottom of the stairs.

They execute a slow turn, realizing it's dusk. And that they can see the four Quadrants stretched out in all their contrasting glory. The browns and greens of Earth, the endless blues of Water, the mountains of Air, and the razed soil of the Scorchlands. All separate and disconnected.

All beautiful.

"This is a good place," Aura says somberly.

Hayze nods. Atmos's goodbye will be at the heart of the Quadrants. The heart of the four Elements.

He carefully walks forward, finding the tin feels sturdy. Reaching the center of the roof, he gently lowers Atmos, laying his body on the warm tin. Hayze steps back, not surprised when Aura slips her arms around his waist. He draws her in tightly, soaking up the comfort as he offers his own. Without conscious thought, he presses a kiss to the crown of her head, the need to do it still alive in his veins. Aura rests her head against his shoulder, sighing.

For long moments, they hold onto everything they hold dear.

Everything they can't afford to lose.

Each other.

Then, wordlessly, they separate. Their gazes fall to the wrapped body lying in wait. It's time for Atmos to be honored in the only way they can.

Hayze and Aura lift their hands. It's an unspoken agreement that they need to do this properly. Quickly. So they breathe in, allowing their palms to heat. Then heat some more.

When they unleash their Element, the flames are white in the scorching center and pale blue at the flickering edges. Atmos's body incinerates in a blink. There's no charring, no sickly burning flesh, only a fragile tendril of smoke.

All that remains is a smattering of ash, so faint and light the particles never have a chance to settle on the rusted tin. The breeze picks them up, almost playing with them, carrying Atmos in a way he wasn't able to while alive.

It's Air that takes him away. Air that lifts him to the twilight sky and beyond.

Air that honors his life.

Hayze and Aura lower their hands, then sink into each other's arms. Both their cheeks are wet. Both their souls carry pain, yet also the promise they're the ones who can end it.

They're alive. They have each other.

And they carry the power of Fire.

What are they going to do with their gifts?

"Hayze, look," Aura whispers, pointing toward the horizon on their left.

Massive trees cover most of Terra, creating an undulating carpet of green. But it's beyond the wall that Aura's indicating toward. Clouds are moving in over the Quakelands, low and heavy. The flash periodically with lightning they can't hear, yet Hayze feels like a jolt to his heart. Gray mist hangs below them, telling him it's raining.

"Eterna's predictions," he says, his voice just as hushed as Aura's.

As if he doesn't want the words to be heard, let alone be true.

They've already experienced flooding in Terra. He almost lost Aura. Seeing her disappear under the surface, watching the raging torrent take her away had fractured his heart. Only holding her again, feeling her breathe, had healed the cracks in his chest.

Yet, that scenario will be repeated over and over in the Quakelands with countless lives.

Without the possibility of surviving because Pace and

Tempo won't be there. There will be no healing for the people of Terra.

The image of the safezone no longer able to be its namesake slams through Hayze. It had flown through the air as if Mother Nature had struck it herself. It's not just the rising waters the people of the Quakelands will have to survive. And gale force winds are something they're not equipped to escape.

"Sweet fractal," Aura gasps.

She's looking further to the left. At their home Quadrant.

A sandstorm is gusting over the Scorchlands, making Hayze's stomach tighten even more. There's no fire, but he knows how fast an inferno can build in his home Quadrant. All it takes is a spark and it won't be sand being buffeted around by the wind. Fueled by it.

It'll be a merciless firestorm.

The images they saw in the Sect below could come true.

And if they do...

Hayze and Aura's parents won't survive what's coming.

He tugs her in tight and she slips in front of him, her back to his chest. Neither of them can take their gaze off the billowing clouds of pale yellow as they roll over the Scorchlands. Everyone would be taking shelter in their bunkers, assuming they'll be safe.

"We can't even warn them," Aura whispers.

Because they're here, at the top of the Sect. Watching and knowing what's coming.

With the power to stop it.

"We're the Solution." Hayze chokes out the words, finding them jagged and bitter.

Aura grips his arms where they're wrapped around her shoulders. "We're the Solution."

Once the words are said, both chaos and peace erupt and

settle within Hayze. His mind rebels as his heart accepts. His breath hitches and escapes in a rush.

Aura turns so she's facing him, the same battle of unease and calm playing across her face. "This is what we were born to do, Hayze."

In some ways, because the leaders created them for this.

But far more because they found a love that defined their childhood. One that was taken from them, wiped by an alternate reality, stolen as if it meant nothing.

And then rose from the ashes, stronger than ever.

Hayze leans down as Aura pushes up. Their lips brush, barely touching as their breaths shiver and tangle. This kiss is fragile, beautiful, cherished.

Like the lives of every soul depending on them.

With an exhale, their mouths connect. Their lips fuse. And their hearts thud in unison. Aura's hands move up to grip Hayze's hair. His fingers clasp her jaw, spreading over her still-wet cheeks. They hold each other as the kiss deepens, as their bodies blur the line of where one starts and the other finishes.

This kiss is powerful. Consuming.

Homage to everything they're fighting for.

They lose themselves to the feelings, to the promise of what they have for long moments. Passion and desire flare, love and longing become an action, not just an emotion. They touch and taste, offer and accept.

Promise and pledge.

When they finally pull apart, they press their foreheads together. They're at the pinnacle of the world they're committed to save. The four Quadrants surround them. The Sect is below them.

Yet it's their love that holds them. That is their foundation.

"We need to accept the leaders' offer," Hayze says, the quiet words laced with conviction.

Aura nods, closes her eyes for the space of a heavy heartbeat, then opens them again. Blue pools gaze at him, steady and sure. "On our own terms."

No more Games.

No more wrong in the name of right.

It's time to heal and save and liberate.

And an alliance with the leaders is the only way. In fact, it could be the start of the lives he and Aura dream of.

Unity is the Solution.

When the world they were born into is founded on division.

Four Quadrants.

Four Elements.

And one future that depends on whether they fail or succeed.

THE END

Ready for the epic conclusion to Elemental Games?

Check out Elemental Solution now!

http://mybook.to/ElementalSolution

BOOK FOUR - ELEMENTAL SOLUTION

ELEMENTAL GAMES

Elemental powers. Deadly games. No escape.

The ultimate enemy has been uncovered. Except the threat is far more devastating than they expected. Which is going to make it even harder to defeat.

Winning this war will require more than just Elemental powers. It's time for the Quadrants to unite.

Fire. Water. Air. Earth.

Together, everyone is stronger. Can Aura and Hayze uncover the truth in time to stop the evil? Because time means everything in a world that means nothing...

Without love.

The epic conclusion to an intoxicating thrill ride packed with twists, romance and nail-biting action! Lovers of Maze Runner and Hunger Games will devour Elemental Solution. One-click your copy now.

Grab your copy now!
http://mybook.to/ElementalSolution

WANT TO STAY IN TOUCH?

If you'd like to be the first for to hear all the news from Tamar and Heidi, be sure to sign up to our newsletter. Subscribers receive bonus content, early cover reveals and sneaky snippets of upcoming books. We'd love you to join us!

SIGN UP HERE:

https://sendfox.com/tamarandheidi

ABOUT THE AUTHORS

Tamar Sloan hasn't decided whether she's a psychologist who loves writing, or a writer with a lifelong fascination with psychology. She must have been someone pretty awesome in a previous life (past life regression indicated a Care Bear), because she gets to do both. When not reading, writing or working with teens, Tamar can be found with her husband and two children enjoying country life in their small slice of the Australian bush.

Heidi Catherine loves the way her books give her the opportunity to escape into worlds vastly different to her own life in the burbs. While she quite enjoys killing her characters (especially the awful ones), she promises she's far better behaved in real life. Other than writing and reading, Heidi's current obsessions include watching far too much reality TV with the excuse that it's research for her books.

MORE SERIES TO FALL IN LOVE WITH...

ALSO BY TAMAR SLOAN AND HEIDI CATHERINE

The Thaw Chronicles

The Sovereign Code

ALSO BY TAMAR SLOAN

Keepers of the Grail

Keepers of the Light

Keepers of the Chalice

Keepers of Excalibur

Zodiac Guardians

Descendants of the Gods

Prime Prophecy

ALSO BY HEIDI CATHERINE

The Kingdoms of Evernow

The Soulweaver

www.ingramcontent.com/pod-product-compliance
Lightning Source LLC
Chambersburg PA
CBHW031938240626
47153CB00003B/779